this girl

Also by Colleen Hoover

Slammed
Point of Retreat
Hopeless

this girl

A novel

Colleen Hoover

ATRIA PAPERBACK

NEW YORK LONDON TORONTO SYDNEY NEW DELHI

ATRIA PATERBACK

A Division of Simon & Schuster, Inc.
1230 Avenue of the Americas
New York, NY 10020

A Very Long Poem by Marty Schoenleber III

First Atria Paperback edition August 2013

ATRIA PAPERBACK and colophon are trademarks of Simon & Schuster, Inc.

For information about special discounts for bulk purchases, please contact Simon & Schuster Special Sales at 1-866-506-1949 or business@simonandschuster.com.

The Simon & Schuster Speakers Bureau can bring authors to your live event. For more information or to book an event, contact the Simon & Schuster Speakers Bureau at 1-866-248-3049 or visit our website at www.simonspeakers.com.

Manufactured in the United States of America

40 39 38 37 36 35 34 33 32

Library of Congress Cataloging-in-Publication Data

Hoover, Colleen.
  This girl : a novel / by Colleen Hoover. — First ATRIA pbk ed.
    pages   cm
  1. Life change events—Fiction. I. Title.
  PS3608.O623T45 2013
  813'.6—dc23   2013014139

ISBN 978-1-4767-4653-1
ISBN 978-1-4767-4654-8 (ebook)

For my mother

this girl

1.

the honeymoon

IF I TOOK every romantic poem, every book, every song, and every movie I've ever read, heard, or seen and extracted the breathtaking moments, somehow bottling them up, they would pale in comparison to this moment.

This moment is incomparable.

She's lying on her side facing me, her elbow tucked under her head, her other hand stroking the back of mine that's lying between us on the bed. Her hair is spread out across the pillow, spilling down her shoulder and across her neck. She's staring at her fingers as they move in circles over my hand. I've known her almost two years now, and I've never seen her this content. She's no longer solely carrying the weight that's been her life for the last two years, and it shows. It's almost as if the moment we said "I do" yesterday, the hardships and heartaches we faced as individuals were meshed, making our pasts lighter and easier to carry. From this point on I'll be able to do that for her. Should there be any more burdens I'll be able to carry them *for* her. It's all I've ever wanted to do for this girl since the moment I first laid eyes on her.

She glances up at me and smiles, then laughs and buries her face in the pillow.

I lean over her and kiss her on the neck. "What's so funny?"

She lifts her face off the pillow—her cheeks a deeper shade of red. She shakes her head and laughs. "*Us*," she says. "It's only been twenty-four hours and I've already lost count."

I kiss her scarlet cheek and laugh. "I'm done with counting, Lake. I've had about all the countdowns I can handle for a lifetime." I wrap my arm around her waist and pull her on top of me. When she leans in to kiss me, her hair falls between us. I reach to the nightstand and grab her rubber band, then twist her hair into a knot behind her head and secure it. "There," I say, pulling her face back to mine. "Better."

She was adamant about having the robes, but we haven't once used them. Her ugly shirt has been on the floor since I threw it there last night. Needless to say, this has been the best twenty-four hours of my life.

She kisses down my jaw and traces a trail with her lips up to my ear. "You hungry?" she whispers.

"Not for food."

She pulls back and grins. "We've still got another twenty-four hours to go, you know. If you want to keep up with me you need to replenish your energy. Besides, we somehow missed lunch today." She rolls off me, reaches into the nightstand, and pulls out the room service menu.

"No burgers," I say.

She rolls her eyes and laughs. "You'll never get over that." She scrolls the menu and points at it with her finger, holding it up. "What about beef Wellington? I've always wanted to try that."

"Sounds good," I say, inching closer to her. She picks up the phone to dial room service. The whole time she's on the phone I kiss up and down her back, forcing her to stifle her laughs as she tries to maintain her composure while ordering. When she hangs up the phone, she slides underneath me and pulls the covers over us.

"You have twenty minutes," she whispers. "Think you can handle that?"

"I only need ten."

THE BEEF WELLINGTON did not disappoint. The only issue now is that we're too stuffed and too tired to move. We've turned the TV on for the first time since I walked her over the threshold, so I think it's safe to say we're due for at least a two-hour break.

Our legs are intertwined and her head is on my chest. I'm running my fingers through her hair with one hand and stroking her wrist with the other. Somehow trivial things like lying in bed watching TV have become euphoric when we're tangled together like this.

"Will?" She pulls herself up onto her elbow and looks at me. "Can I ask you something?" She runs her hand across my chest, then rests it on top of my heart.

"I do about twelve laps a day on the University track, plus one hundred sit-ups twice a day," I say. She arches an eyebrow, so I point to my stomach. "Weren't you asking about my abs?"

She laughs and playfully punches me. "No, I wasn't asking about your *abs*." She leans down and kisses me on the stomach. "They *are* nice, though."

I stroke her cheek and pull her gaze back to mine. "Ask me anything, babe."

She sighs and drops her elbow and lays her head back onto the pillow, staring up at the ceiling. "Do you ever feel guilty?" she says quietly. "For feeling this happy?"

I scoot closer to her and lay my arm across her stomach. "Lake. Don't ever feel guilty. This is exactly what they'd want for you."

She looks at me and forces a smile. "I know it's what they'd want for me. I just . . . I don't know. If I could take back everything that happened, I would do it in a heartbeat if it meant I could have them back. But doing that would mean I never would have met you. So sometimes I feel guilty because I . . ."

I press my fingers to her lips. "Shh," I say. "Don't think like that, Lake. Don't think about *what ifs*." I lean in and kiss her on the forehead. "But I do know what you mean if that helps. It's counterproductive thinking about it, though. It is what it is."

She takes her hand in mine and intertwines our fingers, then brings them to her mouth and kisses the back of my hand. "My dad would have loved you."

"My mom would have loved *you*," I say.

She smiles. "One more thing about the past, then I'll stop bringing it up." She looks at me with a slightly evil grin on her face. "I'm so glad that bitch Vaughn dumped you."

I laugh. "No doubt."

She smiles and releases her fingers from mine. She turns toward me on the bed and looks at me. I pull her hand to my mouth and kiss the inside of her palm.

"Do you think you would have married her?"

I laugh and roll my eyes. "Seriously, Lake? Do you really want to talk about this right now?"

She smiles sheepishly at me. "I'm just curious. We've never really talked about the past before. Now that I know you aren't going anywhere, I feel more comfortable talking about it. Besides, there are a lot of things I want to know about you," she says. "Like how it felt when she broke up with you like she did."

"That's an odd thing to want to hear about on your honeymoon."

She shrugs her shoulders. "I just want to know everything about you. I've already got your future, now I want to get to know your past. Besides," she grins. "We've got a couple of hours to kill before your energy is fully replenished. What else are we going to do?"

I'm too exhausted to move right now and as much as I can pretend I'm not keeping count, nine times in twenty-four hours must be some sort of record. I roll over onto my stomach and prop a pillow under my chin, and then begin to tell her my story.

the breakup

"GOODNIGHT, CAULDER." I flip off the light and hope he doesn't crawl out of bed again. It's our third night with it being just the two of us here. He was too scared to sleep by himself last night so I let him sleep with me. I'm hoping it doesn't become a habit, but I would completely understand if it did.

I still can't wrap my head around all that's happened in the last two weeks, much less the decisions I've made. I hope I'm doing the right thing. I know my parents want us to be together, I just don't think they approve of my dropping my scholarship to make it happen.

Why do I keep referring to them in the present tense?

This is really going to be an adjustment. I make my way into my bedroom and drop onto the bed. I'm too exhausted to even reach over and turn off the lamp. As soon as I close my eyes, there's a light tap on my bedroom door.

"Caulder, you'll be fine. Go back to sleep," I say, somehow dragging myself off the bed again to coax him back to his room. He has successfully slept alone for seven years; I know he's capable of doing it again.

"Will?" The door opens and Vaughn walks in. I had no idea she was coming over tonight, but I'm thankful she's here. She seems to know exactly when I need her the most. I walk to her and close the bedroom door, then wrap my arms around her.

"Hey," I say. "What are you doing here? I thought you were heading back to campus today."

She places her hands on my forearms and pushes back, giving me the most pitiful smile I've ever seen. She walks over to my bed and sits, avoiding eye contact the entire time. "We need to talk."

The look on her face sends a chill up the back of my neck. I've never seen her look so distraught before. I immediately sit on the bed beside her and bring her hand to my mouth and kiss it. "What's wrong? You okay?" I brush a loose strand of hair behind her ear just as the tears begin to fall. I wrap my arms around her and pull her to my chest. "Vaughn, what's wrong? Tell me."

She doesn't say anything. She continues to cry so I give her a moment. Sometimes girls just need to cry. When the tears finally begin to subside, she straightens back up and takes my hands, but still doesn't look me in the eyes.

"Will . . ." She pauses. The way she says my name, the tone of her voice . . . it sends panic straight to my heart. She looks up at me but can't hold her stare, so she turns away.

"Vaughn?" I say hesitantly, hoping I'm misreading her. I place my hand on her chin and pull her gaze back in my direction. The fear in my voice is clear when I speak. "What are you doing, Vaughn?"

She almost looks relieved that I seem to have caught on to her intentions. She shakes her head. "I'm sorry, Will. I'm so sorry. I just can't do this anymore."

Her words hit me like a ton of bricks. *This?* She can't do *this* anymore? When did we become a *this*? I don't respond. What the hell do I say to that?

She senses the shock in my demeanor, so she squeezes my hands and whispers it again. "I'm so sorry."

I pull away and stand up, turning away from her. I run my hands through my hair and take a deep breath. The anger building inside me is suddenly coupled by tears that I have no intention of letting her see.

"I just didn't expect any of this, Will. I'm too young to be a mom. I'm not ready for this kind of responsibility."

She's really doing this. She's really breaking up with me. Two weeks after my parents die and she's breaking my heart all over again? Who *does* that? She's not thinking straight. It's just shock . . . that's all. I turn around and face her, not caring that she can see how much this is affecting me.

"I didn't expect this either," I say. "It's okay, you're just scared." I sit back down on the bed beside her and pull her to me. "I'm not asking you to be his mom, Vaughn. I'm not asking you to be *anything* right now." I squeeze her tighter and press my lips against her forehead; an action that immediately causes her to start crying again. "Don't do this," I whisper into her hair. "Don't do this to me. Not right now."

She turns her head away from me. "If I don't do this now, I'll never be able to do it."

She stands up and tries to walk away, but I pull her back to me and wrap my arms around her waist, pressing my head against her stomach.

"Please."

She runs her hands over my hair and down my neck, then bends forward and kisses the top of my head. "I feel awful, Will," she whispers. "*Awful.* But I'm not about to live a life that I'm not ready for, just because I feel sorry for you."

I press my forehead against her shirt and close my eyes, soaking in her words.

She feels *sorry* for me?

I release my arms from around her and push against her

stomach. She drops her hands and takes a step back. I stand up and walk to the bedroom door, holding it open, indicating she needs to leave. "The last thing I want is your pity," I say, looking her in the eyes.

"Will, don't," she pleads. "Please don't be mad at me." She's looking up at me with tears in her eyes. When she cries, her eyes turn a glossy, deep shade of blue. I used to tell her they were the exact same color as the ocean. Looking into her eyes right now almost makes me *despise* the ocean.

I turn away from her and grip both sides of the door, pressing my head against the wood. I close my eyes and try to hold it in. It feels like the pressure, the stress, the emotions that have been building up for the last two weeks—it feels like I'm about to explode.

She gently places her hand on my shoulder in an attempt to console me. I shrug it off and turn around to face her again. "Two *weeks*, Vaughn!" I yell. I realize how loud I'm being, so I lower my voice and step closer to her. "They've been dead for *two weeks*! How could you possibly be thinking about *yourself* right now?"

She walks past me through the doorway, toward the living room. I follow her as she grabs her purse from the couch and walks to the front door. She opens the door and turns to face me before she leaves. "You'll thank me for this one day, Will. I know it doesn't seem like it right now, but someday you'll know I'm doing what's best for us."

She turns to leave and I yell after her, "What's best for *you*, Vaughn! You're doing what's best for *you*!"

As soon as the door closes behind her I break down. I rush back to my bedroom and slam the door, then turn around and punch it over and over, harder and harder. When I can't feel my hand anymore, I squeeze my eyes shut and press my forehead against the door. I've had so much to process these past two weeks—I don't know how to process this, too.

What the hell has happened to my *life*?

I eventually make my way back to the bed and sit with my elbows on my knees, head in my hands. My mom and dad are smiling at me from the confines of the glass frame on my nightstand, watching me unfold. Watching as the culmination of all that has happened these last two weeks slowly tears me apart.

Why weren't they better prepared for something like this? Why would they risk leaving me with all of this responsibility? Their ill-preparedness has cost me my scholarship, the love of my life, and now, quite possibly, my entire future. I snatch the picture up and place my thumbs over their photograph. With all my force, I squeeze until the glass cracks between my fingertips. Once it's successfully shattered—just like my life—I rare back and throw it as hard as I can against the wall in front of me. The frame breaks in two when it meets the wall and shards of glass sprinkle the carpet.

I'm reaching over to turn off my lamp when my bedroom door opens again.

"Just leave, Vaughn. *Please*."

I look up and see Caulder standing in the doorway, crying. He looks terrified. It's the same look I've seen so many times since the moment our parents died. It's the same look he had when I hugged him good-bye at the hospital and made him leave with my grandparents. It's the same look that rips my heart in two every time I see it.

It's a look that immediately brings me back down to earth.

I wipe my eyes and motion for him to come closer. When

he does, I wrap my arms around him and pull him onto my lap, then hug him while he quietly cries into my shirt. I rock him back and forth and stroke his hair. I kiss him on the forehead and pull him closer.

"Want to sleep with me again tonight, Buddy?"

2.

the honeymoon

"WOW," LAKE SAYS in disbelief. "What a selfish bitch."

"Yeah. Thank God for that," I say. I clasp my hands together behind my head and look up at the ceiling, mirroring Lake's position on the bed. "It's funny how history almost repeated itself."

"What do you mean?"

"Think about it. Vaughn broke up with me because she didn't want to be with me just because she felt sorry for me. *You* broke up with me because you thought I was with you because I felt sorry for *you.*"

"I didn't break up with you," she says defensively.

I laugh and sit up on the bed. "The hell you didn't! Your exact words were, 'I don't care if it takes days, or weeks, or months.' That's a breakup."

"It was not. I was giving you time to think."

"Time I didn't need." I lie back down on my pillow and face her again. "It sure felt like a breakup."

"Well," she says, looking at me. "Sometimes two people need to fall apart to realize how much they need to fall back together."

I take her hand and rest it between us, then stroke the back of it with my thumb. "Let's not fall apart again," I whisper.

She looks me in the eyes. "Never."

There's vulnerability in the way she looks at me in silence. Her eyes scroll over my face and her mouth is curled up into a slight grin. She doesn't speak, but she doesn't have to. I know in these moments, when it's just her and me and nothing else, that she truly, soul-deep loves me.

"What was it like the first time you saw me?" she asks. "What was it about me that made you want to ask me out? And tell me everything, even the bad thoughts."

I laugh. "There weren't any bad thoughts. *Naughty* thoughts, maybe. But not bad."

She grins. "Well then tell me those, too."

the introduction

I HOLD THE phone to my ear with my shoulder and finish buttoning my shirt. "I promise, Grandma," I say into the phone. "I'm leaving straight from work on Friday. We'll be there by five but right now we're running late, I need to go. I'll call you tomorrow."

She says her good-byes and I hang up the phone. Caulder walks through the living room with his backpack slung across his shoulder and a green, plastic army helmet on his head. He's always trying to sneak random accessories to school. Last week when I dropped him off, he was out of the car before I even noticed he was wearing a holster.

I reach out and snatch the helmet off his head and toss it onto the couch. "Caulder, go get in the car. I've got to grab my stuff."

Caulder heads outside and I scramble to gather all the papers scattered across the bar. I was up past midnight grading. I've only been teaching eight weeks now, but I'm beginning to understand why there's a teacher shortage. I shove the stack of papers inside my binder, then shove it into my satchel and head outside.

"*Great*," I mutter as soon as I see the U-Haul backing up across the street. This is the third family to move into that house in less than a year. I'm not in the mood to help people move again, especially after only four hours of sleep. I hope they'll be finished unloading by the time I get home today, or I'll feel obligated to help. I turn around and lock the door behind me, then quickly head for the car. When I open the car door, Caulder isn't inside. I groan and throw my stuff in the seat. He always picks the worst times to play hide-and-seek; we're already ten minutes late.

I glance in the backseat, hoping he's hiding in the floorboard again, but I catch sight of him in the street. He's laughing and playing with another little boy who looks about his age. *This is a plus.* Maybe having a neighbor to play with will get him out of my hair more often.

I start to call his name when the U-Haul catches my eye again. The girl driving can't be any older than me, yet she's confidently backing up the U-Haul without any help. I lean against my car door and decide to watch her attempt to navigate that thing around those gnomes. This should be interesting.

I'm quickly proven wrong and she's parked in the driveway in no time flat. Rather than hop out to inspect her parking job, she kills the engine and rolls down her window, then props her leg up on the dash.

I don't know why these simple actions strike me as odd. *Intriguing*, even. She drums her fingers on the steering wheel, then reaches up and tugs at her hair, letting down her ponytail. Her hair spills down around her shoulders and she massages her scalp, shaking her hair out.

Holy hell.

Her gaze falls on the boys playing in the street between us, and I can't help but let my curiosity get the best of me. Is she his sister? His mom? She doesn't look old enough to have a child that age, but I'm also at a visual disadvantage being all the way across the street. And why is she just sitting in the U-Haul?

I realize I've been staring for several minutes when someone pulls up beside her in a Jeep.

"Please don't let it be a guy," I whisper aloud to myself, hoping it's not a boyfriend. Or worse, a *husband*.

Why would I even care? The last thing I need right now is a distraction. Especially someone who lives right across the street.

I breathe a surprising sigh of relief when the person who steps out of the Jeep isn't a man. She's an older woman, maybe her mother. The woman shuts her door and walks up to greet the landlord, who's standing in the entryway. Before I can talk myself out of it, I'm walking toward their house. I suddenly have the urge to help people move today, after all. I cross the street, unable to take my eyes off the girl in the U-Haul. She's watching Caulder and the other little boy play, and hasn't once glanced in my direction. I don't know what it is about her that's pulling me in. That look on her face . . . she looks sad. And for some reason, I don't like it.

I'm standing unnoticed on the passenger side of the U-Haul, staring at her through the window, practically in a trance. I'm not staring because of the fact that she's attractive, which she *is*. It's that look in her eyes. The *depth*. I want to know what she's thinking.

No, I *need* to know what she's thinking.

She diverts her attention out her window and says something to the boys, then opens the door to get out. I suddenly realize I'm about to look like an idiot just standing in her driveway, staring. I glance across the street at my house and contemplate how I can get back over there without her seeing me. Before I have a chance to make a move, Caulder and the other little boy run around the U-Haul and smash into me, laughing.

"She's a zombie!" Caulder yells after I grab hold of them by their shirts. The girl rounds the U-Haul and I can't help but laugh. She's got her head cocked to the side and she's walking stiff-legged after them.

"Get 'em!" I yell to her. They're trying to fight to get away so I strengthen my grip. I look back up at her and we lock eyes.

Wow. Those *eyes*. They're the most incredible shade of green

I've ever seen. I try to compare the color to something, but nothing comes to mind. It's so unique, it's like her eyes have just invented their own hue.

Studying her features, I conclude she can't be the boy's mom. She looks my age. At the least, maybe nineteen or twenty. I need to find out her name. If I know her name I can look up her Facebook page and at least see if she's single.

Christ. This is the last thing I need in my life right now. A *crush.*

I feel like she knows what I'm thinking, so I force myself to break our gaze. The boy takes my moment of distraction and uses it to his advantage. He breaks free and slices at me with an imaginary sword, so I look back up at the girl and mouth *"help."*

She yells *"brains"* again and lunges forward, pretending to bite Caulder on top of the head. She tickles them until they melt onto the concrete driveway, then she stands back up and laughs. Her cheeks flush when she meets my gaze again and she contorts her mouth into an uncomfortable grimace, like she's suddenly embarrassed. Her unease disappears just as fast as it appeared and is replaced by a smile that suddenly makes me want to know every single minute detail about her.

"Hey, I'm Will," I say, extending my hand out to her. "We live across the street." She places her hand in mine. It's soft and cold, and the moment I wrap my fingers around hers, the physical contact sends a shockwave straight through me. I don't remember the last time a girl has had this kind of immediate effect on me. It must be my lack of sleep last night.

"I'm Layken," she says, her uneasiness once again masking her smile. "I guess I live . . . *here.*" She glances at the house behind her, then back to me.

She doesn't look too pleased about the fact that she lives

"here." That same look she had while sitting in the U-Haul consumes her features again and her eyes suddenly grow sadder. Why does that look affect me so much?

"Well, welcome to Ypsilanti," I say, wanting desperately to make that look go away. She looks down and it occurs to me that I'm still awkwardly shaking her hand, so I quickly pull it away from hers and shove my hands in my jacket pockets. "Where are you guys moving here from?"

"Texas?" she says.

Why does she say it like a question? Did I just ask a stupid question? I did. I'm making stupid small talk.

"Texas, huh?" I say. She nods her head, but doesn't come back with a response. I suddenly feel like an intrusive neighbor. I don't know what else to say without making it even more awkward, so I figure my best move at this point is to retreat. I bend over and grab Caulder by the feet, throwing him over my shoulder, then tell her I've got to get him to school. "There's a cold front coming through tonight. You should try to get as much unloaded today as you can. It's supposed to last a few days, so if you guys need help unloading this afternoon, let me know. We'll be home around four."

She shrugs. "Sure, thanks."

Her words are laced with the slightest hint of a southern drawl. I didn't know how much I liked southern accents until now. I continue across the street and help Caulder into the car. While he's climbing inside, I glance back across the street. The little boy is stabbing her in the back and she lets out a fake cry and falls to her knees. Her playful interaction with him is just one more thing that intrigues me about her. After he jumps on her back, she glances up and catches me staring at her. I shut Caulder's door and walk to my side. Before I get in, I muster a smile and wave, then climb into the car with an overwhelming urge to punch myself.

AS SOON AS the bell for third period rings, I open the lid to my coffee and pour two extra packets of sugar in. I'm about to need it. There's something about some of the students in third period that rub me the wrong way. Especially Javier. That kid is such a jackass.

"Morning, Mr. Cooper," Eddie says, taking her seat. She's as bubbly as ever. I've never seen Eddie in a bad mood, come to think of it. I need to figure out her secret, since the coffee obviously isn't doing it for me today.

"Morning, Eddie."

She turns and kisses Gavin on the cheek, then settles into her desk. They've been dating since right after I graduated. They're probably the only two people that *don't* annoy the hell out of me in here. Well, them and maybe Nick. Nick seems okay.

After the students are all seated, I instruct them to get out their books. The entire time I'm giving my lecture on the elements of poetry, my mind keeps wandering to the new neighbor.

Layken.

I like that name.

AFTER SIX HOURS and only a few dozen thoughts of the new neighbor later, Caulder and I finally pull into the driveway. I shut my car door and open the back door to remove the box of papers. When I turn back around, Layken's little brother has appeared out of nowhere and he's standing right in front of me, staring silently. It seems as though he's waiting on an introduction. Several seconds pass without him moving a muscle or blinking. Are we in a standoff? I shift the box to my left arm and reach out my hand.

"I'm Will."

"Kel is name my," he says.

I stare at him blankly. *Was that even English?*

"I can talk backwards," he says, explaining the clutter of words that just came out of his mouth. "Like this. Backwards talk can I."

Interesting. Someone possibly weirder than Caulder? I didn't think it was possible.

"Kel . . . you meeting . . . nice . . . was . . . it well," I say, a little slower than when he does it. He grins, then runs across the street with Caulder. I glance at their house and see that the U-Haul is now parked in the street with the latch shut. I'm disappointed they've already unloaded it; I was actually looking forward to helping.

I spend the rest of the evening working overtime for free . . . another side effect of being a teacher. I decide after my shower to make a living room detour to glance across the street for about the tenth time, but I don't see her.

"Why do you keep looking out the window?" Caulder asks from behind me.

His voice startles me and I snatch the living room curtain shut. I didn't realize he was sitting on the couch. I walk over to him and pull on his hand, then shove him toward the hallway. "Go to bed," I say.

He spins around before he closes his bedroom door behind him. "You were looking out the window to see if you could see that girl, weren't you? Do you like Kel's sister?"

"Goodnight, Caulder," I say, ignoring his question.

He grins and closes the door to his room. Before I head to my own bedroom, I walk to the window one more time. When I open the curtain, someone is standing in the window across the street with the curtains partially open. They suddenly snatch shut and I can't help but smile, wondering if she's just as curious about me as I am about her.

"IT'S COLD, IT'S cold, it's cold, it's cold, it's cold," Caulder says, jogging in place while I unlock the car doors. I crank the engine and turn the heat up, then head back inside to get the rest of my things while Caulder waits in the car. When I open the door to head back outside, I stop in my tracks when I see Layken standing in her entryway. She bends down and gathers a handful of snow to inspect it, then quickly drops it. She stands up and steps outside, closing the door behind her. I shake my head, knowing exactly what's about to happen. It's snowing and she isn't even wearing a jacket over her pajama bottoms and shirt. I don't know what she's doing, but she won't last long out here. She's not in Texas anymore. She begins to make her way to the driveway when my gaze falls on her feet.

Is she wearing house shoes? Seriously? Before I can even yell a warning, she's flat on her back.

Southerners. They just don't *get* it.

She doesn't move at first. She lies still in the driveway, staring up at the sky. A rush of panic overcomes me, thinking she may be hurt, but then she begins to pull herself up. As much as I don't want to come off like a bumbling idiot again, I head across the street to make sure she doesn't need my help.

The look on her face when she pulls one of the gnomes out

from beneath her makes me laugh. It's almost like she's blaming the poor guy for her fall. She pulls her arm back to throw him when I stop her.

"That's not a good idea!" I yell, making my way up her driveway. She tilts her head up and looks at me with a death grip on the gnome. "Are you okay?" I ask, still laughing. I can't help but laugh, she looks so pissed!

Her cheeks redden and she glances away. "I'll feel a lot better after I bust this damn thing."

I take the gnome out of her hands when I reach her. "You don't want to do that, gnomes are good luck." I place the freshly injured gnome back in his spot before she destroys him completely.

"Yeah," she says, inspecting her shoulder. "Real good luck."

I immediately feel guilty when I see the blood on her shirt. "Oh, my god, I'm so sorry. I wouldn't have laughed if I knew you were hurt." I assist her up and get a better look at the amount of blood coming from her injury. "You need to get a bandage on that."

She looks back to her house and shakes her head. "I wouldn't have any clue where to find one at this point."

I glance at our house, knowing I have a full supply of bandages in the first-aid kit. I'm hesitant to offer them, though, since I'm already running late for work as it is.

I'm looking at my house, struggling with my indecision, when all five of my senses are suddenly flooded. The slightest smell of vanilla that permeates the air around me . . . the sound of her accent when she speaks . . . the way her close proximity wakes up something inside me that's long been dormant. *Holy hell*. I'm in trouble.

Work can wait.

"You'll have to walk with me. There are some in our kitchen." I take my jacket off and wrap it around her shoulders, then help her across the street. I'm sure she can walk on her own, but for some reason I don't want to let go of her arm. I like helping her. I like the way she feels leaning against me. It seems . . . *right*.

Once we're inside my house, she follows me through my living room as I head to the kitchen to find a bandage. I pull the first-aid kit out of the cabinet and remove a Band-Aid. When I glance back at her, she's looking at the pictures on our wall. The pictures of my mom and dad.

Please don't ask me about them. *Please.*

This is not a conversation I want to have right now. I quickly say something to deflect her attention away from the pictures. "It needs to be cleaned before you put the bandage on it." I roll up my sleeves and turn on the faucet, then wet the napkin. I catch myself taking my time when I know I should be in a hurry. For whatever reason, I just want to drag this time out with her. I don't know why I feel like my desire to know her better has suddenly turned into a *need* to know her better. I turn back around and she darts her eyes away from me when I look at her. I don't really understand her sudden embarrassed look, but it's cute as hell.

"It's fine," she says, reaching for the napkin. "I can get it."

I hand her the napkin and reach for the bandage. It's awkwardly quiet as I fidget with the wrapper. For some reason, her presence makes the house seem eerily empty and quiet. I never notice the silence when I'm alone, but the lack of conversation occurring right now is uncomfortably obvious. I think of something to say to fill the void.

"So, what were you doing outside in your pajamas at seven o'clock in the morning? Are you guys still unloading?"

She shakes her head and tosses the napkin into the trash can. "Coffee," she says, matter-of-fact.

"Oh. I guess you aren't a morning person." I'm secretly hoping that's the case. She seems sort of pissy. I'd like to blame it on her lack of caffeine, rather than on indifference toward me. I take a step closer to place the bandage on her shoulder. I briefly pause before touching her and take in a silent breath, preparing for the rush I seem to get every time I touch her. I put the bandage in place and pat it softly, securing the edges with pressure from my fingertips. Her skin prickles and she wraps her arms around herself, rubbing her forearms up and down.

I gave her chills. This is good.

"There," I say, giving it one last, unnecessary pat. "Good as new."

She clears her throat. "Thanks," she says, standing up. "And I *am* a morning person, *after* I get my coffee."

Coffee. She needs coffee. *I've* got coffee.

I quickly walk over to the counter where the remaining brew is still warm in the pot. I grab a cup out of the cabinet and fill it up for her, then set it on the counter in front of her. "You want cream or sugar?"

She shakes her head and smiles at me. "Black is fine. Thanks," she says. I lean across the bar and watch as she brings the coffee to her lips. She blows softly into the cup before pressing her lips to the brim and sips, never taking her eyes off mine.

I've never wanted to be a coffee cup so bad in my life.

Why do I have to go to *work*? I could stay here and watch her drink coffee all day. She's looking right at me, probably wondering what the hell I'm doing staring at her so much. I straighten back up and look down at my watch. "I need to go, my brother is waiting in the car and I've got to get to work. I'll walk you back. You can keep the cup."

She looks down at the cup and reads it. I didn't even notice I gave her my father's cup. She runs her fingers across the letters and smiles. "I'll be okay," she says as she stands to leave. "I think I've got the whole walking erect thing down now." She walks through the living room and is opening the front door when I spot my jacket lying across the back of my couch. I reach over and grab it.

"Layken, take this. It's cold out there." She tries to refuse but I shake my head and make her take my jacket. If she takes the jacket, she'll eventually have to bring it back, which is exactly what I'm hoping will happen. She smiles and pulls my jacket over her shoulders, then she heads across the street.

When I reach my car I turn to watch her make her way back to her house. I like the way she looks, engulfed by my jacket over her pajamas. Who knew pajamas and Darth Vader house shoes could be so damn sexy?

"Layken!" I yell. She turns around just before she reaches her front door. "May the force be with you!" I laugh and hop in the car before she can say anything.

"What took you so long? I'm f-f-f-freezing," Caulder says.

"Sorry," I say. "Layken hurt herself." I back the car up and pull out onto the street.

"What happened?" he asks.

"She tried to walk on the frozen concrete in Darth Vader house shoes. She busted it and cut herself."

Caulder giggles. "She has Darth Vader house shoes?"

I smile at him. "I know, right?"

3.

the honeymoon

"I LOVE HEARING this," she says, grinning next to me on the bed. "So you thought I was cute, huh?"

"No, I didn't think you were cute. I thought you were absolutely beautiful," I correct her. I brush the hair out of her face and she leans into my hand and kisses my palm. "What did you think about me?" I ask.

She smiles. "I tried *not* to. I was attracted to you, but I had so much going on and we'd been in Michigan all of five minutes when we met. Circumstances just kept bringing us back together, though. Every minute I was around you, I just fell harder and harder in crush with you."

"In *crush*?" I laugh.

She grins. "I was *so* in crush with you, Will. Especially after you helped me with the bandage. And after our trip to the grocery store."

"I'd have to say we were *both* in crush after that trip."

crush

I ATTEMPT TO go over my lesson plans for the next week but I can't even concentrate. I try to pinpoint exactly what it is about her that completely consumes my mind, but I can't figure it out. After the incident with the bandage this morning, she was all that went through my head at work. I wish she would just do or say something stupid so this hold she has on me would break. It's weird.

I've never been so consumed by the thought of someone in my entire life. This is the last thing I need right now, but somehow it's the only thing I *want*.

Caulder bursts through the front door, laughing. He slips his shoes off and walks across the living room shaking his head. "That Darth Vader girl asked me how to get to the grocery store," he says. "I don't know how to drive. She's so dumb." He walks to the refrigerator and opens it.

I stand up. "Is she still out there?" I rush to the front door and see her Jeep parked in the street. I quickly pull my shoes on, then run outside before she drives away. I'm relieved when I see her fiddling with the GPS. It'll buy me some time.

I wonder if she would care if I went with her to the store.

Of course she would. That would be awkward.

"That's not a good idea," I say as I approach her car, then lean through the window.

She glances up at me, a smile hiding in the corners of her mouth. "What's not a good idea?" She begins to insert the GPS into its holder.

Shit. What's not a good idea? I didn't think this through.

I say the first lie that pops into my head. "There's quite a bit of construction going on right now. That thing will get you lost."

Just as she opens her mouth to respond, a car pulls up beside her and a woman leans over the seat and speaks to Layken through the window. This has got to be her mother; they're practically identical. Same accent and everything.

I continue to lean through the window, using her distraction as an opportunity to study her. Her hair is a deep brown, but not as dark as her mother's. Her nail polish is chipped. It looks like she picks at it, which somehow makes me like her even more. Vaughn never left the house unless her hair and nails were perfect.

Kel jumps out of the other car and invites Caulder, who is now standing next to me, over. Caulder asks if he can go, so I grab the handle of Layken's car door without worrying about possible consequences. *The hell with it.*

"Sure," I reply to him. "I'll be back in a little while, Caulder. I'm riding with Layken to the store." I open her door and climb inside without second-guessing my actions. She shoots me a look, but it seems more like an amused one than an irritated one. I take this as another good sign. "I don't give very good verbal directions. Mind if I go with you?"

She laughs and puts the car into gear, glancing at the seat belt I've already fastened. "I guess not."

The closest grocery store is only two blocks away. That's not nearly enough time with her, so I decide to take her the long way. It'll give me more of a chance to get to know her.

"So, Caulder is your little brother's name?" she asks as she turns off our street. I like how she says Caulder's name, drawing out the *Caul* a little bit more than necessary.

"One and only. My parents tried to have another baby for years. They eventually had Caulder, when names like Will weren't that cool anymore."

"I like your name," she says. She smiles at me and her cheeks redden, then she quickly darts her eyes back to the road.

Her embarrassment makes me laugh. Was that a compliment? Did she just flirt with me? *God, I hope so.*

I instruct her to turn left. She flips the blinker on, then brings her hand up to her hair, running her fingers through it all the way down to the ends; an action that causes me to gulp. When both of her hands are on the steering wheel again, I reach over and brush her hair behind her shoulders, then pull back the collar of her shirt.

I look at her bandage, wanting her to believe this is the reason I'm touching her, when really I just needed to feel her hair. When my fingers graze her skin, she flinches. It seems like I make her nervous. I'm hoping it's in a good way. "You're going to need a new bandage soon," I say. I pull her shirt back up and pat it.

"Remind me to grab some at the store," she says. She grips the steering wheel tightly and keeps her eyes focused on the road. She's probably not used to driving in the snow. I should have offered to drive.

The next few moments are quiet. I catch myself staring at her, deep in thought. I wonder how old she is. She doesn't look older than me, but it would suck if she is. Sometimes girls don't date guys who are younger than them. I should really find out more about her.

"So, Layken," I say casually. I place my hand on her headrest and glance behind me at all the boxes still in the back of the Jeep. "Tell me about yourself."

She cocks an eyebrow at me, then turns her attention back to the road. "Um, no. That's so cliché."

Her unexpected response makes me laugh under my breath. She's *feisty*. I like that, but it still doesn't answer any of my questions. I glance to her CD player and lean forward. "Fine. I'll figure you out myself," I say as I hit eject. "You know, you can tell a lot about a person by their taste in music." I pull the CD out of the player and hold my breath as I prepare to read it. *Please don't let her be into Nickelback.* I would have to jump out of the car. When I read the handwritten label, I laugh. *"Layken's shit?* Is shit descriptive here, or possessive?"

She snatches the CD out of my hands and inserts it back into the player. "I don't like Kel touching my shit, okay?"

And that's when it happens . . . the most beautiful sound in the world. Sure, the *song* is beautiful. *All* Avett Brothers songs are beautiful. But the sound I'm hearing is the sound of commonality. The sound of similarity. The sound of my favorite band that I've been listening to nonstop for two years . . . coming from her speakers.

What are the chances?

She immediately leans forward and turns down the volume. I unconsciously grab her hand to stop her. "Turn it back up, I know this."

She smirks at me like there isn't a shred of truth to what I just said. "Oh, yeah? What's it called?" she challenges.

"It's the Avett Brothers," I say. She arches her eyebrow and looks at me inquisitively as I explain the song. The fact that she apparently loves this band as much as I do stimulates a feeling deep in the pit of my stomach that I haven't felt in years.

Good lord, I've got butterflies.

She glances down at my hand still clasped on top of hers.

I pull my hand back and run it down my pants, hoping it didn't make her uncomfortable. I'm almost positive she's blushing again, though. That's a good sign. That's a *really* good sign.

The entire rest of the way to the grocery store, she tells me all about her family. She mostly talks about the recent death of her father and her birthday gift from him. She continues talking about her father and everything her family has been through this year. It explains that distant look she gets in her eyes sometimes. I can't help but feel somewhat connected with her, knowing she can relate on some level with what I've been through the last few years. I tense up at the thought of having to tell her about my parents right now.

I can feel the conversation on her end coming to a close, so I point her in the actual direction of the grocery store, hoping it will deflect the parental subject before it becomes my turn to share. When we pull into the parking lot, I'm both relieved *and* anxious. Relieved that I didn't have to explain my situation with Caulder to her, but anxious at the thought that I know the conversation is inevitable. I just don't want to scare her off yet.

"Wow," she says. "Is that the quickest way to the store? That drive took twenty minutes."

I swing the door open and wink at her. "No, actually it's not." I step out of the car, impressed with myself. It's been so long since I've been into a girl, I wasn't sure if I still had any game. She's got to realize I'm flirting with her. I like her. She seems to like me, but she's not as forward as I am, so I'm not sure. I'm definitely not one to play games, so I decide to just go with it. I grab her hand, tell her to run, and pull her faster toward the entrance. I do this partly because we're getting soaked, but mostly because I just wanted an excuse to grab her hand again.

When we get inside she's soaking wet and laughing. It's the first time I've really heard her laugh. I like her laugh.

There's a strand of wet hair stuck to her cheek, so I reach up and wipe it away. As soon as my fingers touch her skin, her eyes lock with mine and she stops laughing.

Damn, those eyes. I continue to stare at her, unable to look away. She's beautiful. *So* damn *beautiful*.

She breaks our stare and clears her throat. Her reaction is somewhat guarded, like I may have made her feel uncomfortable. She hands me the grocery list and grabs a cart. "Does it always snow in September?" she asks.

We just had a seriously intense, slightly awkward moment . . . and she's asking me about the *weather*? I laugh.

"No, it won't last more than a few days, maybe a week. Most of the time the snow doesn't start until late October. You're lucky."

She looks at me. *"Lucky?"*

"Yeah. It's a pretty rare cold front. You got here right in time."

"Huh. I assumed most of y'all would hate the snow. Doesn't it snow here most of the year?"

It's official. The southern accent is my absolute favorite now. *"Y'all?"* I laugh.

"What?" she says defensively.

I shake my head and smile. "Nothing. I've just never heard anyone say 'y'all' in real life before. It's cute. So southern belle."

She laughs at my comment. "Oh, I'm sorry. From now on I'll do like you Yankees and waste my breath by saying 'all you guys.'"

"Don't," I say, nudging her shoulder. "I like your accent, it's perfect."

She blushes again, but doesn't look away. I look down at the grocery list and pretend to read it, but I can't help but notice she's staring at me. *Intensely* staring. Almost like she's trying to figure me out or something.

She eventually turns her head and I steer her in the direction of the foods on her list.

"Lucky Charms?" I say, eyeing her as she grabs three huge boxes of the cereal. "Is that Kel's favorite?"

She grins at me. "No, actually it's mine."

"I'm more of a Rice Krispies fan myself." I take the boxes of cereal from her and throw them into the cart.

"Rice Krispies are boring," she says.

"The hell they are! Rice Krispies make Rice Krispies treats. What can your cereal do?"

"Lucky Charms have shooting star marshmallows in them. You get to make a wish every time you eat one."

"Oh, yeah?" I laugh. "And what are you gonna wish for? You've got three boxes, that's a lot of wishes."

She folds her arms across the handle of the cart and leans forward while she pushes it. She gets that same distant look in her eyes again. "I'd wish I could be back in Texas," she says quietly.

The sadness in her answer makes me want to hug her. I don't know what it is about Michigan that makes her feel this way. I just have an overwhelming need to console her. "What do you miss so much about Texas?"

"Everything," she says. "The lack of snow, the lack of concrete, the lack of people, the lack of . . ." She pauses. "The lack of unfamiliarity."

"Boyfriend?"

I say it without even thinking. It's like I lose my filter when I'm around her. She shoots me a look of confusion, almost as though she doesn't want to misinterpret my question.

"You miss your boyfriend?" I clarify.

She smiles at me, erasing the troubled look that consumed her features just seconds ago. "No boyfriend," she says.

I smile back at her. *Nice.*

I DECIDE TO take her the quick route home. I would have taken her the long way again, just to spend more time with her, but I figure she actually needs to know how to get to the grocery store in the event I can't invite myself along on the next trip. When we pull into her driveway I hop out and make my way around to the rear of the Jeep. When she pops the hood, I pull it open and watch as she gathers her things together. It surprises me how disappointed I am that we're about to part ways again. I hate the thought that once these groceries are unloaded, I'm going to have to go back home. I want to spend more time with her.

When she meets me at the back of the Jeep, she smiles and places her hand over her heart. "Why! I never would have been able to find the store without your help. Thank you so much for your hospitality, kind sir."

Oh.

My.

God.

That is the hottest damn southern impression I've ever heard. And that *smile*. And that nervous *laughter*. Everything she does pierces my heart. It's all I can do to stop myself from grabbing her face and kissing the hell out of her right here and now. Looking down at her, watching her laugh . . . God, I've never wanted to kiss a girl so bad in my entire life.

"*What*?" she says nervously. She can obviously see the internal struggle behind my expression.

Don't do it, Will.

I ignore my better judgment and step forward. Her eyes remain locked on mine as I cup her chin with my free hand. My bold move causes a small gasp to pass between her lips, but she makes no move to pull away. Her skin is soft beneath my fingertips. I bet her lips are even softer.

My eyes scroll over her features, admiring their beautiful simplicity. She doesn't shy away. In fact, she looks a little bit hopeful, like she would welcome my lips on hers.

Don't kiss her. Don't do it. You'll screw this up, Will.

I attempt to silence the voice in my head, but it ultimately wins out. It's way too soon. *And* it's broad daylight. Her mother's home, for Christ's sake! *What am I thinking?*

I slide my hand around to the back of her neck, then kiss her on her forehead, instead. I take a step back and reluctantly drop my hand. I have to remind myself to breathe. Being this close to her is suffocating, but in the best way.

"You're so cute," I say, attempting to make light of the moment. I grab a few sacks out of the back of the Jeep and quickly head to the front door before she comes to her senses and punches me. I can't believe I just kissed her on the forehead! I've only known the girl for two days!

I set the bags down and head back to the Jeep just as her mother makes her way outside.

I feel nothing but relieved over my decision not to kiss her when I realize we would have been interrupted. A humiliating thought.

I reach my hand out to introduce myself. "You must be Layken and Kel's mom. I'm Will Cooper. We live across the street."

She smiles a welcoming smile. She seems nice; not intimidating at all. It's amazing how much Layken looks like her.

"Julia Cohen," she says. "You're Caulder's older brother?"

"Yes, Ma'am. Older by twelve years."

She stares at me for a moment. "So that makes you . . . twenty-one?"

I'm not sure, because it happens so fast, but I could swear she glances behind me and winks at Layken. She returns her focus back in my direction and smiles again.

"Well, I'm glad Kel and Lake were able to make friends so fast," she says.

"Me, too."

Julia releases my hand and turns toward the house, grabbing the sacks in the entryway.

Lake. She calls her *Lake.* I might like that even more than Layken. I reach in and grab the last two sacks out of the back of her Jeep.

"Lake, huh? I like that." I hand her the sacks and shut the back. "*So,* Lake," I say, leaning against her car. I fold my arms across my chest and take a deep breath. This part is always the hardest. The "asking out" part.

"Caulder and I are going to Detroit on Friday. We'll be gone until late Sunday, family stuff," I say. "I was wondering if you had any plans for tomorrow night, before I go?"

She grins at me, then makes a face like she's trying to stifle the grin. I wish she wouldn't do that. Her smile is breathtaking.

"Are you really going to make me admit that I have absolutely no life here?" she says.

That wasn't a no, so I take it as a yes. "Great. It's a date then. I'll pick you up at seven-thirty." I immediately turn and head back to my house before she can object. I didn't officially *ask* her out. In fact, it was more like I just *told* her. But . . . she sure didn't object. That's a good sign. That's a *really* good sign.

4.

the honeymoon

LAKE PULLS HERSELF up onto her elbows and rests her chin in her hands.

"You're really enjoying this," I say.

She's smiling. "I don't think I ever told you, but when you kissed me on the forehead that day it was the best kiss I'd ever had. Up to that point, anyway," she says, falling back against her pillow.

I lean in and replicate the forehead kiss, except this time I don't stop there. I plant tiny pecks all the way down to the tip of her nose, then I pull back. "Mine, too," I say, looking into the eyes that I get to wake up to every morning for the rest of my life. At the risk of sounding cheesy, I've got to be the luckiest man in the world.

"Now I want to know all about our date." She puts her hands behind her head and relaxes, waiting for me to spill it.

I lie back on my pillow and think back to that day. The day that I fell for my wife.

the first date

I HAVEN'T BEEN in this good a mood in over two years. I also haven't been this nervous about a girl in over two years. In fact, I haven't even been on a single *date* in two years. A double load, a full-time job and a child really interfere with the whole dating scene.

There's half an hour left before Caulder and I have to leave for school, so I decide to do a little cleaning since I'll be with Lake tonight. I'm hesitant to take her to Club N9NE on our first date. Slam poetry is so much a part of me; I don't know how I'd take it if she didn't connect with it. Or worse, if she hated it.

Vaughn was never into it. She loved Club N9NE on any other night, just not slam night. Thursdays were usually the one night of the week we didn't spend together. I realize this moment is the first moment Vaughn has even crossed my mind since the moment I met Lake.

"Caulder, go make sure your room's clean. Maya's watching you tonight," I say as he emerges from the hallway. He rolls his eyes and backtracks into the bedroom. "Clean *is* it," he mumbles.

He's been talking backward since he met Kel a few days ago. I just ignore him half the time. It's too much to keep up with.

I take the overloaded bag out of the kitchen trash can and begin to head outside with it, but I pause at the hallway. Something about the picture of Caulder and me with our dad in the front yard catches my eye. I take a step forward and get a closer look. I've never noticed it before this moment, probably because it actually has meaning now . . . but in the background right over my father's shoulder, you can see the gnome with the red hat from across the street. The same gnome Lake fell on and broke. The gnome is staring right at the camera with a smirk on his face, almost like he's posing.

I glance at the rest of the pictures on the wall, recalling the moments they were all captured. I used to hate looking at these pictures. I hated the way it would make me feel and how much I would miss them when I looked into their eyes. It doesn't hurt as much anymore. Now when I look at them, I mostly recall the good memories.

Seeing their pictures brings the realization back to the forefront of my mind that Lake has no idea of the responsibilities I have in my life. I need to tell her tonight. It's better to get it out now, that way if she can't handle it, I won't be too far gone. It'll be a lot easier to be rejected by her tonight, before whatever it is I'm feeling toward her becomes even more intense.

I close the lid to the trash can and pull it to the curb. When I near the end of the driveway, I see the back door to Lake's Jeep is open. She's leaning all the way across the seat, searching for something. When she finds what she's looking for, she climbs out of the backseat with a coffeepot in her hands. She's still wearing pajamas and her hair is piled on top of her head in a knot.

"That's not a good idea," I say, heading across the street toward her.

She jumps when she hears my voice, then spins around to face me and grins. "What am I doing wrong *this* time?" She shuts the door to the Jeep and walks toward me.

I point to the coffeepot. "If you drink too much coffee this early in the morning, you'll crash after lunch. Then you'll be too exhausted to go out with your hot date tonight."

She laughs. Her smile is fleeting, though. She looks down at her pajamas, then runs her hands over her hair with a slight look of panic in her eyes. She's silently freaking out about the way she looks, so I ease her mind. "You look great," I assure her. "Bed hair looks really good on you."

She smiles, then leans against her car. "I know," she says confidently, looking down at her pajamas. "This is what I'm wearing on our date tonight. You like?"

I slowly look her up and down, then shake my head no. "Not really," I say, eyeing her boots. "I'd prefer it if you wore the house shoes."

She laughs. "I'll do that, then. Seven-thirty, right?"

I nod and smile back at her. We're about four feet apart, but the way her eyes are piercing into mine makes it feel like she's just inches away. She smiles at me with an unfamiliar sparkle in her eye. Unlike the last two days, she actually looks *happy* right now.

We continue to stare at each other, neither of us speaking . . . or walking away. There's a long silence, but it's not awkward. The way she's watching me this time seems more confident. More at ease.

More hopeful.

I decide to give in before the awkwardness *does* set in, so I take a couple of steps backward toward my house. "I have to get to work," I say. "I'll see you tonight."

She lifts her hand and waves good-bye before turning toward her house. Not just a normal back-and-forth wave, either. It's a fingers up and down *flirty* wave.

Wow. Who knew a simple wave could be so damn *hot*?

"Lake?"

She glances back at me, the corners of her mouth hinting at a smile. "Yeah?"

I point to her pajamas. "I really am digging this unwashed,

straight-out-of-bed look. Just make sure you brush your teeth before I pick you up tonight, because I'm gonna kiss you." I wink at her and turn back toward my house before she can respond.

"GOOD MORNING, MRS. Alex," I say, careful not to sound too friendly. I have to watch every word that comes out of my mouth around this woman; she takes it all the wrong way. The *inappropriate* way. I walk past her desk and into the mailroom, then grab the contents from inside my box. When I exit the mailroom, she's already rushing toward me.

"Did you get my note? I left you a sticky note." She glances down at the stack of papers I'm holding.

I look at the papers in my hands and shrug. "I don't know yet. I just checked my box five seconds ago."

Mrs. Alex isn't known for her kind demeanor, except toward *me*. Her obvious favoritism has become a running joke among the staff. A joke that I'm the butt of. She's at least twenty years older than me, not to mention married. However, it doesn't stop her from blatantly displaying her affection, which is why I only come to the mailroom once a week now.

"Well, I wrote you a message. Your faculty advisor called and needs to schedule a meeting with you." She grabs the stack of papers out of my hands and spreads them out on her desk, looking for the note she wrote. "He said he needs to do your quarterly observation. I swear I put it right on top."

I reach forward and swipe the contents of my mailbox back into a stack. "Thank you. I'm running late, so I'll look through it later. I'll let you know if I don't find it."

She smiles and waves good-bye as I back away from her.

Oh, shit. It was a *flirty* wave. I've got to quit coming in here.

"Have a great day," I say, turning to leave as fast as I can. I'm relieved when the door to the administration office closes behind me. I'm really going to have to get someone else to check my mail from now on.

"You really need to stop leading her on like that," Gavin says. I look up and he's staring through the window at Mrs. Alex.

I roll my eyes. "Nothing has changed since high school, Gavin. It's even worse now that I'm a teacher here."

Gavin looks past me and waves at Mrs. Alex through the window and smiles at her. "She's still watching you. Maybe you should flex your muscles; give her a little gun show. Or at least give her a nice view while you're walking away."

The thought of Mrs. Alex admiring me from behind makes me a little too uncomfortable, so I change the subject and walk toward my first-period class. "You and Eddie going to Club N9NE tonight? I haven't seen you guys there in a couple of weeks."

"Maybe. Why? You doing one?"

I shake my head. "No, not tonight," I say. "We'll be there a little after eight, though. My sitter isn't available until seven-thirty, so we'll probably miss the sac."

He stops in his tracks just as we reach my classroom door. "*We?* Who's we? Does Will Cooper have a *date?*" He cocks an eyebrow and waits for my reply.

I don't usually hang out with students outside of work, but Gavin and Eddie have been showing up at Club N9NE every now and then for a few months. We sometimes sit together, so I've gotten to know them pretty well. When you're teaching at twenty-one years old, it's sort of difficult to completely cut off socialization with people who are practically your age.

"So? Who is she?" he says. "Who's the elusive girl that may just be the end to Will Cooper's dry spell?"

I open the door to the classroom and lose the smile as I switch on teacher-mode. "Get to class, Gavin."

He laughs and salutes me, then heads down the hallway.

"THANKS AGAIN, MAYA," I say as I head through the living room. "There's cash on the table. I ordered pizza about fifteen minutes ago." I grab my keys and shove my wallet into my pocket. "He's been talking backward a lot so just ignore it. He'll talk frontward if he has anything important to say."

"You paying me double?" she says, falling onto the sofa with the remote in hand. "I didn't agree to watch that other kid."

"He's just the neighbor," I say. "He'll go home soon. If he doesn't, then yeah . . . I guess I'll pay you extra." I've turned to head outside when the boys make their way back into the house. Kel stops in the doorway and puts his hands on his hips, looking up at me.

"Are you my sister's boyfriend?"

I'm thrown off by his directness. "Um, no. Just her friend."

"She told my mom you were taking her on a date. I thought only boyfriends took girls on dates."

"Well," I pause. "Sometimes boys take girls on dates to see if they *want* them to be their girlfriend."

I notice Caulder standing beside me, taking in the conversation as if he's just as curious. I wasn't prepared to have to explain the rules of dating right now.

"So it's like a test?" Caulder asks. "To see if you want Layken to be your girlfriend?"

I shrug and nod. "Yeah, I guess you could say that."

Kel laughs. "You aren't gonna like her. She burps a lot. And she's bossy. And she never lets me drink coffee, so she probably won't let you have any either. And she has really bad taste in music and sings way too loud and leaves her bras all over the house. It's gross."

I laugh. "Thanks for the warning. You think it's too late to back out now?"

Kel shakes his head, missing my sarcasm completely. "No, she's already dressed so you have to take her now."

I sigh, pretending to be annoyed. "Well, it's just a few hours. Hopefully she won't burp a lot and boss me around and steal my coffee and sing to her really bad music and leave her bra in my car."

Or hopefully she *will*.

Kel walks past me into the house. "Good luck," he says, his voice full of pity. I laugh and shut the door behind me. I'm halfway to my car when Lake opens her front door and walks to the driveway.

"You ready?" I yell to her.

"Yes," she yells back.

I wait for her to walk to my car, but she doesn't. She *looks* ready. Why is she just standing there?

"Well, come on then!" I yell.

She still doesn't move. She folds her arms across her chest and stands still. I throw my hand up in defeat and laugh. "What are you doing?"

"You said you would pick me up at seven-thirty," she yells. "I'm waiting for you to pick me up."

I grin and get in the car, then back up into her driveway. When I get out and open her door, I notice she's not wearing the house shoes. I was sort of hoping she was serious this morning. It's not quite dark yet, which is unfortunate since I can't stop staring at her. She curled her hair and put on just a touch of makeup. She's wearing jeans and a purple shirt that brings out the hue of her eyes, making them even harder to look away from. She looks . . . *perfect*.

Once we're both in the car, I reach behind me and grab the bag out of the backseat. "We don't have time to eat, so I made us grilled cheese." I hand her the sandwich and a drink. I'm hoping she's not too upset that we aren't going out to eat. We just don't have time. I almost went to her house earlier to let her know we weren't, in case she didn't eat, but I decided to throw something together at the last minute instead. I sort of wanted to see how she'd react to not being taken on a typical date. Maybe it's a little mean, but she's smiling, so she doesn't seem to mind.

"Wow. This is a first." She puts her sandwich on her knee and twists open her soda. "And where exactly are we going in such a hurry? It's obviously not a restaurant."

I take a bite of my sandwich and pull out of her driveway. "It's a surprise. I know a lot more about you than you know about me, so tonight I want to show you what *I'm* all about."

She grins at me. "Well, I'm intrigued," she says before she takes a bite of her sandwich.

I'm relieved she doesn't press me further about where we're going. It would be sort of hard to explain that I'm taking her to a club on a Thursday night to watch a bunch of people recite poetry. It doesn't sound near as appealing as it actually *is*. I'd rather let her experience it for the first time in person without having preconceived notions.

When we finish our sandwiches, she puts the trash in the

backseat and shifts in her seat so that she's facing me. She casually rests her head against the headrest. "What are your parents like?"

I glance out my window, not wanting her to see the reluctance in my expression. It's the exact thing I was hoping she wouldn't ask about until the drive home, at least. I'd hate for this to be the first thing we talk about. It would put a somber mood on the whole night. I take a deep breath and exhale, hoping I'm not appearing as uncomfortable on the outside as I'm feeling on the inside.

How the hell can I redirect this conversation?

I decide to play the game Caulder and I play sometimes on the drive to our grandparents. I hope she won't think it's too cheesy, but it'll pass the time and may even help me get to know her better.

"I'm not big on small talk, Lake. We can figure all that out later. Let's make this drive interesting." I adjust myself in the seat and prepare to explain the rules to her. When I turn to look at her, she's staring at me with a repulsed look on her face.

What the hell did I say? I replay my last sentence in my head and realize how it sounded. I laugh when it dawns on me that she completely misconstrued what I just said. "Lake, no! I just meant let's talk about something besides what we're *expected* to talk about."

She expels a breath and laughs. "Good," she says.

"I know a game we can play. It's called, '*would you rather.*' Have you played it before?"

She shakes her head. "No, but I would *rather* you go first."

I feel like if I use some of the ones Caulder and I have used it would be cheating, so I take a few seconds to think of a new one. "Okay," I say when I come up with one. I clear my throat. "Okay, would you rather spend the *rest* of your life with *no* arms; or would you rather spend the rest of your life with arms you couldn't *control*?"

I remember when Caulder and I tried to get Vaughn to play this game on our way to Detroit once; she rolled her eyes and told us to grow up. I watch Lake, hoping for a different reaction, and she just stares at me straight-faced like she's actually contemplating an answer.

"Well," she says. "I guess I would rather spend the rest of my life with arms I couldn't control?"

"What? Seriously?" I laugh, glancing over at her. "But you wouldn't be controlling them! They could be flailing around and you'd be constantly punching yourself in the face! Or worse, you might grab a knife and stab yourself!"

She laughs. *Damn, I love that laugh.*

"I didn't realize there were right and wrong answers," she says.

"You suck at this. Your turn."

She smiles at me, then furrows her brows, facing forward and leaning back into her seat. "Okay, let me think."

"You have to have one ready!"

"Jeez, Will! I heard of this game for the first time thirty barely seconds ago. Give me a second to think of one."

I reach over and squeeze her hand. "I'm teasing."

It wasn't my intention to keep holding on to her hand, but for some reason it feels right, so I don't let go. It's so natural, like we didn't even contemplate the move. I'm still staring at our interlocked fingers when she continues with her turn, unfazed. I like how much she seems to be enjoying the game. I like how she seemed to prefer the grilled cheese sandwiches to a restaurant. I like girls who don't mind the simple things every now and then. I like that we're holding hands.

We play a few more rounds and the bizarre things she comes up with could give Caulder a run for his money. The half-hour drive to the club seems like it takes five minutes. I decide to ask one final question as we're pulling into the parking lot. I pull into a space and reach over with my left hand to kill the engine so that I don't have to move my right hand from hers. I glance over at her. "Last one," I say. "Would you rather be back in Texas right now? Or here?"

She looks down at our fingers that are interlocked and grazes her thumb across my hand. Her reaction to my question isn't a negative one. In fact, it almost seems just the opposite when her lips crack a smile and she looks back up. Just when she opens her mouth to respond, her attention is pulled to the sign on the building behind me and her smile fades.

"Uh, Will?" she says hesitantly. "I don't dance." She pulls her hand from mine and begins to open her door, so I do the same.

"Uh, neither do *I*."

We both exit the vehicle, but the fact that she didn't answer that last question isn't lost on me. I grab her hand when we meet at the front of the car and I lead her inside. When we walk through the doors I make a quick scan of the room. I know a lot of the regulars here and I'm hoping I can at least find a secluded area in order for us to have some privacy. I spot an empty booth in the back of the room and lead her in that direction. I want her to be able to get the full experience without the constant interruption of conversation from other people.

"It's quieter back here," I say. She's looking around with curiosity in her eyes. She asks about the younger audience when she notices pretty quickly that this isn't a regular club-going crowd. She's observant.

"Well, tonight it's not a club," I say. She scoots into the booth first and I slide in right next to her. "It's slam night. Every Thursday they shut the club down and people come here to compete in the slam."

She breaks her gaze from the table of kids and looks at me, the curiosity still present in her eyes. "And what's a slam?"

I pause for a second and smile at her. "It's poetry," I say. "It's what I'm all about." I wait for the laughter, but it doesn't come. She looks directly at me, almost like she didn't understand what I said.

I start to repeat myself when she interrupts. "Poetry, huh?" She continues to smile at me, but in a very endearing way. Almost like she's impressed. "Do people write their own or do they get it from other authors?"

I lean back in my seat and look at the stage. "People get up there and pour their hearts out just using their words and the movement of their bodies. It's amazing. You aren't going to hear any Dickinson or Frost here."

When I look at her again, she actually looks intrigued. Poetry has always been such a huge part of my life; I was worried she wouldn't understand it. Not only does she understand it, she seems *excited* about it.

I explain the rules to her regarding the competition. She asks a lot of questions, which puts me even more at ease. When I've explained everything to her, I decide to grab us drinks before the sac comes on stage.

"You want something to drink?"

"Sure," she says. "I'll take some chocolate milk."

I expect her to laugh at her joke, but she doesn't.

"Chocolate milk? Really?"

"With ice," she says, matter-of-fact.

"Okay. One chocolate milk on the rocks coming right up."

I exit the booth and walk over to the bar to order our drinks, then turn around and lean against the bar and watch her. This feeling I get when I'm with her . . . I've missed it. I've missed that feeling of *feeling*. Somehow, she's the first person in the last two years of my life who gives me any sense of hope about the future.

I realize as I'm watching her that I've made a huge mistake. I've been comparing what her reaction to things might be based on what Vaughn's reactions were in the past. It's not fair to Lake to assume she would be turned off by the simplicity of the date or by the game we played on the drive here. It's not fair to Lake that I assume she wouldn't like poetry simply because Vaughn didn't. It's also unfair of me to assume she would push me away if she knew that I was Caulder's guardian.

This girl isn't anything *like* Vaughn.

This girl isn't anything like *any* girl I've known. This girl is . . .

"She's cute." Gavin's voice jerks me out of my thoughts. I look over at him and he's leaning against the bar next to me, watching me watch Lake. "What's her name?" He turns around and orders two drinks from the waitress.

"Layken," I say. "And yeah. She *is* cute."

"How long have you guys been dating?" he asks, turning back to me.

I look down at my watch. "Going on forty-five minutes."

He laughs. "*Shit*. The way you were looking at her I would have guessed a hell of a lot longer. Where'd you meet her?"

The bartender hands me my change and the receipt for our drinks. I glance down at the receipt and laugh. It actually says, "*Chocolate milk—rocks*." I fold the receipt and put it in my wallet.

"Actually," I say as I turn back to Gavin, "she's my new neighbor. Just moved in three days ago."

He shakes his head and looks back in her direction. "You better hope it works out. That could get really awkward, you know."

I nod. "Yeah, I guess so. But I have a good feeling about her."

Before he walks away he points to the front of the room. "Eddie and I are over there. I'll try to keep her occupied so you two can have your privacy. If she sees you here with a girl, she'll be over there in a second trying to be her new best friend."

I laugh, because he's right. "Thanks." I grab our drinks and head back to the booth, relieved that I won't have to deal with introductions tonight. I don't know if I'm ready for that.

5.

the honeymoon

LAKE SITS UP on the bed and glares at me. "What the *hell*, Will? Gavin knew? He's known this whole time?"

I laugh. "Hey, you and Eddie weren't the only ones keeping secrets."

She shakes her head in disbelief. "Does Eddie know he knew?"

"I don't think so. Unlike some people, Gavin can keep a secret."

She narrows her eyes and rolls back onto her pillow, dumbfounded. "I can't believe he knew," she says. "What did he say when I showed up in your poetry class?"

"Well, I could go ahead and tell you all about that day, but that would mean I would be skipping over our first kiss. You don't want to hear about the rest of our date?"

She grins. "You know I do."

falling

"WHAT'S THE SAC?" she says when I return with the drinks.

"Sacrifice. It's what they use to prepare the judges." I slide back into the booth but make it a point to scoot in closer this time. "Someone performs something that isn't part of the competition so the judges can calibrate their scoring."

"So they can call on anyone? What if they had called on me?" she asks. She looks terrified at the thought.

"Well, I guess you should have had something ready," I tease.

She laughs, then puts one of her elbows on the table, turning toward me. She runs her hand through her hair, sending a slight scent of vanilla in my direction. She watches me for a moment, her smile spreading up to her eyes. I love this peaceful look about her right now.

We're sitting so close together I can feel the heat of her body against mine, parts of us touching. Our thighs, her hip against mine, our hands just inches apart. Her gaze shifts from my eyes down to my lips and, for the first time tonight, I feel the *first kiss* pressure. There's something about her lips that makes me want to kiss them when she's in such close proximity. I remind myself that even though I'm just "Will" tonight, I've got at least one student who is more than likely intermittently spying on us.

The quiet moment between us causes her to blush and she looks back to the stage, almost as if she could sense that I was struggling with the desire to kiss her. I reach over and take her hand in mine and bring it under the table, placing it on my leg. I look down at it as I slowly stroke her fingers. I stroke up her wrist and want so bad to keep trailing up her arm, straight to her lips . . . but I don't. I circle back down to her fingertips, wishing more than anything that we weren't in public right now. I don't know what it is about her that completely enthralls me. I also don't know what it is with her that gets me to spout things I would normally be more reserved about.

"Lake?" I continue tracing up and over her hand with my fingertips. "I don't know what it is about you . . . but I like you." I interlock her fingers with mine and turn my attention toward the stage so she doesn't think I expect a response from her. I smile when I see her grab for her glass and quickly down her chocolate milk. She definitely feels it, too.

When the sac walks up to the stage, Lake's whole demeanor changes. It's almost as if she forgets I'm even here. She leans forward attentively when the woman begins her piece and she doesn't remove her attention from the performer the entire time. I'm so drawn to the emotion in Lake's expression that I can't take my eyes off *her*. As I watch her, I attempt to decipher the reason behind the intense connection I feel with her. It's not like we've spent that much time together. Hell, I hardly even know her. I still don't even know what her major is, what her middle name is, much less her birthday. Deep down, I know none of it matters. The only thing that matters right now is this moment, and this moment is definitely my sweet for the day.

As soon as the sac is finished with her poem, Lake pulls her hand from mine and wipes tears from her eyes. I put my arm around her and pull her to me. She accepts my embrace and rests her head against my shoulder.

"Well?" I ask. I rest my chin on top of her head and stroke her hair, taking in another wave of vanilla. I'm beginning to love the smell of vanilla almost as much as southern accents.

"That was unbelievable," she whispers.

Unbelievable. That was the exact word I used to describe it to my father the first time I saw it.

I fight the urge to lift her chin and pull her lips to mine, knowing I should wait until we're in private. The need is so overwhelming, though; my heart is at war with my conscience. I lean forward and press my lips against her forehead and close my eyes. It'll have to do for now.

We sit in the same embrace as several more poets perform. She laughs, she cries, she sighs, she aches, and she *feels* every single piece performed. By the time the final poet for round one comes onto the stage, it's obvious that it's too late. I was hoping to put everything out in the open between us before things became more serious. Little did I know it would happen this fast. I'm too far gone. There's no way I can stop myself from falling for this girl now.

I keep my attention on the stage, but I can't help but watch Lake out of the corner of my eye as she watches the performer prepare at the microphone. She's holding her breath again as he steps up to the microphone.

"This poem is called *A Very Long Poem*," the performer says. Lake laughs and leans forward in her seat.

> This poem is very long
> So long, in fact, that your attention span
> May be stretched to its very limits
> But that's okay
> It's what's so special about poetry
> See, poetry takes time
> We live in a time

Call it our culture or society
It doesn't matter to me 'cause neither one rhymes
A time where most people don't want to listen
Our throats wait like matchsticks waiting to catch fire
Waiting until we can speak
No patience to listen
But this poem is long
It's so long, in fact, that during the time of this poem
You could've done any number of other wonderful
things
You could've called your father
Call your father
You could be writing a postcard right now
Write a postcard
When was the last time you wrote a postcard?
You could be outside
You're probably not too far away from a sunrise or a
sunset
Watch the sun rise
Maybe you could've written your own poem
A better poem
You could have played a tune or sung a song
You could have met your neighbor
And memorized their name
Memorize the name of your neighbor
You could've drawn a picture (or, at least, colored one in)
You could've started a book
Or finished a prayer
You could've talked to God
Pray

When was the last time you prayed?

Really prayed?

This is a long poem

So long, in fact, that you've already spent a minute

with it

When was the last time you hugged a friend for a

minute?

Or told them that you love them?

Tell your friends you love them

. . . no, I mean it,

tell them

Say, *I love you*

Say, *you make life worth living*

Because that is what friends do

Of all of the wonderful things that you could've done

During this very, very long poem

You could have connected

Maybe you are connecting

Maybe we're connecting

See, I believe that the only things that really matter

In the grand scheme of life are

God and people

And if people are made in the image of God

Then when you spend your time with people

It's never wasted

And in this very long poem

I'm trying to let a poem do what a poem does:

Make things simpler

We don't need poems to make things more

complicated

We have each other for that
We need poems to remind ourselves of the things that
really matter
To take time
A long time
To be alive for the sake of someone else for a single
moment
Or for many moments
'Cause we need each other
To hold the hands of a broken person
All you have to do is meet a person
Shake their hand
Look in their eyes
They are you
We are all broken together
But these shattered pieces of our existence don't have
to be a mess
We just have to care enough to hold our tongues
sometimes
To sit and listen to a very long poem
A story of a life
The joy of a friend and the grief of a friend
To hold and be held
And be quiet
So, *pray*
Write a postcard
Call your parents and forgive them and then thank
them
Turn off the TV
Create art as best as you can

Share as much as possible, especially money
Tell someone about a very long poem you once heard
And how afterward it brought you to them

SHE WIPES ANOTHER tear from her eye when the performer steps away from the microphone. She begins clapping with the rest of the crowd, completely engrossed in the atmosphere. When she finally relaxes against me again, I take her hand in mine. We've been here close to two hours now and I'm sure she's tired, based on the week she's had. Besides, I never stay for all of the performances, since I have work on Fridays.

I begin to stand up to lead her out of the booth when the emcee makes one last appeal for performers. She turns to me and I can see her thoughts written clearly across her face.

"Will, you can't bring me here and not perform. Please do one? Please, please, please?"

I had no intention of doing a poem tonight. *At all.* But oh, my God—that look in her eyes. She's really going to make me do this, I can already tell. There's no *way* I can say no to those eyes. I lean my head against the back of the booth and laugh. "You're killing me, Lake. Like I said, I don't really have anything new."

"Do something old then," she suggests. "Or do all these people make you *nervous?*"

She has no idea how often I perform and how natural it feels to me now. It's almost as natural as breathing. I haven't been nervous about taking the stage since the first time I took it five years ago.

Until now, anyway.

I lean in closer and look her directly in the eyes. "Not all of them. Just *one* of them."

Our faces are so incredibly close right now; it would be so easy to do it. Just a couple more inches and I could taste her. Her smile fades and she bites her bottom lip as her gaze slowly drops to my mouth again. I can tell by the look in her eyes that she wants me to kiss her just as much. The unfamiliar nerves that have occupied my stomach have now multiplied and I'm quickly losing my self-control. As soon as I start to lean in, she clasps her hands under her chin and resumes her plea.

"Don't make me beg."

For a moment, I had forgotten she even asked me to perform. I pull back and laugh. "You already *are*."

She doesn't pull her hands away from her chin and she's looking up at me with the most adorable expression. An expression I already know I'll never be able to say no to. "All right, all right," I say, easily giving in. "But I'm warning you, you asked."

I pull my wallet out of my pocket and take the money out, holding it up in the air. "I'm in!"

When the emcee recognizes me, I slide out of the booth and begin making my way to the stage. I'm not prepared for this at all. Why did I not think she would ask me to perform? I should have written something new. I'll just do my "go-to" piece about teaching. It's easy enough. Besides, I don't even think I've discussed my profession with her; this might be a fun way to do it.

I reach the stage and adjust the microphone, then look out over the audience. When we lock eyes, she perches her elbows on the table and rests her chin in her hands. She waves her flirty wave at me as her smile spreads across her face. The way she looks at me sends a pang of guilt straight to my heart. She's looking at me right now in the same way that I've been looking at her.

With *hope*.

It hits me with that look that I shouldn't waste this opportunity on a poem about my profession. This is my opportunity to put it all out there . . . to use my performance as a way to let her know who I really am. If her feelings for me are half what mine already are for her, then she deserves to know what she may be getting herself into.

"What's the name of your piece tonight, Will?"

Without breaking our gaze, I look straight into her eyes from up on the stage and reply, *"Death."*

The emcee exits the stage and I take a deep breath, preparing to say the words that will either make or break the possibility of a future with her.

Death. The only thing inevitable in life.
People don't like to *talk* about death because
it makes them *sad.*
They don't want to *imagine* how life will go on
without them,
all the people they love will briefly grieve
but continue to *breathe.*
They don't *want* to imagine how life will go on
without *them,*
Their children will still *grow*
Get married
Get *old* . . .
They don't want to *imagine* how life will *continue* to
go on without them,
Their material things will be *sold*
Their medical files stamped *"closed"*
Their name becoming a *memory* to everyone they *know.*

They don't *want* to *imagine* how life will go on
without them, so *instead* of accepting it *head-on*, they
avoid the subject *altogether*,
hoping and *praying* it will *somehow* . . .
pass them by.
Forget about them,
moving on to the *next* one in line.
No, they didn't *want* to imagine how life would
continue to go on . . .
without them.
But death
didn't
forget.
Instead they were met *head-on* by death,
disguised as an *eighteen-wheeler*
behind a cloud of *fog.*
No.
Death didn't *forget* about *them.*
If they *only* had been *prepared*, *accepted* the
inevitable, laid out their *plans*, understood that it
wasn't just *their* lives at hand.
I may have legally been considered an adult at the age
of nineteen, but I still felt very much
all
of just nineteen.
Unprepared
and *overwhelmed*
to suddenly have the *entire life* of a seven-year-old
In my *realm.*
Death. The only thing inevitable in *life.*

• • •

I TAKE A step away from the microphone, feeling even more nervous than when I began. I completely laid it all out there. My whole life, condensed into a one-minute poem.

When I step off the stage and make my way to our booth, she's wiping tears from her eyes with the back of her hand. I'm not sure what she's thinking, so I walk slowly in order to give her a moment to absorb my words.

When I slide into the booth she looks sad, so I smile at her and try to break the tension. "I warned you," I say as I reach for my drink. She doesn't respond, so I'm not sure what to say at this point. I become uncomfortable, thinking maybe this wasn't the best way to go about telling her my life story. I guess I sort of put *her* on the spot, too. I certainly hope she doesn't feel like she has to tell me how sorry she feels for me. I hate pity more than anything.

Just when I start to regret my choice in performance, she reaches out and takes my free hand in hers. She touches me so gently—it's like she's telling me what she's thinking without even speaking. I set my drink down on the table and turn to face her. When I look into her eyes, it's not pity I see at all.

She's still looking at me with hope in her eyes.

This girl just became privy to everything I've been scared to tell her about my life. The death of my parents, the anger I held toward them, the amount of responsibility I now face, the fact that I'm all Caulder has—and she's still looking at me with hope in her tear-filled eyes. I reach to her face and wipe away a tear, then lightly trace my thumb across the wet trail running down her cheek. She places her hand on top of mine and slowly pulls it to her mouth. She presses her lips into the center of my palm without breaking her gaze from mine, causing my heart to catch in my throat. She just somehow managed to convey every single thought and emotion she's feeling through this one simple gesture.

I suddenly don't care where we are or who might be watching us. I have to kiss her. I *have* to.

I take her face in my hands and lean in closer, ignoring the part of my conscience that is screaming for me to wait. She closes her eyes, inviting me in. I hesitate, but as soon as I feel her breath fall on my lips, I can't hold back. I close the gap between us, lightly pressing my lips against her bottom lip. It's even softer than it looks. Somehow the background noise has completely faded and all I can hear is the sound of my own heartbeat, pulsating throughout my entire body. I slowly move my lips up to her top lip, but as soon as I feel her mouth begin to part, I reluctantly pull away. As much as I want to kiss her with everything I've got, I'm also vaguely aware that we're in public, and I've got at least two students here tonight. I decide to save the better kiss for later, because if we do this right now, I know I won't want to stop.

"Patience," I whisper, mustering up all the self-control I've got. I stroke her cheek with my thumb and she smiles at me in understanding. Still holding her face in my hands, I close my eyes again and press my lips against her cheek. She sucks in a breath as I release my hold and slide my hands down her arms, trying to remember how to breathe again. I'm unable to pull away from her, so I press my forehead against hers and open my eyes. It's in this moment that I know she's feeling exactly what I'm feeling. I can see it in her eyes.

"Wow," she exhales.

"Yeah," I agree. "Wow."

We hold each other's stare for a few more seconds. When

the emcee begins announcing the qualifiers for round two I'm quickly brought back to reality. There is no way I can sit here any longer without pulling her onto my lap and kissing the hell out of her. I figure in order to avoid that, my best course of action would be to just leave.

"Let's go," I whisper. I take her hand as we slide out of the booth and I lead her to the exit.

"You don't want to stay?" she says after we walk outside.

"Lake, you've been moving and unpacking for days. You need sleep."

As soon as I say it, she yawns. "Sleep does sound good."

When we reach the car I open the door for her, but before she gets in, I wrap my arms around her and pull her to me. It's a movement that occurs so quickly, I don't even think about it beforehand. Why does she have that effect on me? It's like my conscience just goes out the window when she's around.

As much as I know I should let go before it gets awkward, I can't. She returns my embrace, then rests her head against my chest and sighs. We stand there, neither one of us speaking or moving, for several minutes. There's not a single kiss passed between us, not a single graze of my hand across her skin, not a single word spoken . . . yet somehow, this is the most intimate moment I've ever shared with anyone.

Ever.

I don't want to let go, but as soon as I look up and see Gavin and Eddie exiting the club, I pull back and motion for her to climb inside. Now is not the time for an Eddie introduction.

As we're pulling out of the parking lot, she leans her head against the window and sighs.

"Will? Thank you for this."

I reach over and take her hand in mine. All I really want to do is thank *her*, but I don't respond. I had a lot of hope for tonight, but she far exceeded my expectations. She's exhausted and I can tell she's about to fall asleep. She closes her eyes and I drive home in silence and let her sleep.

When I pull into her driveway, I expect her to wake up, but she doesn't. I kill the engine and reach over to shake her awake, but the peacefulness in her features stops me. I watch her sleep as I try to sift through everything I've been feeling. How can I possibly feel like I care about someone after only knowing her a matter of days?

I loved Vaughn, but I can honestly say we never connected this way. On this sort of emotional level, anyway. I can't remember feeling this way since . . . well, *ever*. It's new. It's scary. It's exciting. It's nerve-racking. It's calming. It's every single emotion I've ever felt balled up into an intense urge to grab hold of her and never let go.

I lean closer and press my lips against her forehead while she sleeps. "Thank *you* for this," I whisper.

When I walk around and open her door, she wakes up. I help her out of the car and we're both silent as we make our way to her front door, hand in hand. Before she goes inside, I pull her to me again. She rests her head against my chest and we resume the same embrace from outside the club. I can't help but wonder if this feels as natural to her as it does to me.

"Just think," she says. "You'll be gone three whole days. That's the same length of time I've known you."

I laugh and squeeze her tighter. "This will be the longest three days of my life." We continue to hold on to each other, neither of us wanting to let go, because maybe we realize it really *will* be the longest three days of our lives.

I notice her glance toward the window like she's worried someone's watching us. As much as I want to give in to the insatiable need I have to kiss her, I give her a quick peck on the cheek, instead. I release her and slowly walk back to my car. When her fingers release from mine, her arm drops to her side and she smiles a smile that quickly causes me to regret not kissing her better. As soon as I'm in my car, I conclude that there is absolutely no way I'll be able to sleep tonight if I don't rectify this.

I roll down my window. "Lake, I've got a pretty long drive home. How about one for the road?"

She laughs, then walks to my car and leans through the window. I slip my hand behind her head and pull her to me. The second our lips meet, I'm a goner. She parts her lips and at first, our kiss is slow and sweet. She reaches through the window and runs her hands through my hair, pulling me closer, and it completely drives me insane. My mouth becomes more urgent against hers and for a brief second, I contemplate canceling my trip this weekend. Now that I've finally tasted her, I know I won't be able to go three days without it. Her lips are everything I've been imagining they would be. The door between us is pure torture. I want to pull her through the window and onto my lap.

We continue kissing until we get to a point where we both realize that either she needs to climb inside the car with me, or we need to come to a halt. We simultaneously slow down and eventually stop, but neither of us pulls away.

"Damn," I whisper against her lips. "It gets better every time."

She smiles and nods in agreement. "I'll see you in three days. You be careful driving home tonight." She presses her lips against mine again, then pulls away.

I regretfully back out of the driveway and into my own, wishing more than anything I wasn't about to leave town for the next three days. When I exit my car she's making her way back up her driveway. I watch as she gathers her hair and pulls it up in a knot, securing it with a band while she nears her front door. Her hair looks good like that. It looked great down, too. As I'm admiring the view, it dawns on me that I never even complimented her on how great she looked tonight.

"Lake!" I yell. She turns around and I jog back across the street to her. "I forgot to tell you something." I wrap my arms around her and whisper into her hair, "You look beautiful tonight." I kiss her on top of the head, then release her and walk back to my house. When I reach my door, I turn around and she's still standing in the same spot watching me. I smile at her and go inside, then immediately head straight for the window. When I pull back the curtain, I see her twirl back toward her house and practically skip inside.

"What are you looking at?" Maya says.

Her voice startles me and I snatch the curtain shut and turn around. "Nothing." I take my jacket off and step on the heel of my shoe to ease my foot out of it. "Thanks, Maya. You want to watch him again next Thursday?"

She stands up and heads to the front door. "Don't I always?" she says. "But I'm not watching that weird one again." She shuts the door behind her and I throw myself on the couch and sigh. This was by far the best date I've ever been on, and I have a feeling they're only going to get better.

6.

the honeymoon

LAKE SMILES, THINKING back on how blissfully happy we both were after that date. "I had never had a night like that in my life," she says. "Everything about it was perfect, from beginning to end. Even the grilled cheese."

"Everything except the fact that I failed to mention my occupation."

She frowns. "Well, yeah. That part sucked."

I laugh. "Sucked is an understatement for how I felt in that hallway," I say. "But, we got through it. As tough as it was, look at us now."

"Wait," she says, pressing her fingers to my lips. "Don't jump ahead. Start from where you left off. I want to know what you were thinking when you saw me in the hallway that day. My god, you were so pissed at me," she says.

"*Pissed* at you? Lake, you thought I was mad at *you*?"

She shrugs.

"*No*, babe. I was *anything* but pissed at you."

oh, shit

MY THREE-DAY WEEKEND. What can I say about my three-day weekend other than it was the longest, most treacherous three days of my entire life. I was distracted the entire time thinking about her. I could have kicked myself for not getting her phone number before I left; at least we could have texted. My grandfather apparently noticed the difference in my attention span during the course of the visit. Before we left their house last night, he pulled me aside and said, "So? Who is she?"

Of course I played dumb and denied having met someone. What would he think if he knew I went on one date with this girl, and she already had me in a stupor? He laughed when I denied it and he squeezed my shoulder. "Can't wait to meet her," he said.

I usually dread Monday mornings, but there's a different air about today. Probably because I know I'll get to see her after work today. I slide the note under the windshield wiper of her Jeep, then head back across the street to my car. As soon as I place my fingers on the door handle, I have second thoughts. I'm being way too forward. Who says, "I can't wait to see you" in a note after one date? The last thing I want to do is scare her off. I walk back to her Jeep and lift the wiper blade to remove the note from her windshield.

"Leave it."

I spin around and Julia is standing in their entryway, holding a cup of coffee between her hands. I look down at the note, then back at the Jeep, then back at Julia, not really knowing what to say.

"You should leave it," she says, pointing to the note in my hand. "She'll like it." She smiles and heads back into the house, leaving me completely and utterly embarrassed in her driveway. I place the note back under the windshield wiper and make my way back across the street, hoping Julia is right.

"I TOLD YOU last week he was coming," Mrs. Alex says in a defensive tone of voice.

"No, you said he *called* about coming. You never told me it was today."

She turns to her computer and begins typing. "Well, I'm telling you now. He'll be here at eleven o'clock to observe your fourth-period class." She reaches to her printer and removes a freshly printed form. "And you'll have a new student in your next class. I just registered her this morning. Here's her information." She hands me the form and smiles. I roll my eyes and shove the form into my satchel, suddenly dreading the remainder of the day.

I walk in a hurry to third period considering I'm already five minutes late. I look down at my watch and groan. *An eleven o'clock observation?* That's just an hour from now. All I have scheduled for my classes today are section tests. I wasn't prepared to lecture at all, much less in front of my faculty advisor. I'll just have to use this period to prepare something last-minute.

God, could this day get any worse?

When I round the corner to Hall D, the day somehow gets one hundred percent better as soon as I lay eyes on her.

"Lake?"

She's got her hands in her hair, pulling it up into a knot again. She spins around and her eyes widen when she sees me. She pulls a sheet of paper from between her lips and smiles, then immediately wraps her arms around my neck.

"Will! What are you doing here?"

I return her hug, but the sheet of paper that just flashed in front of my face has left my entire body feeling like an immobile solid block of concrete.

She's holding a schedule.

I suddenly can't breathe.

She's holding a *class* schedule.

This can't be good.

Mrs. Alex said something about enrolling a new student.

Oh, shit.

Holy shit.

I immediately begin to internally panic. I wrap my fingers around her wrists and pull her arms away from my neck before someone sees us. *Please let me be wrong. Please.*

"Lake," I say, shaking my head—trying to make sense of this. "Where . . . what are you doing here?"

She lets out a frustrated sigh and thrusts the schedule into my chest. "I'm trying to find this stupid elective but I'm lost," she whines. "Help me!"

Oh, shit. What the hell have I done?

I take a step back against the wall, attempting to give myself space to think. Space to *breathe*.

"Lake, no . . ." I say. I hand her back the schedule without even looking at it. There's no need to look at it. I know exactly where her "stupid elective" is. I can't seem to process a coherent thought while looking at her, so I turn around and clasp my hands behind my head.

She's a *student*?

I'm her *teacher*?

Oh, shit.

I close my eyes and think back to the past week. Who have I told? Who saw us together? Gavin. *Shit*. There's no telling who else may have been at Club N9NE. And Lake! She's about to figure this out any second. What if she thinks I was trying to hide this from her? She could go straight to administration and end my career.

As soon as the thought crosses my mind, she picks up her backpack and begins to storm off. I reach out and pull her to a stop. "Where are you going?" It's obvious she's pissed and I hope her intentions aren't to report me.

She rolls her eyes and sighs. "I get it, Will," she says. "I *get* it. I'll leave you alone before your girlfriend sees us." She pulls her arm out of my grasp and turns away from me.

"Girlfr—*no*. No, Lake. I don't think you *do* get it." I wait for her to process what's happening. I would just come out and say it, but I *can't*. I don't think I could say it out loud if I wanted to.

The sound of footsteps closing in on us diverts her attention away from me. Javier suddenly rounds the corner and comes to a quick stop when he sees me in the hallway.

"Oh, man, I thought I was late," he says.

If Lake hasn't figured it all out by now, she's about to.

"You *are* late, Javier," I reply. I open the door to my classroom and wave him inside. "Javi, I'll be there in a few minutes. Let the class know they have five minutes to review before the exam." I slowly close the door behind me and look down at the floor. I can't look at her. I don't think my heart can take what she's about to feel. There's a brief moment of silence before she quietly gasps. I raise my eyes to hers and the disappointment on her face tears my heart in two. She *gets it* now.

"Will," she whispers painfully. "Please don't tell me . . ."

Her voice is weak and she tilts her head slightly to the side, slowly shaking her head back and forth. She isn't angry. She's *hurt*. I'd almost rather her be pissed right now than feel the way she's feeling. I look up at the ceiling and rub my hands over my face in an attempt not to punch the damn wall. How could I be so stupid? Why wasn't my profession the first thing I thought to share with her? Why did I not see this as a possibility? I continue to pace, hoping beyond all hope that *I'm* the one not getting it. When I reach the lockers in front of me, I tap my head against them, silently cursing myself. I've really screwed it up this time. For both of us. I drop my hands and reluctantly roll around to face her.

"How did I not *see* this? You're still in *high school*?"

She backs up to the wall behind her and leans against it for support. "*Me?*" she says in defense. "How did the fact that you're a teacher not come up? *How* are you a teacher? You're only twenty-one."

I realize I'm going to have to answer a lot of her questions. My teaching situation isn't particularly normal, so I understand her confusion. But we can't do this here. Not right now.

"Layken, listen." I realize when her name falls off my tongue that I didn't call her "Lake." I guess that's probably best at this point. "There has apparently been a huge misunderstanding between the two of us." I look away from her when I finish my sentence. An overwhelming feeling of guilt overcomes me when I look into her eyes, so I just don't. "We need to talk about this, but now is definitely not the right time."

"I agree," she whispers. It sounds like she's attempting not to cry. I couldn't take it if she cried.

The door to my classroom opens and Eddie walks out into the hall, looking directly at Lake. "Layken, I was just coming to look for you," she says. "I saved you a seat." She looks at me, then back at Lake, leaving no traces or hint that she's put two and two together. *Good.* That just leaves Gavin to contend with. "Oh, sorry, Mr. Cooper. I didn't know you were out here."

I stand straight and walk toward the classroom door. "It's fine, Eddie. I was just going over Layken's schedule with her." I pull the door open wider and wait for Lake and Eddie to make their way into the room. I'm thankful it's a test day. There's no *way* I would be able to lecture right now.

"Who's the hottie?" Javier asks when Lake slides into her seat.

"Shut it, Javi!" I snap. I am so not in the mood for his smart-ass comments right now. I reach over and grab the stack of tests.

"Chill out, Mr. Cooper. I was paying her a compliment." He leans back in his chair and gives Lake a slow, full-body glance that makes my blood boil. "She's hot. Look at her."

I point to the classroom door. "Javi, get out!"

He snaps his focus back to me. "Mr. Cooper! Jeez! What's with the temp? Like I said, I was just . . ."

"Like *I* said, get out! You will not disrespect women in my classroom!"

He snatches his books off his desk. "Fine. I'll go disrespect them in the hallway!"

After the door shuts behind him, I cringe at my own behavior. I've never lost my temper in a classroom before. I look back at the students and everyone is watching Lake, waiting on some sort of reaction from her. Everyone except Gavin. His eyes are burrowing a hole right through me. I give him a slight nod, letting him know that I acknowledge the fact that we obviously have a lot to discuss. For right now, though, it's back to the task at hand.

"Class, we have a new student. This is Layken Cohen," I say, quickly wanting to brush what just happened under the rug. "Review is over. Put up your notes."

"You're not going to have her introduce herself?" Eddie asks.

"We'll get to that another time," I say, holding up the papers. "Tests."

I begin passing out the tests. When I reach Gavin's desk, he looks up at me inquisitively. "Lunch," I whisper, letting him know I'll explain everything then. He nods and takes his test, finally breaking eye contact.

When I pass out all but one of the tests, I reluctantly walk closer to her desk. "Lake," I say. I quickly clear my throat and correct myself. "Layken, if you have something else to work on, feel free. The class is completing a chapter test."

She straightens up in her desk and looks down at her hands. "I'd rather just take the test," she says quietly. I place the paper on her desk, then make my way back to my seat.

I spend the rest of the hour grading papers from the first two classes. I occasionally catch myself peeking in her direction, trying hard not to stare. She just keeps erasing and rewriting answers over and over. I don't know why she chose to take the test; she hasn't been here for any of the lectures. I break my gaze from her paper and look up. Gavin is glaring at me again, so I dart my eyes down at my watch right when the dismissal bell rings. Everyone quickly files to the front of the room and places their papers on my desk.

"Hey, did you get your lunch switched?" Eddie asks Lake.

I watch as Eddie and Lake converse about her schedule and I'm secretly relieved that Lake has already found a friend. I'm not so sure I like that it's Eddie, though. I don't have a problem with Eddie. It's just that Gavin knows way too much now and I'm not sure if he would tell Eddie or not. I hope not. I glance back down to my desk as soon as Eddie begins to walk away from Lake. Rather than exiting the classroom, she heads straight to my desk. I look up at her and she removes something from her purse. She shakes a few mints into her hand and lays them on my desk.

"Altoids," she says. "I'm just making assumptions here, but I've heard Altoids work wonders on hangovers." She pushes the mints toward me and walks away.

I stare at the mints, unnerved that she assumed I have a hangover. I must not be as good at hiding my emotions as I thought I was. I'm disappointed in myself. Disappointed I lost my temper, disappointed I didn't use my head when it came to the whole situation with Lake, disappointed that I now have this huge dilemma facing me. I'm still staring at the mints when Lake walks to the desk and places her paper on top of the pile.

"Is my mood that obvious?" I say rhetorically. She takes two of the mints and walks out of the room without saying a word. I sigh and lean back in the chair, kicking my feet up on the desk. This is by far the second-worst day of my life.

"I can't wait that long, man." Gavin walks back into the room and closes the door behind him. He throws his backpack on the desk in front of me, then scoots it closer and climbs into it. "What the *hell*, Will? What were you thinking?"

I shake my head and shrug my shoulders. I'm not ready to talk about this right now, but I do owe him an explanation. I bring my feet down from the desk and rest my head in my hands, rubbing my temples with my fingers. "We didn't know."

Gavin laughs incredulously. "Didn't know? How the hell could you not *know*?"

I close my eyes and sigh. He's right. How did we not know? "I don't know. It just . . . it never came up," I say. "I was out of town all weekend. We haven't spoken since our date Thursday. It just . . . somehow it never came up." I shake my head, sorting through my thoughts as they're flowing from my lips. I'm a jumbled mess.

"So you *just* found out she's a student? Like, *just* now?"

I nod.

"You didn't have sex with her, did you?"

His question takes a moment to register. He takes my silence as an admission of guilt and he leans forward and whispers, "You had sex with her, didn't you? You're gonna get fired, man."

"No, I didn't have sex with her!" I snap.

He continues to glare at me, attempting to analyze my demeanor. "Then why are you so upset? If you didn't have sex with her, you can't really get in trouble. I doubt she'll report it if all you did was kiss her. Is that what you're worried about? That she'll report you?"

I shake my head, because that's not at all what I'm worried about. I could see in Lake's demeanor that the thought of reporting me never even crossed her mind. She was upset, but not with me.

"No. No, I know she won't say anything. It's just . . ." I run my hand across my forehead and sigh. I have no idea how to handle this. No idea. "Shit," I say, exasperated. "I just need to think, Gavin."

I run my fingers through my hair and clasp my hands behind my head. I don't think I've ever been this confused and overwhelmed in my life. Everything I've worked for could possibly be going to hell today simply because of my stupidity. I've got three months left until graduation, and there's a good chance if this gets out, I've just ruined my entire career.

What confuses me though is the fact that it's not my career that has me in a jumbled mess right now. It's *her*. These emotions are a direct result of *her*. The main reason why I'm so upset right now is that it feels like I somehow just broke her heart.

"Oh," Gavin says quietly. "*Shit*."

I look up at him, confused by his reaction. "What?"

He stands up and points to me. "You *like* her," he says. "*That's* why you're so upset. You already fell for her, didn't you?" He grabs his backpack and starts walking backward toward the door, shaking his head. I don't even bother denying it. He saw the way I was looking at her the other night.

When the classroom door opens and several students begin to file in, he walks back to my desk and whispers, "Eddie doesn't know anything. I didn't recognize anyone else at the slam, so don't worry about that part of it. You just need to figure out what you need to do." He turns toward the classroom door and exits . . . just as my faculty advisor enters.

Shit!

IF THERE'S ONE thing I've learned how to do well in my life, it's adapt.

I somehow made it through the observation unscathed and somehow made it to the end of last period without bashing my fists into a wall. Whether or not I'll make it through the rest of the day just knowing I'm right across the street from her is still up in the air.

When Caulder and I pull into the driveway, she's sitting in her Jeep. She's got her arm over her eyes and it looks like she's crying.

"Can I go to Kel's?" Caulder asks when he climbs out of the car.

I nod. I leave my things in the car and shut my door, then slowly make my way across the street. When I reach the back of her car, I pause to gather my thoughts. I know what needs to be done, but knowing something and accepting it are two completely different things. I asked myself over and over today what my parents would have done in this situation. What would *most* people do in this situation? Of course, the answer is obviously to do the right thing. The responsible thing. I mean, we went on one date. Who would quit a job over *one* date?

This shouldn't be this hard. Why is this so hard?

I walk closer and lightly tap on her passenger window. She jerks up and flips the visor down and looks in the mirror, attempting to wipe away traces of her heartache. When the door unlocks, I open it and take a seat. I shut the door behind me and adjust the seat, then prop my foot on the dash. My gaze falls to the note that I left under her wiper this morning. It's unfolded, lying on her console. When I wrote the words, *see you at four o'clock*, this isn't how I envisioned four o'clock at all. I glance up at her and she's avoiding looking at me. Just seeing her causes my words to catch in my throat. I have no idea what to say. I have no idea where her head is right now.

"What are you thinking?" I finally ask.

She slowly turns toward me and pulls her leg up into the seat. She wraps her arms around it and rests her chin on top of her knee. I've never wanted to be a knee so bad in my entire life.

"I'm confused as hell, Will. I don't *know* what to think."

Honestly, I don't know what to think, either. *God, I'm such an asshole.* How could I have let this happen? I sigh and look out the passenger window. I can't for the life of me hold my composure if I keep looking into those eyes.

"I'm sorry," I say. "This is all my fault."

"It's nobody's fault," she says. "In order for there to be fault, there has to be some sort of conscious decision. You didn't know, Will."

I *didn't* know. But it's my own damn fault that I didn't know.

"That's just it, Lake," I say, turning to face her. "I should have known. I'm in an occupation that doesn't just require ethics inside the classroom; they apply to all aspects of my life. I wasn't aware because I wasn't doing my job. When you told me you were eighteen, I just assumed you were in college."

She looks away and whispers, "I've only been eighteen for two weeks."

That sentence. If that sentence could have just been spoken a few days ago, this entire situation would have been avoided. Why the *hell* didn't I just ask her when her birthday was? I close my eyes and rest my head against the seat, preparing to explain my unique situation to her. I want her to have a better understanding of why this can't work between us.

"I student teach," I say. "Sort of."

"Sort of?"

"After my parents died, I doubled up on all my classes. I have enough credits to graduate a semester early. Since the school was so shorthanded, they offered me a one-year contract. I have three months left of student teaching. After that I'm under contract through June of next year." I look over at her and her eyes are closed. She's shaking her head ever so slightly like she doesn't comprehend what I'm saying, or she just doesn't want to hear it.

"Lake, I need this job. It's what I've been working toward for three years. We're broke. My parents left me with a mound of debt and now college tuition. I can't quit now."

She darts her eyes toward me, almost like I've insulted her.

"Will, I understand. I'd never ask you to jeopardize your career. You've worked hard. It would be stupid if you threw that away for someone you've only known for a week."

Oh, but I would. If you would just ask me to . . . I would.

"I'm not saying you would ask me that. I just want you to understand where I'm coming from."

"I do understand," she says. "It's ridiculous to assume we even have anything worth risking."

She can deny it all she wants, but whatever it is that I'm feeling, I know she's feeling it, too. I can see it in her eyes. "We both know it's more than that."

As soon as the words leave my lips, I immediately regret them. This girl is my *student*. S-T-U-D-E-N-T! I've *got* to get this through my *head*.

We're both silent. The lack of conversation only invites the emotions we've been trying to suppress. She begins to cry, and despite the fact that my conscience is screaming at me, I can't help but console her. I pull her to me and she buries her face in my shirt. I want so bad to push the thought out of my head that this is the last time I'm going to hold her like this—but I know it's true. I know once we separate, it's over. There's no way I can continue to be around her with the way she consumes my every thought. I know, deep down, that this is good-bye.

"I'm so sorry," I whisper into her hair. "I wish there was something I could do to change things. I have to do this right for Caulder. I'm not sure where we go from here, or how we'll transition."

"Transition?" she says. She brings her eyes to meet mine and they're full of panic. "But—what if you talk to the school? Tell them we didn't know. Ask them what our options are."

She doesn't realize it, but that's all I've been trying to figure out for the last five hours. I've been thinking of any and all possible scenarios to change the outcome for us. There just *isn't* one.

"I can't, Lake. It won't work. It *can't* work."

She pulls apart from me when Kel and Caulder come out of her house. I reluctantly release my hold from around her, knowing it's the last time I'll hold her. This is more than likely the last time we'll have a conversation outside school. In order for me to do the right thing, I know that letting her go completely is the only way. I need to distance myself from her.

"Layken?" I say hesitantly. "There's one more thing I need to talk to you about."

She rolls her eyes like she knows it's something bad. She doesn't respond, though. She just waits for me to continue.

"I need you to go to administration tomorrow. I want you to withdraw from my class. I don't think we should be around each other anymore."

"Why?" she says, turning to face me. The hurt in her voice is exactly what I was afraid I would hear.

"I'm not asking you to do this because I want to avoid you. I'm asking you this because what we have isn't appropriate. We have to separate ourselves."

The hurt in her eyes is replaced by a look of incredulity. "Not appropriate?" she says, disbelievingly. "*Separate* ourselves? You live across the street from me!"

The hurt in her voice, the anger in her expression, the heartache in her eyes; it's too much. Seeing her hurt like this and not being able to console her is unbearable. If I don't get out of this car right now, my hands will be tangled in her hair and my lips will be meshed with hers in a matter of seconds. I swing open the door and get out.

I just need to breathe.

She opens her door, too, and looks at me over the hood of her car. "We're both mature enough to know what's appropriate, Will. You're the only person I know here. Please don't ask me to act like I don't even know you," she pleads.

"Come on, Lake. You aren't being fair. I can't do this. We can't *just* be friends. It's the only choice we have."

She has no idea how close I came to *not* being her friend just now. There's no possible way I can be around this girl and continue to do the right thing. I'm not that strong.

She opens her car door and reaches inside to grab her things. "So, you're saying it's either all or nothing, right? And since it *obviously* can't be *all*!" She slams the door and walks toward her house. She stops short and kicks over the gnome with the broken red hat. "You'll be rid of me by third period tomorrow!" She slams her front door, leaving me a heartbroken, emotional wreck in her driveway.

The last thing I wanted out of this was to upset her even more. I pound my fists against the top of her Jeep, pissed at myself for putting her in this situation to begin with. "Dammit!" I yell. I spin and turn to head home, but instead come face to face with Kel and Caulder. They're both staring at me, wide-eyed.

"Why are you so mad at Layken?" Kel asks. "Are you not gonna be her boyfriend?"

I glance back to Lake's house and clasp my hands behind my head. "I'm not mad at her, Kel. I'm just—I'm mad at myself." I drop my arms and turn back around to head home. They step apart as I pass between them. I hear them following me when I retrieve my things from my car. I'm still being followed when I walk inside and set the box down on the bar, so I turn around and look at the boys.

"What?" I say with a clear amount of annoyance. They both look at each other, then back at me.

"Um. We just wanted to ask you something," Caulder says nervously. He slides into one of the bar stools and rests his chin in his hand. "Maya said if Layken becomes your girlfriend and you marry her, me and Kel will be brothers of law."

Both boys are looking at me with hopeful expressions.

"It's brothers-*in*-law, and Layken's not going to be my girlfriend," I say. "We're just friends."

Kel steps around me and climbs into the other seat at the bar. "She burped too much, didn't she? Or did she leave her bra in your car? I bet she wouldn't let you have coffee, would she?"

I force a fake smile and step toward the stack of papers. "You nailed it," I say. "It was the coffee. She's so stingy."

Kel shakes his head. "I knew it."

"Well," Caulder says. "You could try going on another date to see if you like her better. Me and Kel want to be brothers."

"Layken and I aren't going on another date. We're just friends." I glance at both of them with a serious expression. "Drop it." I sit down and pull out my pen, then grab the test off the top and flip it over.

It's *her* test.

Of course it would be hers. I stare at it, wondering how in the hell this is going to get any easier. Just seeing her handwriting makes my pulse race. Makes my heart ache. I lightly trace her name with the tip of my finger. I'm pretty sure it's the most beautiful handwriting I've ever seen.

"Please?" Caulder says.

I flinch, having forgotten they were even standing here. I have *got* to stop thinking about her like this. She's a *student*. I slap her test facedown on the pile and stand up.

"Kel, do you like pizza?"

He shakes his head. "No. I *love* pizza."

"Go ask your mom if you can chill with us tonight. We need a boy's night."

Kel jumps out of his chair and they both run toward the front door. I take a seat at the bar again and drop my head into my hands.

This entire day is definitely my suck.

I REST MY hand on the door to the administration office, almost second-guessing my entrance. I'm not in the mood for Mrs. Alex today. Unfortunately, she sees me through the glass window and waves. Her *flirty* wave. I suck it up and reluctantly open the door.

"Good morning, Will," she says in her annoying singsong voice.

I know I was "Will" to her just a couple of years ago, but it wouldn't hurt her to extend me the courtesy that she extends to all the other teachers here. I don't bother arguing, though. "Morning." I shove a form across the desk toward her. "Can you have this signed by Mr. Murphy and fax it to my faculty advisor?"

She takes the form and places it in a tray. "Anything for you," she says and smiles. I give her a quick smile in return, then spin toward the exit, very conscious of my own ass this time.

"Oh, by the way," she calls after me. "That new student I registered yesterday just came by to drop your class. I guess she isn't a big fan of poetry. You'll need to sign the form I gave her before I can make it official. She's probably on her way to your classroom right now."

"Thanks," I mumble, exiting the office.

This is going to be impossible. It's not like I can just erase the fact that Lake exists. I'll more than likely see her at work on a daily basis, whether in passing . . . in the lunchroom . . . in the parking lot. I'll definitely see her at home every day considering her house is the first thing I see when I walk out my own front door. Or look out my window. Not that I'll be doing that.

Kel and Caulder are becoming inseparable, so I'll eventually have to interact with her regarding them. Trying to avoid her isn't going to work. Lake is absolutely right . . . it isn't going to work at all. I kept trying to tell myself over and over last night that what she said wasn't true, but it is. I wonder if the only other alternative would be to try and at least be her friend. We're obviously going to have to work through this situation somehow.

When I round the corner to my classroom, she's standing next to my door with the transfer form pressed against the wall, attempting to forge my name. My first instinct is to turn around and walk away, but I realize these are the exact types of situations we're going to have to learn to confront.

"That's not a good idea," I say, before she forges my name. If anyone could recognize my handwriting, it would be Mrs. Alex.

Lake spins around and looks at me. Her cheeks flush and she darts her eyes down to my shirt, embarrassed. I walk past her and unlock the door, then motion for her to enter the classroom. She walks to my desk and smacks her form down.

"Well, you weren't here yet, I thought I'd spare you the trouble," she says.

She must not have had her coffee today. I pick up the form and look it over. "Russian Lit? That's what you chose?"

She rolls her eyes. "It was either that or Botany."

I pull my chair out and take a seat, preparing to sign the form. As soon as the tip of my pen meets the paper, it occurs to me that in a way, I'm being incredibly selfish. She chose poetry as an elective before she even knew I would be teaching it. She chose poetry because she loves it. The fact that the thoughts I have about her make me uncomfortable is an extremely selfish reason to force her into Russian Literature for the rest of the year. I hesitate, then lay the pen back down on the paper.

"I thought a lot last night . . . about what you said yesterday. It's not fair of me to ask you to transfer just because it makes me uneasy. We live a hundred yards apart; our brothers are becoming best friends. If anything, this class will be good for us, help us figure out how to navigate when we're around each other." I reach into my satchel and pull out the test she somehow made a perfect score on. "Besides, you'll obviously breeze through."

She takes the test from my hands and looks down at it. "I don't mind switching," she says quietly. "I understand where you're coming from."

I put the lid back on the pen and scoot my chair back. "Thanks, but it can only get easier from here, right?"

She nods her head unconvincingly. "Right," she says.

I know I'm completely wrong. She could move back to Texas today and I would still feel too close to her. But once again, it's not my feelings that should matter at this point. It's hers. I've screwed her life up enough in the past week; the last thing I want to do is shove Russian Lit on top of that. I crumple up her transfer form and chuck it toward the trash can. When it misses, she walks over and picks it up, then throws it in.

"I guess I'll see you third period, Mr. Cooper," she says as she exits the room.

The way she refers to me as "Mr. Cooper" makes me scowl. I hate the fact that I'm her teacher.

I'd so much rather be her *Will*.

7.

the honeymoon

LAKE HASN'T MOVED a muscle in the last fifteen minutes. She's been soaking in every word I've said. Recalling the day we met and our first date was actually fun. Recalling the things that tore us apart is grueling.

"I don't like talking about this anymore," I say. "It looks like it's making you sad."

Her eyes widen and she turns her body toward me. "Will, no. I love hearing your thoughts on everything that happened. I actually feel like it helps me understand a lot of your actions better. I don't know why I felt like you sort of blamed me."

I kiss her softly on the lips. "How could I blame you, Lake? All I wanted was you."

She smiles and rests her head on my forearm. "I can't believe my mom told you to leave me that note," she says.

"God, Lake. That was so embarrassing. You have no idea."

She laughs. "She really liked you, you know. At first, I mean. She *loved* you in the end. It was the in-between where her feelings about you sort of waned."

I think about the day Julia found out, and how worried she must have been for Lake. To have everything going on in her life like she did, then have to watch your daughter deal with heartache? Unimaginable.

"Remember when she found out you were my teacher?" Lake says. "The look on your face when she was walking up the driveway toward you, it was awful. I was so afraid you would think I told her because I was mad at you."

"I was so scared of her that day, Lake. She could be really intimidating when she wanted to be. Of course after we talked again later that night, I saw a more vulnerable side to her, but still. I was scared to death of her."

Lake jerks up on the bed and looks at me. "What do you mean when y'all talked *again*?"

"Later that night when she came back to my house. Did I never tell you that?"

"No," she says abruptly, almost like I've deceived her. "Why did she come back? What did she say?"

"Wait, let me start from the beginning. I want to tell you about the night before she found out," I say. "I slammed a poem about you."

She perks up. "No way! How come you never told me?"

I shrug. "I was hurt. It wasn't a positive piece."

"I want to hear about it, anyway," she says.

this *girl*

I'M HOPING THIS situation is like dieting, where they say day three is when the cravings start to subside. I really hope that's the case. The fact that she sits two feet from me in class makes my mind feel like a damn hurricane. It takes everything in me not to look at her during third period. In fact, I spend the entire time in my class trying *not* to look at her. I've been fairly successful, which is good considering Gavin still watches me like a hawk. At least it felt like he was today, anyway. I've never so looked forward to a weekend off in my life.

One. More. Day.

"I might be a little late tonight, Maya. I'm performing so I may stay until it's over."

She plops down on the sofa with a carton of ice cream. "Whatever," she says.

I grab my keys and head out the front door. No matter how hard I try not to, I glance across the street during my short walk to the car. I could swear I see her living room curtain snap shut. I stop and stare for a minute, but it doesn't move again.

I'M ONE OF the first to arrive, so I take one of the seats toward the front of the room. I'm hoping the energy from the crowd will distract me long enough to get out of this funk. I'm almost embarrassed to admit it, but I feel more heartbroken over this entire situation with Lake than I did when Vaughn dumped me. I'm sure a lot of that heartache was lost in the heartache from losing my parents, so maybe it just seems different for that reason. How could ending things with a girl who wasn't even my girlfriend to begin with possibly cause this much distress?

"Hey, Mr. Cooper," Gavin says. He and Eddie pull out their chairs and sit at the table with me. Unlike last week, I actually welcome their distraction tonight.

"For the last time, Gavin, call me Will. It's weird hearing you say that when we're not in class."

"Hey, *Will*," Eddie says sarcastically. "You doing one tonight?"

I had planned on performing, but seeing Gavin has me second-guessing my choice. I know most of the pieces I perform are metaphorical, but he'll see right through this one. Not that it matters; he already knows how I feel.

"Yeah," I say to Eddie. "I'm doing a new one."

"Cool," she says. "Did you write it for that girl?" She turns around and scans the room. "Where is she? I thought I saw you leaving with someone last week." She returns her focus to me. "Was she your girlfriend?"

Gavin and I immediately look at each other. He makes a face that tells me he didn't say anything to Eddie. I try to steady my expression when I respond.

"Just a friend."

Eddie pushes her bottom lip out and pouts. "Friend, huh? That sucks. We really need to hook you up with someone." She leans forward onto the table and puts her chin in her hands while studying me. "Gavin, who can we hook Will up with?"

He rolls his eyes. "Why do you always think you have to hook everyone up? Not everyone feels the need to be in a relationship every second of their lives." He's obviously trying to squelch the subject and I appreciate him for that.

"I don't try to hook *everyone* up," she says. "Just the people who clearly need it." She looks back at me. "No offense, Will. It's just—you know. You never date. It might do you some good."

"Enough, Eddie," Gavin snaps.

"*What?* Two people, Gavin! I've mentioned finding dates for two people this week. That's not excessive. Besides, I think I may have figured out someone for Layken."

When Eddie says her name, I immediately shift in my chair. So does Gavin.

"I think I'm gonna try to get Nick to ask her out," she says, thinking aloud.

Before Gavin can respond, the sac is called to the stage. I'm relieved the subject is off the table now, but I can't deny the twinge of jealousy that just made its way into my stomach.

What did I expect would be the outcome of all this? Of course she's going to date other people. She's got her entire senior year of school left; it would be crazy if she *didn't* date. But still, it doesn't mean I'll be happy when she does.

"I'll be back," I say, excusing myself from the table. It's been five minutes and I already need a breather from Eddie.

When I return from the bathroom, the sac has already finished performing. As soon as I sit back down, the emcee calls me to the stage to perform first.

"Break a leg," Gavin says when I stand back up.

"That's theater, Gavin," Eddie says, hitting him on the arm.

I ascend the steps and take my place in front of the microphone. I've noticed in the past that if I concentrate and really put my emotions into writing, performing can actually be therapeutic. I really need to find some relief after all that's happened this week.

"My piece is called *This Girl*." I do my best to avoid Gavin's glare, but it's obvious by his expression that he knows the poem is about Lake as soon as the title passes my lips. I close my eyes and inhale a deep breath, then begin.

I dreamt about this girl last night.

Wow.

This *girl.*

In my *dream* I was standing on the edge of a *cliff*

Looking *down* over a *vast, barren valley below*

I wasn't wearing any *shoes* and the rocks were

crumbling beneath my *toes.*

It would have been so *easy* to take a step back,

To *move* away from the *ledge,*

Away from a *certain inevitable life* that had *somehow*

been *determined* for me

a life that had *somehow* become my only option.

It had been my life for *two years* and I *accepted* that.

I had not *embraced* it,

But I *had* accepted it.

It was where I belonged.

As much as it didn't *appeal* to me, as much as I *yearned*

for the *rivers* and *mountains* and *trees,*

As much as I *yearned* to hear their *songs* . . .

To hear their . . . *poetry?*

It was apparent that what *I* yearned for

wasn't *decided* by me . . .

it was decided *for* me.

So . . . I did the only thing I could do.

The only thing I *should* do.

I prepared myself to *embrace* this life.

I sucked it up and took a *deep* breath. I placed my

hands on the edge of the *cliff* and began to *lower*

myself onto the *rocks* protruding from the *edge.* I

burrowed my *fingers deep* into the *crevices* and *slowly*

began lowering myself *down*.

Down into the *vast*,

barren

valley

that had become

my

life.

But *then* . . .

Then this *girl* . . .

Holy *hell*, this *girl* . . .

She appeared out of *nowhere*, standing *directly* in front

of me on the edge of that *cliff*. She looked *down* at me

with her *sad eyes* that ran a *million* miles *deep* . . .

and she *smiled* at me.

This girl *smiled* at me.

A *look* that cut *straight* to my *core* and *pierced* through

my *heart* like a *million* of Cupid's arrows,

One right on top of the *other*, on top of the *other*, on

top of the *other*

Straight . . .

Into . . .

My *heart* . . .

Now *this* is the part of the dream where *most* girls

would bend down and grab my *hands*, telling me not

to *go* . . . not to *do* it. *This* is the part of the dream

where *most* girls would grab my *wrists* and *brace*

themselves with their *feet* as they *pulled* me *up* with

every ounce of strength in their *being*. *This* is the part

of the dream where *most* girls would *scream* at the top
of their *lungs* for help, doing *anything* and *everything*
they could to *save* me . . .

To *rescue* me

from that

vast,

barren

valley

below.

But *this* girl.

This girl wasn't most girls.

This girl . . .

This girl did something even *better.*

First, she sat down on the edge of the *cliff* and *kicked*
off her shoes and we both watched as they *fell* and *fell*
and *fell* and *continued* to *fall* until they landed in a
heap. One shoe right on top of the other in that *vast,*
barren valley below.

Then she *slid* a rubber *band* off her *wrist,*

Reached behind her . . .

And pulled her *hair*

into a *knot.*

And then this girl

This *girl* . . .

She *placed* her *hands* right next to *mine* on the *edge*
of that *cliff* and she *slowly* began to *lower* herself *off*
of it. She poked her *bare feet* into *whatever* crevice
she could *find* next to mine. She dug the *fingers* of her
right hand into the *cracks* between the *rocks,* then
placed her *left* hand

directly . . .

on *top . . .*

of *mine*.

She looked down at the *vast, barren valley below* us,

then she looked back up at me and she *smiled*.

She *smiled*.

She *looked* at me and *smiled* and said . . .

"Are you *ready?*"

And I *was*.

I *finally* was.

I had never been more *ready* in my *life*.

Yeah . . .

This *girl*.

My mother would have *loved* this girl.

Too bad she was just a *dream*.

I CLOSE MY eyes and tune out the noise of the crowd while I wait for my lungs to find their rhythm again. When I descend the stage and take a seat back at the table, Eddie stands up, wiping tears from her eyes. She looks down at me and frowns.

"Would it kill you to do something *funny* for once?" She storms toward the bathroom, I'm assuming to fix her makeup.

I look at Gavin and laugh, but he's staring back at me with his arms folded in front of him on the table. "Will, I think I've got an idea."

"Pertaining to . . ."

"You," he says. He gestures toward the stage, "and your . . . situation."

I lean forward. "What about my *situation*?"

"I know someone," he says. "She works with my mom. She's your age, cute, in *college*."

I immediately shake my head. "No. No chance," I say, leaning back into the booth.

"Will, you can't be with Layken. If your poem had anything to do with her, which I'm thinking it had *everything* to do with her, then you need to find a way to get over this. If you don't, you'll end up screwing up your entire career over *this girl*. A girl you went on *one* date with. One!"

I continue to shake my head at his reasoning. "I'm not looking for a girlfriend, Gavin. I wasn't even looking for anything when I met Lake. I'm fine with where I am right now; I definitely don't need to add even more female drama into the picture."

"You won't be adding more drama. You'll be filling an obvious void in your life. You need to date. Eddie was right."

"What was I right about?" Eddie says, returning to her seat.

Gavin gestures toward me. "About Will. He needs to date. Don't you think he and Taylor would hit it off?"

Eddie perks up. "I didn't even think about her! Yes! Will, you're gonna love her," she says excitedly.

"I'm not letting you guys set me up." I grab my jacket. "I've got to get back home. See you guys in class tomorrow."

Eddie and Gavin both stand. "I'll get her number tomorrow," Eddie says. "Is next Saturday night okay? You two could double date with us."

"I'm not going." I walk away without turning back or giving in.

8.

the honeymoon

"OKAY," LAKE SAYS. "Two things. One. That poem was . . . heart-breakingly *beautiful*."

"Just like its subject," I say. I lean in to kiss her but she brings her hand up and pushes my face away.

"Two," she says, narrowing her eyes. "Gavin and Eddie tried to set you up with someone?" She huffs and sits up on the bed. "Good thing you didn't agree to it. I don't care how screwed up our situation was, there's no way I would have dated anyone else considering the way I felt about you."

I quickly change the subject before she realizes that, although I didn't *agree* to it, Eddie is pretty damn persistent.

"Okay, now for Friday night," I say, successfully taking her mind off the date. "Your mom."

"Yeah," she says, finding a comfortable spot next to me and throwing her leg over mine. "My mom."

secrets

"PASTA AGAIN?" CAULDER whines. He grabs his plate of food from the counter and takes it to the bar and sits.

"If you don't like it, learn how to cook."

"*I* like it," Kel says. "My mom cooks a lot of vegetables and chicken. That's probably why I'm so small, because I'm malnoure-dish."

I laugh and correct him. "It's mal*nourished*."

Kel rolls his eyes. "That's what I said."

I grab my own bowl and fill it with pasta . . . *again*. We do have pasta at least three times a week, but there are only two of us. I don't see the point in making expensive meals when it's just me and a nine-year-old most of the time. I take a seat at the bar across from the two boys and fill all of our glasses with tea.

"Suck and sweet time," Caulder says.

"What's suck and sweet?" Kel asks.

As soon as Caulder starts to explain, there's a knock at the front door. When I reach the door and open it, I'm surprised to find Julia standing in the entryway. Her presence has definitely become more intimidating since the first day I met her; especially after this afternoon when she found out about me being a teacher.

She looks up at me straight-faced, with her hands in the pockets of her scrub top.

"Oh. Hey," I say, trying not to appear as nervous as I am. "Kel just started eating. If you want, I'll send him home as soon as he's done."

"Actually," she says. She glances over my shoulder at the boys, then looks back at me and lowers her voice to a whisper. "I really wanted to talk to you if you have a few minutes."

She seems a little bit nervous, which just makes me ten times more nervous. "Sure." I step aside and motion for her to come in.

"You guys can eat in your room, Caulder. I need to talk to Julia."

"But we haven't said our suck and sweet for today," Caulder says.

"Do them in your room. I'll tell you mine later."

The boys pick up their bowls and drinks and head to Caulder's room, closing the door behind them. When I turn back to Julia her mouth is curled up in a smile.

"Suck and sweet?" she says. "Is that your way of getting him to tell you his good and bad for the day?"

I smile and nod. "We started it about six months ago." I take a seat on the same couch as her. "It was his therapist's idea. Although the original version wasn't called suck and sweet. I sort of ad-libbed that part to make it sound more appealing to him."

"That's sweet," she says. "I should start doing that with Kel."

I give her a slight smile but don't respond. I'm not really sure what she's doing here or what her intentions are, so I silently wait for her to continue. She takes a deep breath and focuses her gaze on the family picture hanging on the wall across from her.

"Your parents?" she says, pointing to the picture.

I relax into the couch and look up at the picture. "Yeah. My mom's name was Claire. My dad's name was Dimas. He was half Puerto Rican—named after his maternal grandfather."

Julia smiles. "That explains your natural tan."

It's obvious she's trying to deflect for some reason. She continues to stare at the picture. "Do you mind if I ask how they met?" she says.

Just a few hours ago she was ready to rip my head off after

finding out I'm Lake's teacher; now she's trying to get to know me? Whatever's going on with her, I'm in no position to question her, so I just go along with it.

"They met in college. Well, my mom was in college. My dad was actually a member of a band that played on her campus. He didn't go to college until a few years after they met. My mom was on a campus crew that would help set up their shows and they got to know each other. He asked her out and the rest is history. They married two years later."

"What'd they do for a living?"

"Mom was in human resources. Dad was a . . . he taught English." Just saying the word *teacher* in front of her makes me uncomfortable. "Not the best-paying jobs but they were happy."

She sighs. "That's what counts."

I nod in agreement. There's an awkward silence that follows while she slowly scans the pictures on the walls around us. I feel like she wants to bring up everything from earlier today, but maybe she doesn't know how.

"Listen, Julia." I turn toward her on the couch. "I really am sorry about what happened between Lake . . . between *Layken* and me. The position I've put her in isn't fair to her and I feel terrible. It's completely my fault."

She smiles and reaches across the couch, then pats the top of my hand. "I know it wasn't intentional, Will. What happened was an unfortunate misunderstanding; I know that. But . . ." She sighs and shakes her head. "As much as I like you and think you're a great guy . . . it's just not right. She's never been in love before and it scares me when I think about the way she looked when she walked through that front door last Thursday night. I know she wants to do the right thing, but I also know she would do anything to get back to that moment. It's the first time I've seen her that happy since before her father died."

Hearing her validate that Lake's feelings were just as intense as mine makes this whole thing even harder. I know she's only trying to make a point, but it's a point I'd rather not hear.

"What I'm trying to say is . . . this is in your hands, Will. I know she's not strong enough to deny her heart what it wants, so I need you to promise me that you *will*. You've got more at stake here than she does. This isn't a fairy tale. This is reality. If you two end up following your hearts and not your heads, it'll end in disaster."

I shift on the couch and attempt to think of a way to respond. Julia is obviously the type of person who can see through bullshit, so I know I need to be up front with her.

"I like her, Julia. And in some odd way, I care about her. I know I've only known her for a little over a week now, but . . . I do. I care about her. And that's exactly why you don't have anything to worry about. I want nothing more than to help Layken get past this—whatever it is she's feeling. I know the only way to do that is to keep our relationship strictly professional from now on. And I promise you, I will."

I hear the words coming from my mouth, and I would like to admit that I'm being one hundred percent honest with her. But if I'm being one hundred percent honest with *myself*, I know I'm not that strong. Which is why I have to keep my distance.

Julia rests her elbow against the back of the couch and lays her head on it. "You're a good person, Will. I hope one day she'll be lucky enough to find someone half as good as you. I just don't want her finding it yet, you know? And definitely not under these circumstances."

I nod. "I don't want that for her right now, either," I say quietly. And that response is for certain the truth. If there's anything I know for sure, it's that I don't want to burden Lake with all of my responsibilities. She's young and, unlike me, she still has a chance at an untainted future. I don't want to be the one to take that from her.

Julia leans back into the couch and looks at the picture of my parents again. I watch her while she stares at it. I can see now where Lake gets that distant gaze. I wonder if they were ever despondent before Lake's father passed away, or if it's a natural reaction after someone close to you dies. It makes me wonder if maybe I'm just as despondent when I think about my own parents.

Julia's hand goes up to her cheek and she wipes at newly formed tears in her eyes. I don't know why she's crying, but I instantly feel her sadness. It exudes from her.

"What was it like for you?" she whispers, still staring at the picture.

I face forward again and look at their picture. "What was *what* like?" I ask. "Their death?"

She nods, but doesn't look at me. I lean back and fold my arms across my chest, resting my head against the back of the couch again. "It was . . ." I realize I've never talked to anyone about what it was like for me. Other than the slam I've performed about their death, I've never spoken about it to a single person. "It was as if every single nightmare I've ever had throughout my entire life became reality in that single instant."

She squeezes her eyes shut and clamps her hand over her mouth, quickly turning away.

"Julia?"

She's unable to control her tears now. I scoot closer to her on the couch and put my arm around her and pull her to me. I know she isn't crying because of what I said. She's crying because of something else entirely. There's something bigger going on here than just me and Lake. Something much bigger. I pull back and look at her.

"Julia, tell me," I say. "What's wrong?"

She pulls away and stands up, heading toward the door. "I need to go," she says through her tears. She walks out the front door before I have a chance to stop her. When I make it outside, she's standing on my patio crying uncontrollably. I walk over to her, unsure of what to do. Unsure if I'm in the position to do anything, even if I wanted to.

"Look, Julia. Whatever this is, you need to talk about it. You don't have to tell me, but you need to talk about it. Do you want me to go get Layken?"

She darts her eyes up to mine. "No!" she says. "Don't. I don't want her to see me upset like this."

I place my hands on her shoulders. "Is everything okay? Are you okay?"

She breaks her gaze from mine, indicating I've hit the nail on the head. She's not okay. She steps away from me and wipes her tears away with her shirt. She inhales a few deep breaths, attempting to stop more tears from flowing.

"I'm not ready for them to know, Will. Not yet," she whispers. She hugs herself tightly and glances at her house. "I just want them to have a chance to settle in. They've been through so much already this year. I can't tell them yet. It'll break their souls."

She doesn't come out and say it, but I can hear it in her voice. She's sick.

I wrap my arms around her and hug her. I hug her for what she's going through, for what she's been through. I hug her for Lake, I hug her for Kel, and I hug her for Caulder and myself. I hug her because it's all I know to do.

"I won't say anything. I promise." I don't even know how to begin to put myself in her shoes in order to empathize. I can't imagine how hard this must be for her. To know that both of your children are possibly going to be left in the world without you? At least my parents didn't know what was about to happen to them before it happened. At least they didn't have to carry around the burden that Julia is carrying.

She finally pulls away and wipes at her eyes again. "Just send Kel home when he's finished eating. I need to get to work."

"Julia," I say. "If you ever feel like talking about it . . ."

She smiles, then turns and walks away. I'm left standing in front of my house with the emptiest feeling in the world. Knowing what's about to become of Lake's life—it makes me want to protect her even more. I've been in her shoes before and I wouldn't wish it on my worst enemy. I sure as hell don't wish it on the girl I'm falling in love with.

9.

the honeymoon

LAKE SLIDES OFF the bed and walks to the bathroom, wiping her eyes. This is such a bad idea. This is exactly why I don't like bringing up the past.

"Lake," I say, following after her. She's looking into the bathroom mirror, dabbing a tissue to her eyes. I stand behind her and wrap my arms around her waist, resting my head on her shoulder. "I'm sorry. We don't have to talk about it anymore."

She looks at my reflection in the mirror. "Will," she whispers. She turns around to face me and wraps her arms around my neck. "It's just that I had no idea. I didn't know you already knew she was sick."

I pull her to me. "I couldn't really come out and say it, you know. We weren't even speaking at that point. Besides, I would have never betrayed your mom."

She laughs into my shirt, causing me to pull back and look at her. "*What?*" I ask, confused about why she's laughing through her tears.

"Believe me," she says. "I know how your promises to my

mom work. We had to suffer the consequences of that last promise you made for an entire year." She throws her tissue into the trash can and grabs my hand, leading me back to the bed.

"I wouldn't call it suffering," I say, thinking back on last night. "In fact, I'm pretty sure it was worth all the waiting."

She places her hand between her cheek and the pillow and we turn toward each other. I run my fingers through her hair and tuck it behind her ears, then kiss her on the forehead.

"Speaking of suffering," she says. "You just wait until I see Gavin and Eddie again. I can't believe they tried to set you up."

I pull my hand away from her face and rest it on the bed between us. For some reason, I feel like I can't touch her when I'm withholding truth. I break eye contact and roll onto my back. If she's going to bring this up to Eddie, I might as well get it all out in the open now. Otherwise, we'll *all* suffer.

"Um . . . Lake?" I say hesitantly. As soon as her name comes out of my mouth, she shakes her head and scoffs at me.

"You didn't," she says, her words laced with disappointment. She's way too perceptive.

I don't respond.

My silence prompts her to jerk up and grab my jaw, forcing me to look at her.

"You went on a *DATE*?" she says in disbelief.

I place my hand on her cheek in a heartening gesture, hoping my touch will soothe the words about to come out of my mouth. She jerks her face away from my hand and sits up on her knees, placing her hands on them.

"Are you *serious*?"

I laugh a nervous laugh, attempting to make light of the situation. "Lake, you know how forceful Eddie can be. I didn't want to go. Besides, it was just one date."

"Just one date?" she says. "Are you saying you can't develop feelings for someone after just one date?" She spins around on the bed and stands up, dropping down into the desk chair beside the bed. She folds her arms across her chest, shaking her head again. "Please tell me you didn't kiss her."

I scoot toward her until I'm sitting on the edge of the bed. I reach forward and take her hands in mine and look her in the eyes. "I love you," I say. "And I'm here. With you. *Married* to you. Who cares what happened on one silly date more than two years ago?"

"You *KISSED* her?" she says, jerking her hands back. She places her foot on the bed between my legs and pushes against it, rolling her and the chair several feet away from me.

"She kissed *me*," I say defensively. "And it was . . . God, Lake. It was nothing like kissing you."

She glares at me.

"Okay," I say, wiping the smirk off my face. "Not funny. But seriously, you're making a big deal out of nothing. Besides, you agreed to go out with Nick that next week. Remember? What's the difference?"

"What's the *difference*?" she says, enunciating each word carefully. "I didn't *go* on a date with him. I didn't *kiss* him. That's a pretty damn big difference."

I lean forward and grab the arms of her chair and pull her back to me until she's flush against my legs. I place my hands on her cheeks and force her to look at me. "Layken Cooper, I love you. I've loved you since the second I laid eyes on you and I haven't stopped loving you for a second since. The entire time I was out with Taylor, all I was thinking about was *you.*"

She crinkles up her nose. "*Taylor?* I didn't need to know her name, Will. Now I'll have a distaste for Taylors for the rest of my life."

"Like I have distaste for Javiers and Nicks?" I say. She grins, but quickly forces the smile away, still trying to punish me with her ineffective scowl.

"You're so cute when you're jealous, babe." I lean forward and softly press my lips to hers. She sighs a quiet, defeated sigh into my mouth and relents, parting her lips for me. I run my hands down her arms and to her waist, then pull her out of the chair and on top of me as I lean back onto the bed.

I place one hand on the small of her back, pressing her against me, and my other hand I run through her hair, grabbing the back of her head. I kiss her hard as I roll her onto her back, proving to her she has absolutely nothing to be jealous of. As soon as I'm on top of her, she places her hands on my cheeks and forces my face away from hers.

"So your lips touched someone else's lips? *After* our first kiss?"

I fall back onto the bed beside her. "Lake, *stop* it. Stop thinking about it."

"I can't, Will." She turns to me and makes that damn pouty face she knows I can't refuse. "I have to know details. In my head all I can picture is you taking some girl out on this perfect date and making her grilled cheese sandwiches and playing "*would you rather*" with her and sharing seriously intense moments with her, then kissing the hell out of her at the end of the night."

Her description of our first date makes me laugh. I lean over and press my lips to her ear and whisper, "Is that what I did to you? I kissed the *hell* out of you?"

She pulls her neck away and shoots me a glare, letting me know she isn't backing down until she gets her way. "Fine," I groan, pulling back. "If I tell you all about it will you promise to let me kiss the hell out of you again?"

"Promise," she says.

the *other* date

WHEN THE DISMISSAL bell rings, Lake is the first out of the classroom again. The tension in the air between us is so thick, it's like she has to run outside just to breathe. I walk to my desk and take a seat while the rest of the students file out.

"Saturday night. Seven o'clock good for you?" Gavin says. I look up at him and he's staring at me, waiting for a response.

"Good for *what*?"

"For Taylor. We're going on a double date and Eddie won't take no for an answer."

"No."

Gavin stares at me for a few seconds, finding it difficult to comprehend my answer. It was a pretty clear *no*, so I'm not sure what the problem is.

"*Please?*" he says.

"Puppy dog eyes only work on your girlfriend, Gavin."

He slumps his shoulders and lands in the desk in front of me. "She's not gonna let it go, Will. Once Eddie gets something in her head, it's way less painful to just go along with it."

I shake my head. "No. I'm not going," I say firmly. "Besides, you're the one who *put* this idea in her head. You should have to suffer the consequences, not me."

Gavin leans back in his chair and runs his hands over his face, defeated. As soon as I feel victorious, he shoots forward in his seat. "If you don't go, I'll tell."

I lean back in my chair and glare at him. "You'll tell *what*?"

He glances at the door, then back at me, ensuring our privacy. "I'll go to Principal Murphy and I'll tell him you went out with a student. I'm sorry it has to come to blackmail, Will, but you don't know Eddie when she gets an idea in her head. You *have* to do this for me."

Did he really just threaten to blackmail me?

I pick up my pen and pull my lesson plan in front of me, breaking eye contact with him. "Gavin, you won't tell," I say, laughing.

He groans at my response, because he knows he would never stoop that low. "You're right. I'd never tell. But don't you think you owe it to me for being so trustworthy?" he says. "It's just one date. One tiny favor. What difference can one date make?"

"Depending on who it's with, it can make a *huge* difference," I say. One date with Lake was enough to send my life into a tailspin.

"If it helps, you won't have to do much talking. Taylor and Eddie will completely monopolize the conversation. We can eat our steaks and grunt every few minutes and they'll be none the wiser. Then it'll be over. I swear."

I do owe him a favor. A *huge* favor. He's the only one who knows about my situation with Lake and he's never once given me flak about it. I don't know how Eddie can get her way when she's not even in the room, but I finally relent. I slap my pen down on the desk and sigh, giving him a stern look.

"Fine," I say. "Under one condition."

"Anything," he says.

"I don't want this to get back to Lake. Tell Eddie I'll go, but give her an excuse to keep her quiet. Tell her I'm not supposed to be hanging out with you two after hours or something."

Gavin stands and gathers his things. "Thank you, Will,"

he says. "You're a lifesaver. And hey, you might even like Taylor. Keep an open mind."

I WALK INTO the restaurant and spot the three of them in a booth in the far corner. I take a deep breath, then grudgingly walk toward them. I can't believe I'm going on a date. A date that's not with Lake, the only girl I *want* to be on a date with.

The girl I *can't* be on a date with.

Gavin's words, *"keep an open mind,"* linger in my head. I've been completely consumed by thoughts of Lake since I met her almost three weeks ago. I've made the right choice by not continuing something that could ruin my career, but now I just need to figure out how to accept that choice and get her out of my head. Maybe Gavin's right. Maybe I do need to try to move on. It could be better for both of us this way.

When Gavin spots me, he waves and stands up, prompting Taylor to turn around. She's . . . cute. *Really* cute. Her hair is darker than Lake's and shorter, but it fits her well. She's not as tall as Lake, either. She's got a great smile; one of those that seems to be permanently affixed.

I reach the table and smile back at her. Might as well give this a shot.

"Will, Taylor. Taylor, Will," Gavin says, gesturing between us. She smiles and stands up, then gives me a quick hug. General greetings pass around the table and we take our seats. It's odd sitting on the same side of the booth with her. I don't know if I should turn toward her or give my attention to Eddie and Gavin.

"So," she says. "Gavin says you're a teacher?"

I nod. "Student teacher. Until December graduation, anyway."

"You're graduating in December?" she asks, taking a sip of her soda. "How? Isn't that a semester early?"

The waitress walks up to the table and hands me a menu, interrupting the short conversation. "What can I get you to drink?"

"I'll have a sweet tea," I say. The waitress nods and walks away, then Eddie nudges Gavin and pushes his shoulder.

"Sorry, guys, but . . . something just came up," Eddie says. Gavin stands up and pulls his wallet out of his pocket, throwing some cash down on the table.

"This should cover our drinks. You can take Taylor home, right?" he says to me.

"Something came up, huh?" I ask, glaring at both of them. I can't believe they're doing this. I'm *so* going to fail them.

"Uh, yeah," Eddie says, taking Gavin's hand. "So sorry we can't stay. You two have fun."

And they're gone. Just like that.

Taylor laughs. "Wow. *That* wasn't obvious," she says.

I turn back to her and she's grinning, shaking her head. Now it *really* feels odd sitting in the same side of the booth with her. "Well," I say. "This is . . ."

We both say "awkward" at the same time, which causes us to laugh.

"Do you mind if . . ." I point to the other side of the booth and she shakes her head.

"No, please. I've never been a same-side-of-the-booth girl. It's weird."

"I agree," I say, scooting into the seat across from her. The waitress brings my drink and takes our order. It gives us about thirty seconds of distraction before she walks away again, leaving us to fend for ourselves.

Taylor lifts her glass up, motioning to mine. "To awkward first dates," she says. I pick my glass up and clink it against hers.

"So, before all that," she says, waving her hand in the air. "We were talking about how you were graduating a semester early?"

"Yeah . . ." I pause. I don't really feel like going into detail about the real reasons I'm graduating early. I lean back in the booth and shrug. "When I want something, I guess I just focus until I get it. Tunnel vision," I say.

She nods. "Impressive. I've still got a year left, but I'm going into teaching, too. Primary. I like kids."

Our conversation begins to flow better. We talk about college for a while, then when the food comes we talk about that. Then when we run out of things to talk about, she brings up her family. I let her talk about them, but I don't divulge. By the time the bill comes, the conversation is far from awkward. I've only thought about Lake ten times. Maybe fifteen.

Everything seems okay until we're in the car, backing out of the parking lot. Seeing her sitting in the passenger seat, staring out the window; it's reminiscent of just a few weeks ago when Lake was doing the exact same thing, in this exact same spot. But it doesn't feel anything like that. That night with Lake I couldn't keep my eyes off of her while we drove and she slept, her hand still locked with mine. I'm not one to believe that there is only one person right for me in the world. But the tug and pull Lake has on me, even when she isn't in my presence, it makes it feel like she's the *most* right for me. As much as I think Taylor and I would hit it off on a second date, I'm not so sure I'll ever be able to settle for anything less than what I feel for Lake.

We make more small talk and she directs me toward her house. When we pull up into the driveway, the awkwardness immediately sets in. I don't want to lead her on at all, but I also don't want her to think she did anything wrong to turn me off. She was great. The date was great. It's just that my date with Lake was so much more, and now I want nothing less.

I put the car in park and, as awkward as this is going to be, I offer to walk her to her door. When we reach the patio, she turns around and looks up at me with an inviting and welcoming look on her face. This is the point where I need to be honest with her. I don't want to get her hopes up.

"Taylor . . ." I say. "I had a really good ti—" Before I can finish my sentence, her lips are meshed with mine. She doesn't seem like the type to make such bold moves, so the kiss catches me completely off guard. She runs her hands through my hair and I'm suddenly faced with the realization that I don't know what to do with my *own* hands. Do I touch her? Do I push her away? To be honest, the kiss isn't half bad and I catch myself closing my eyes, bringing my hand to her cheek. I know I shouldn't be making comparisons but I can't help it. This kiss is reminiscent of kissing Vaughn. It's not bad . . . pleasant even. But there isn't any emotion in it. No passion. Nothing like what I felt when I kissed Lake.

Lake.

I prepare to pull myself away from her when she finally pulls back herself. I'm relieved I didn't have to be the one to push her away. She takes a step back and covers her mouth in embarrassment. "Wow," she says. "I'm so sorry. I'm not usually that forward."

I laugh. "It's fine. Really, Taylor. It was nice."

I'm not lying; it *was* nice.

"You're just really . . . I don't know," she says, still smiling uncomfortably. "I just wanted to kiss you," she shrugs.

I rub the back of my neck and glance at her front door, then back at her. *How am I going to say this?*

She follows my gaze to her front door, then back to me and smiles. "Oh. You uh . . . You want to come inside?"

Oh, god, oh, god. Why did I look at the door? She thinks I want to come inside now. *Do* I want to come inside? *Shit.* I don't want to come inside. I can't. I wouldn't be thinking about Taylor at all if I went inside.

"Taylor," I say. "I need to be honest with you. I think you're great. I had a great time. If we did this a few months ago, I'd be inside that house with you in a heartbeat."

She can see where I'm headed, so she just nods. "But . . ." she says.

"There's someone else. Someone recent that I can't seem to get past. I agreed to this date because I was hoping that maybe it would somehow help me get over her, but . . . it's too soon."

She looks up at the sky and drops her arms to her side. "Oh, god. I just kissed you. I thought you were feeling it, too, so I kissed you." She covers her face with her hands, embarrassed. "I'm an idiot."

"No," I say, taking a step closer. "No, don't say that. I know this is cliché and it's the last thing you want to hear, but . . . it's not you, it's me. It's completely me. Really. I think you're great and cute and I'm glad you kissed me. Honestly, the timing just really sucks. That's all."

She hugs herself with her arms and looks down at the ground. "If it's just timing," she says quietly, "will you keep my number? In case the timing thing ever gets better?"

"Yeah," I say. "Definitely."

She nods, then looks up at me. "Okay, then," she smiles. "To awkward first dates."

I laugh. "To awkward first dates," I say. She waves and heads inside. Once she's inside her house, I sigh and head back to my car. "Never again, Gavin," I mutter. "Never again."

10.

the honeymoon

"EXCUSE ME FOR a second," Lake says. She pushes herself up and walks to the bathroom, then slams the door behind her.

She's *mad*? *Seriously*? Oh, hell no. I jump up and try to open the bathroom door, but it's locked from the inside. I knock. After several seconds, she swings it open and spins back around toward the shower without looking at me. She turns the shower knob until the water comes to life, then she slips off her shirt.

"I just need a shower," she snaps.

I lean against the doorframe and cross my arms. "You're mad. Why are you mad? Nothing *happened*. I never went out with her again."

She shakes her head and closes the lid to the toilet, then takes a seat on top of it. She slips off her socks one at a time and tosses them to the floor with a jerk of her wrist. "I'm not mad," she says, still avoiding eye contact.

"Lake?" She doesn't look up at me. "Lake? Look at me," I demand.

She inhales a slow breath, then looks up at me through her lashes, her mouth puckered into a pout.

"Three days ago you made a promise to me," I say. "Do you remember what that promise was?"

She rolls her eyes and stands up, unbuttoning her pants. "Of course I remember, Will. It was three freaking days ago."

"What did you promise me you wouldn't do?"

She walks to the mirror and pulls at her ponytail, letting her hair down. She doesn't respond. I take a step closer to her. "What did you promise, Lake? What did we *both* promise each other the night before we got married?"

She grabs her brush off the counter and vigorously combs at her hair. "That we would never carve pumpkins with each other," she mumbles. "That we would talk everything out."

"And what are you doing right now?"

She slams the brush down on the counter and turns to me. "What the hell do you want me to say, Will? Do you want me to admit that I'm not perfect? That I'm jealous? I know you said it didn't mean anything to you, but that doesn't mean it didn't mean something to *me*!" She brushes past me and walks to my suitcase to grab her bottle of conditioner. I lean against the bathroom door again and watch her toss the contents of my suitcase onto the floor while she continues searching for more toiletries.

I don't give her a rebuttal; I have a feeling she isn't finished. Once she gets started like this, it's better if I don't interrupt her. She finds her razor and spins around, continuing her rant.

"And I know you didn't kiss her first, but you didn't *not* kiss her. And you admitted you thought she was cute! And you even admitted that if it weren't for me, you probably would have asked her out again! I hate her, Will. She sounded really, really nice and I hate her for it. It feels like she's been your backup plan in case the two of *us* didn't work out."

She marches toward me again, but this last comment of hers really gets to me. *My backup plan?* I block her way into the bathroom and look down at her, attempting to calm her down before she says something she'll regret.

"Lake, you *know* how I felt about you back then. I never even thought about that girl again. I knew exactly who I wanted to be with. It was just a matter of *when*."

She drops her arms to her side. "Well, that's nice that you had that reassurance, because I sure as hell didn't. I lived every single day feeling like I was going through hell while you were across the street, choosing everything and everyone over *me*. Not to mention all the while going on dates and kissing other girls while I sat home, watching my own mother die right before my eyes."

I step forward and grab her face with both hands. "That's. Not. Fair," I say through clenched teeth. She darts her eyes away from mine, aware of the low blow she delivered. She pulls away from my grasp and walks around me, back into the bathroom. She pushes open the shower curtain and adjusts the water again, letting her pride and stubbornness win.

"That's it? You're leaving it at that?" I say loudly. She doesn't look up at me. I can sense when I need to step away from a situation, and this is one of those times. If I don't walk away, I'll say something I'll regret, too. I punch the door and storm out of the bathroom, then swing open the door to the hallway. I slam the hotel room door and pace back and forth, cursing under my breath. Each time I pass our hotel room, I pause and turn toward it, expecting her to open the door and apologize.

She never does.

She just got in the shower? How in the hell can she say something like that to me and just get in the damn shower without apologizing? God, she's so infuriating! I haven't been this mad at her since that night I thought she was kissing Javi.

I rest my back against our door and slide down to the floor, then take fistfuls of my hair into my hands. She can't seriously be mad about this. We weren't even dating! I try to justify her reasons for reacting the way she is, but I can't. She's acting like an immature high schooler.

"Will?" she says, her voice muffled by the door. She sounds close and I realize she's on the other side of the door at my level. The fact that she knew I was sitting on the floor in front of the door pisses me off even more. She knows me too well.

"What?" I say sharply.

It's silent for a moment, then she sighs. "I'm sorry I said that," she says softly.

I lean my head against the door and close my eyes, taking in a long, deep breath.

"It's just . . . I know we don't believe in soulmates," she says. "There are so many people in this world that can be right for each other. If there weren't, then cheating would never be an issue. Everyone would find their one true love and life would be great—relationships would be a piece of cake. But that's not how it is in reality, and I realize this. So . . . it just hurts, okay? It hurts me to know that there are other women out there in the world that could make you happy. I know it's immature and I was being petty and jealous, but . . . I just want to be your only one. I want to be your soulmate, even if I don't believe in them. I overreacted and I'm sorry," she says. "I'm really sorry, Will."

There's silence on both ends, then I hear the bathroom door shut. I close my eyes and contemplate everything she said. I know exactly how she feels; I've been prone to my own bouts of jealousy in the past when it comes to her. Back when I was her teacher and hearing her agree to that date with Nick, then later seeing Javi kiss her; I lost my mind both times. Hell, I beat the *shit* out of Javi, and Lake wasn't even my girlfriend at the time. Expecting her not to have a reaction when she finds out I kissed someone else in the midst of all our emotional turmoil makes me nothing but a hypocrite. She had a normal reaction just now, and I'm treating her like this is her fault. She's probably in the shower right now, crying. All because of me.

I'm such an *asshole*.

I jump up and slide the key card in, then open the door. I swing open the bathroom door and she's sitting on the edge of the shower, still in her pants and bra, crying into her hands. She looks up at me with the saddest eyes and guilt consumes me. I grab her hand and pull her up. She sucks in a breath like she's scared I'm about to yell at her again, which only makes me feel worse. I slide my hands through her hair and grip the nape of her neck, then look her in the eyes. She can see in my expression that I'm not here to fight.

I'm here to make up.

"Wife," I say, staring straight into her eyes. "Think what you want, but there isn't a single woman in this whole damn universe that I could ever love like I love you."

Our mouths collide so forcefully; she almost falls backward into the shower. I brace my hand against the shower wall with one arm, then pick her up around the waist with the other arm, lifting her over the lip of the tub. I shove her up against the wall, the water from the showerhead falling between us. We're both breathing heavily and I pull her as close against me as she can possibly get while her fingers tug and pull at my hair. My chest heaves with each breath I inhale as we frantically grab and pull and stroke every inch of each other within arm's reach.

I pull her bra up and over her head, then throw it behind me. My hand slides down to the small of her back, my fingers tracing a trail just inside the back of her jeans. She moans and arches her back, pressing herself harder against me. My fingers slowly slide around to the front of her jeans and I lower her zipper. Her pants are soaked, so it takes effort getting them off her, but I eventually do.

I slide my hand all the way up her thigh and I'm met with nothing but smooth skin. I grin against her lips. "Commando, huh?"

She doesn't waste any time pulling my mouth back to hers. I've been standing directly in the stream of water, so my clothes are soaked, making them more challenging to remove than hers were. Especially since she won't release me for a second longer than needed to pull off my shirt. Once my shirt is successfully gone, I lean back into her. She moans into my mouth when our bare skin collides, forcing me to immediately dispose of my pants as well. She grabs them out of my hand and tosses them over my shoulder, then pulls me against her. I reach down and grab her right leg behind the knee and I pull it up to my side.

She smiles. "Now *this* is how I pictured our first shower together," she says.

I take her bottom lip between my teeth, and I give her the best damn shower she's ever had.

"HOLY CRAP," SHE says, falling onto the bed. "That was intense."

Her arms are relaxed above her head, her robe open just far enough to keep my imagination in check. I sit down beside her and stroke her cheek, then run my hand down her neck. She shivers against my touch. I bend over and press my lips to her collarbone. "There's just something about this spot," I say, teasing her neck. "From here . . ." I kiss up her collarbone until I get to the curve in her neck. "To here." I kiss back down again. "It drives me insane."

She laughs. "I can tell. You can't keep your mouth off it. Most guys prefer the ass or the boobs. Will Cooper prefers the *neck*."

I shake my head, disagreeing with her while I continue running my lips across her incredibly smooth skin. "Nope," I say. "Will Cooper prefers the whole *Lake*."

I tug at the tie on her robe until it loosens between my fingertips. I slide my hand inside the robe and graze her stomach with my fingers. She squirms beneath my hand and laughs.

"Will, you can't be serious. It hasn't even been three minutes."

I ignore her and kiss the chills that are breaking out on her shoulder. "You remember the first time I couldn't resist kissing your neck?" I whisper against her skin.

the (first) mistake

IT'S BEEN THREE weeks since Julia told me she was sick, but from watching Lake and listening to Kel on a daily basis, I know she still hasn't told them. I've spoken to Julia a few times, but only in passing. She doesn't seem to want to bring it up again, so I give her that respect.

Having Lake in third period hasn't gotten any easier. I've learned how to adapt and focus more on what I'm teaching, but the fact that she's still just feet from me every day still has the same emotional impact. Every morning she comes to class, I try to watch for any hints or signs that Julia may have revealed everything to her, but every day is the same. She never raises her hand or speaks, and I make it a point never to call on her. I make it a point not to even look at her. It's been getting harder now that Nick seems to be marking his territory. I know it's none of my business, but I can't help but wonder if they're dating. I haven't seen him at her house but I've noticed they sit together at lunch. She always seems to be in a good mood around him. Gavin would know, but as far as he knows I've moved on, so I can't ask him. I really shouldn't even care . . . but I can't help it.

I'm running late when I get to class. When I walk in, the first thing I notice is Nick turned toward Lake. She's laughing again. She's always laughing at his stupid jokes. I like seeing her laugh, but I also hate that he's the reason she's laughing. It immediately puts me in a bad mood, so I decide to cancel the lecture I had planned and give a poetry writing assignment instead. After I lay out the rules and everyone begins on their assignment, I take a seat at my desk. I try to focus on completing a lesson plan, but I can't help but notice Lake hasn't written a single word. I know she doesn't have a problem with the material in class. In fact, she's had the best grades since the day she enrolled. Her lack of effort on this assignment makes me wonder if she has the same concentration problems during third period that I have.

I glance up from staring at the blank paper on her desk and she's staring right at me. My heart catches in my throat and the same emotional and physical responses I try so hard to squelch are suddenly consuming me again. It's the first eye contact we've had in three weeks. I try to look away, but I can't. She doesn't reveal any hint of emotion in her expression. I wait for her to look away, but instead she stares at me with the same intensity that I'm sure I'm returning in my own stare. This silent exchange between us causes my pulse to race just as fiercely as it did when I kissed her.

When the bell rings, I force myself out of my chair and walk to the door to hold it open. When everyone's gone, including Lake, I slam it shut.

What the hell am I thinking? That twenty seconds of whatever the hell that was negated my entire last three weeks of effort. I lean against the door and kick it out of frustration.

AS SOON AS I reach the parking lot after school, I see that the hood to Lake's Jeep is open. I look around, hoping someone else is around to assist her instead. I really don't need to be alone with her right now, especially after what happened in my classroom this morning. I'm finding it harder and harder to resist the thought of her, and this current predicament has trouble written all over it.

Unfortunately, I'm the only one around. I can't just leave her here stranded in a parking lot. I'm sure it would be just as easy to turn around and head inside before she notices me. Someone else will help her eventually. Despite my hesitation, I keep walking forward. When I near her vehicle, she's bludgeoning the battery with a crowbar.

"That's not a good idea," I say. I'm hoping she doesn't bust through the battery before I reach her. She spins around and looks at me, eyeing me up and down, then returns her focus back under the hood like she never even saw me.

"You've made it clear that you don't think a lot of what I do is a very good idea," she says firmly. She's obviously not happy to see me, which is just more confirmation that I should turn around and walk away.

But I don't.

I *can't*.

I reluctantly walk closer and peer under the hood. "What's wrong, it won't crank?" I check the connections on the battery and inspect the alternator.

"What are you doing, Will?" She has an edgy, almost annoyed tone to her voice. I lift my head out from under the hood and look at her. Her features are hard. It's obvious she's put up an invisible wall between us, which is probably a good thing. She seems offended that I'm even offering to help her.

"What does it look like I'm doing?" I break our stare and quickly turn my attention back to the battery cable. "I'm trying to figure out what's wrong with your Jeep," I say. I walk around to the door and attempt to turn the ignition. When it doesn't crank, I turn to exit the Jeep and she's standing right next to me. I'm quickly reminded what it feels like to be in such close proximity to her. I hold my breath and fight back the urge to grab her by the waist and pull her into the Jeep with me.

"I mean, *why* are you doing this? You've made it pretty clear you don't want me to speak to you," she says.

Her obvious annoyance at my presence almost makes me regret having decided to help her after all. "Layken, you're a student stranded in the parking lot. I'm not going to get in my car and just drive away." As soon as the words escape my lips, I regret them. She draws her chin in and glances away, shocked at my impersonal words.

I sigh and get out of the car. "Look, that's not how I meant it," I say as I reach back under the hood.

She steps closer to me and leans against the Jeep. I watch her out of the corner of my eye while I pretend to fidget with more wires. She tugs on her bottom lip with her teeth and stares at the ground, a saddened expression across her face. "It's just been really hard, Will," she says quietly. The softness in her voice now is even more painful to hear than the edginess. I inhale, afraid of what she's about to confess. She takes a deep breath like she's hesitating to finish her sentence, but continues anyway. "It was so easy for you to accept this and move past it. It hasn't been that easy for me. It's all I think about."

Her confession and the honesty in her voice cause me to wince. I grip the edge of the hood and turn toward her. She's looking down at her hands with a troubled expression on her face. "You think this is *easy* for me?" I whisper.

She glances at me and shrugs. "Well, that's how you make it seem," she says.

Now would be the opportune moment to walk away. Walk away, Will.

"Lake, nothing about this has been easy," I whisper. I know beyond a doubt that I shouldn't be saying any of the things I've been dying to say to her, but everything about her draws the truth out of me whether I want to share it or not. "It's a daily struggle for me to come to work, knowing this very job is what's keeping us apart." I turn away from the car and lean against it, next to her. "If it weren't for Caulder, I would have quit that first day I saw you in the hallway. I could have taken the year off . . . waited until you graduated to go back." I turn toward her and lower my voice. "Believe me, I've run every possible scenario through my mind. How do you think it makes me feel to know that I'm the reason you're hurting? That I'm the reason you're so sad?"

I just said way too much. *Way* too much.

"I . . . I'm sorry," she stutters. "I just thought—"

"Your battery is fine," I say as soon as I see Nick round the car next to us. "Looks like it might be your alternator."

"Car won't start?" Nick says.

Layken looks at me wide-eyed, then turns around to face Nick. "No, Mr. Cooper thinks I need a new alternator."

"That sucks," Nick says as he glances under the hood. He looks back up at Lake. "I'll give you a ride home if you need one."

As much as I'd rather punch him than let him take her home, I know it's her only option right now because *I* sure as hell don't need to take her home.

"That would be great, Nick," I say. I shut the hood of the Jeep and walk away before I add to my long list of stupid decisions.

I SHOULD JUST pull the list of stupid decisions back out, because I'm making another one right now.

We've spent the last fifteen minutes frantically searching for Kel and Caulder. I'd assumed they were at her house, she had assumed they were at mine. We finally found them passed out in the backseat of my car, where they still are.

Now, I'm rummaging through my satchel, searching for the keys to her Jeep. I had my mechanic put a new alternator on it this afternoon, then stupidly invited her inside to give her the keys back. I say *stupidly*, because every ounce of my being doesn't want her to leave. My heart is pounding against my chest just being in her presence. I locate the keys and turn around to hand them to her. "Your keys," I say, dropping them into her hand.

"Oh, thanks," she says, looking down at them. I'm not sure what she expected me to hand her, but she seems disappointed that it's just her keys.

"It's running fine now," I say. "You should be able to drive it home tomorrow." I'm hoping she'll be the strong one right now and just leave. I can't bring myself to walk her back to the door, so I make my way back into the living room and sit on the couch. The conversation at her Jeep this afternoon lingers silent and thick in the air between us.

"What? You fixed it?" she says, following me into the living room.

"Well, *I* didn't fix it. I know a guy who was able to put an alternator on it this afternoon."

"Will, you didn't have to do that," she says. Rather than leave like we both know she should, she sits on the couch beside me. When her elbow grazes mine, I bring my hands up and clasp them behind my head. We can't even graze elbows without my wanting to reach over and kiss the hell out of her.

"Thanks, though. I'll pay you back."

"Don't worry about it. You guys have helped me a lot with Caulder lately, it's the least I can do."

She looks down at her hand and twirls the keys around. She runs her thumb over the Texas-shaped keychain and I can't help but wonder if she'd still rather be there right now.

"So, can we finish our conversation from earlier?" she says, still staring down at the keychain.

I already regret having said what I said at her Jeep today. I confessed way too much. I can't believe I told her I would have quit my job if it weren't for Caulder. I mean, it's the truth. As crazy and desperate as it sounds, I would have quit in a heartbeat. I'm not so sure I still wouldn't if she would just ask me to.

"That depends," I say. "Did you come up with a solution?"

She shakes her head and looks up at me. "Well, no," she says. She tosses her keys onto the coffee table and pulls her knee up, turning to face me on the couch. She sighs, almost as if she's afraid to ask me something. She runs her fingers over the throw pillow between us and traces the pattern without looking up at me. "Suppose these feelings we have just get more . . . complex." She hesitates for a moment. "I wouldn't be opposed to the idea of getting a GED."

Her plan is so absurd I almost have to hold back a laugh. "That's ridiculous," I say, shooting a look in her direction. "Don't even think like that. There's no way you're quitting school, Lake."

She tosses the pillow aside. "It was just an idea," she says.

"Well, it was a dumb one."

Things grow quiet between us. The way she's turned toward me on the couch causes every muscle in my body to clench, even my jaw. I'm trying so hard not to turn toward her, to take her in my arms. This entire situation isn't fair. If we were in any other circumstances, a relationship between us would be absolutely fine. Accepted. Normal. The only thing keeping us apart is a damn job title.

It's so hard having to hide how I feel about her when it's just the two of us. It would be so easy to just say *"To hell with it,"* and do what I want to do. I know if I could just get past the moral aspect and the threat of getting caught, I'd do it in a heartbeat. I'd take her in my arms and kiss her just like I've been imagining for the past three weeks. I'd kiss her mouth, I'd kiss her cheek, I'd kiss that line from her ear down to her shoulder that I can't stop staring at. She'd let me, too. I know how hard this has been on her; I can see it in the way she carries herself now. She's depressed. I'm almost tempted to make all of this easier on her and just act on my feelings. If neither of us says anything, no one would know. We could do this secretly until she graduated. If we were careful, we could even keep it from Julia and the boys.

I pop my knuckles behind my head in order to distract myself from pulling her mouth to mine. My heart is erratic just thinking about the possibility of kissing her again. I inhale through my nose and out my mouth, trying to physically calm myself before I do something stupid. Or smart. I can't tell what's right or wrong when I'm around her because what's wrong feels so right and what's right feels so wrong.

Her finger grazes across my neck and the unexpected touch causes me to flinch. She defensively holds up her finger to show me the shaving cream she just wiped off my neck. Without even thinking, I grab her hand to wipe it onto my shirt.

Big mistake.

As soon as my fingers touch hers, whatever conscious thoughts remained get wiped away right along with the shaving cream. My hand remains clasped on top of hers and she relaxes it onto my chest.

I've reached the threshold of my willpower. My pulse is racing, my heart feels like it's about to explode. I can't let go of her hand and I can't stop looking into her eyes. In this moment, absolutely nothing is happening, but then again *everything* is happening. Every single second I silently look at her, holding on to her hand, erases days of willpower and determination I spent keeping my distance. Every ounce of energy I've put into doing the right thing has all been in vain.

"Will?" she whispers without breaking her gaze. The way my name flows from her lips makes my pulse go haywire. She strokes her thumb ever so slightly across my chest—a movement she may not have even been aware of, but one that I feel all the way to my core. "I'll wait for you," she says. "Until I graduate."

As soon as the words come from her lips, I exhale and close my eyes. She just said what I've wanted to hear from her for an entire month. I stroke my thumb across the back of her hand and sigh. "That's a long wait, Lake. A lot can happen in a year."

She scoots closer to me on the couch. She removes her hand from my chest and lightly touches my jaw with the tips of her fingers, pulling my gaze back to hers. I refuse to look into her eyes. I know if I do, I'll give in and kiss her. I slide my fingers down her hand with every intention of stopping at her wrist to pull her hand from my face. Instead, my fingers trail past her wrist and slowly graze up the length of her arm. I need to stop. I need to pull back, but my willpower and my heart are suddenly at war.

I pull my legs off the coffee table in front of me. I'm hoping she pushes me away from her—does what we both know one of us needs to do. When she doesn't, I find myself drawing in closer. I just want to put my arms around her and hold her. I want to hold her like I held her outside Club N9NE before all of this became out of our control. Before it became this overwhelming, convoluted mess.

Before I can stop myself or give myself time to think about it—my lips meet her neck, and all hell breaks loose inside me. She wraps her arms around me and inhales a breath deep enough for the both of us. The feel and taste of her skin against my lips is enough to completely wipe away the rest of my conscience.

To hell with it.

I kiss across her collarbone, up her neck and to her jaw, then take her face in my hands and pull back to look her in the eyes. I need to know we're on the same page. I need to know that she wants this as bad as I do. That she *needs* this as bad as I do.

The sadness in her eyes that has consumed her for the past three weeks is nonexistent right now. There's hope in her eyes again, and I want nothing more than to somehow help her maintain whatever it is she's feeling right now. I slowly lean in and press my lips against hers. The sensation from the kiss both kills me and brings me back to life in the same breath. She quietly gasps, then parts her lips for me, taking a fist of my shirt in her hands, gently pulling me closer.

I kiss her.

I kiss her like it's the first time I've ever kissed her.

I kiss her like it's the *last* time I'll ever kiss her.

Her hands are around my neck—my lips are caressing hers. Holding her in my arms right now feels like I'm taking the first breath I've taken since that moment I saw her standing in the hallway. Every moan from her mouth and every touch of her hands brings me back to life. Nothing and no one can come between us and this moment. Not Caulder, not my morals, not my job, not my school, not Julia.

Julia.

I clench my fists, fighting against the pull to release her when reality hits. The heaviness of the situation comes crashing back down on me like a ton of bricks, forcing itself into the forefront of my mind. Lake has no idea what's about to happen to her life, and I'm allowing myself to complicate it even *more*? With every movement of my mouth against hers, I'm pulling us further and further into a hole we aren't going to be able to crawl out of.

She runs her hands through my hair and begins to lower herself back onto the couch, pulling me with her. I know once our bodies are meshed together on this couch, neither one of us will be strong enough to stop.

I can't *do* this to her. There is so much more going on in her life than she's even aware of. What the hell am I thinking adding this kind of stress to that? I swore to Julia I wouldn't complicate Lake's life, and that's precisely what I'm doing. I somehow find the strength to tear my lips apart from hers and pull away. When I do, we both gasp for air.

"We've got to stop," I say, breathless. "We can't do this." I squeeze my eyes shut and cover them with my forearm, giving myself a minute to regroup. I feel her inching closer to me. She pulls herself onto my lap and forces her lips onto mine again in a desperate plea to keep going. The second our lips meet, I instinctively wrap my arms around her and pull her closer. My conscience is literally screaming at me so loud, I pull her face to mine even harder in an attempt to squelch the internal voice. My mind is telling me to do one thing; my heart and my hands are begging me to do another. She grasps my shirt and slips it over my head, then returns her lips to my mouth where they belong.

In my mind I'm pushing her away, but in reality I've got one hand on her lower back, pulling her against me, and my other hand gripping the nape of her neck. She runs her hands over my chest and I have a huge urge to do the same to her. Just as I grasp the hem of her shirt, I clench my fists and release it. I've already let it go way too far. I've got to put an end to this before I *can't*. It's entirely my responsibility to make sure she doesn't get hurt again, and right now I'm dropping the ball completely.

I push her off me and back onto the couch, then stand up. I've got one chance to prove to her that this is bad. As good as it feels, it's wrong. So wrong.

"Layken, get up!" I demand, taking her hand. I'm so incredibly flustered right now, I don't mean for my reaction to come off so harsh, but I don't know how else to react. I'm so pissed at myself I want to scream, but I struggle with the attempt to calm my nerves. She stands up with a look of embarrassment and confusion across her face.

"This—this can't happen!" I say. "I'm your teacher now. Everything has changed. We can't do this." I can hear the edge in my voice again. I'm trying my best not to come off as angry, but I *am* angry. Not at her, but how can she differentiate? Maybe she shouldn't. Maybe this would be easier for her if she were disappointed in me. Easier for her to let me go.

She sits back down on the couch and drops her face into her hands. "Will, I won't say anything," she whispers. "I swear." She looks back up at me and the sadness in her eyes has returned. All the hope is gone.

The hurt in her voice only solidifies the fact that I'm an asshole. I can't believe I just *did* this to her—led her on like this. She doesn't need this right now.

"I'm sorry, Layken, but it's not right," I say as I pace the floor. "This isn't good for either of us. This isn't good for *you*."

She glares at me. "You don't know what's good for me," she snaps.

I've really screwed this up. *Royally.* I need to fix it now. I need to *end* it now. For good. She can't leave here thinking this is going to happen again. I stop pacing and turn toward her.

"You won't wait for me. I won't let you give up what should be the best year of your life. I had to grow up way too fast; I'm not taking that away from you, too. It wouldn't be fair." I inhale a breath and tell the biggest lie I've ever told. "I don't want you to wait for me, Layken."

"I won't be giving *anything* up," she replies weakly.

The pain in her voice is too much, causing me to have an overwhelming urge to hug her again. I can't take these emotional swings anymore. One minute I'm wanting to kiss the living hell out of her and take her in my arms and protect her from every tear that's about to come her way, then the next minute my conscience kicks in and I want to kick her out of my house. I've hurt her so bad and she has no idea how much worse her life is about to get. Just knowing this makes me hate myself for what I just allowed to happen. *Despise* myself, even.

I grab my shirt and pull it over my head, then move across the living room to the back of the couch. I take a deep breath, feeling slightly more in control the farther away I am from her. I grip the back of the couch and prepare an attempt to rectify a nonrectifiable situation. If I could just get her to understand where I'm coming from, maybe she wouldn't take it so hard.

"My life is nothing but responsibilities. I'm raising a *child*, for Christ's sake. I wouldn't be able to put your needs first. Hell, I wouldn't even be able to put them *second*." I raise my head and meet her eyes. "You deserve better than third."

She stands up and crosses the living room, kneeling on the couch in front of me. "Your responsibilities *should* come before me, which is why I want to wait for you, Will. You're a good person. This thing about you that you think is your flaw—it's the reason I'm falling in love with you."

Whatever was left of my heart before those words left her mouth is in a million pieces now. I can't let her do this. I can't let her feel this way. The only thing I can do to make her stop loving me is to make her start hating me. I bring my hands up to meet her cheeks and I look her in the eyes, then I say the hardest words that I'll ever have to say. "You are *not* falling in love with me. You *cannot* fall in love with me." As soon as I see the tears welling in the corners of her eyes, I have to drop my hands and head toward the front door. I can't watch her cry. I don't want to see what I'm doing to her right now.

"What happened tonight—" I point to the couch. "That can't happen again. That *won't* happen again."

I open the front door and shut it behind me, then lean against the door and close my eyes. I rub my hands over my face and attempt to calm myself down. This is all my fault. I allowed her into my house, knowing how weak I am around her. I kissed her. *I* kissed *her.* I can't believe all of this just happened. Twenty minutes alone with her and I somehow screw her life up even more.

Seeing her sitting on the couch just now, dumbfounded and heartbroken because of my actions and my words . . . I *hate* myself. Pretty sure Lake hates me now, too. I hope it was worth it. Somehow doing the *right* thing in this situation seems completely and utterly *wrong*.

I walk to the car and pull Caulder out. He wraps his arms around my neck without even waking up. Kel opens his eyes and looks around, confused.

"You guys fell asleep in the car. Go home and go to bed, okay?"

He rubs his eyes and crawls out of the car, then makes his way across the street. When I walk back through the front door holding Caulder, Lake is still sitting on the couch, staring at the floor. As much as I want to grab her and tell her I'm so, so sorry for this entire night, I realize she needs this to get past whatever it is going on between us. She *needs* to be angry at me. And Julia needs her to be focused this year. She can't have Lake wrapped up in us when it might be the last year she ever gets to spend with her mom.

"Kel woke up, he's walking home now. You should go, too," I say.

She snatches the keys off the table in front of her and turns to face me. She looks me straight in the eyes; tears streaming down her face. "You're an *asshole*," she says, her words like a bullet of truth straight through my heart. She walks out and slams the door behind her.

I take Caulder to his room and tuck him in, then walk to my bedroom. When I close the door behind me, I lean against it and close my eyes, then slide down the length of the door until I meet the floor. I press the heels of my palms against my eyes, holding back the tears.

God, this *girl*. This girl is the only girl I care about, and I just gave her every reason in the world to hate me.

11.

the honeymoon

"I'M SO, SO sorry, Will," she whispers. She puts her hands over her face and covers her eyes. "I feel horrible. Terrible. And *selfish*. I didn't know how hard it was for you, too. I just thought you kicked me out because I wasn't worth the risk."

"Lake, you didn't know what all was going through my mind. For all you knew I was just some jerk who kissed you, then kicked you out of my house. I never blamed you. And you were absolutely worth the risk. If it weren't for knowing what I knew about Julia, I would have never let you go."

She pulls her hands away from her face and turns to me. "Oh, my god, and those *names*. I never did apologize for that." She rolls on top of me and brings her face inches from mine. "I'm so sorry I called you all those names the next day."

"Don't be," I shrug. "I sort of deserved it."

She shakes her head. "You can't sit here and tell me that didn't piss you off. I mean, I called you thirty different names in front of the entire class!"

"I didn't say it didn't piss me off. I just said I deserved it."

She laughs. "So you *were* mad at me." She lies back down on her pillow. "Let me hear it," she says.

regrets

I'VE GONE AS slowly as possible. I've called on each student, never rushed them, never even timed them. Usually they don't spit them out this fast. Of course, as soon as Gavin finishes his poem, there's still five minutes to spare. I have no choice but to call on her. I waited until last, hoping the bell would ring. I don't know if I'm trying to spare her from having to get up and speak after what happened between us last night, or if I'm scared to death about what she might say. Either way, it's her turn and I have no choice but to call her up.

I clear my throat and attempt to say her name, but it comes out all mangled. She walks to the front of the room and leaves her poem on her desk. I know for a fact she didn't write a single word yesterday in class. And considering the events that transpired in my living room last night, I doubt she was in the right mindset to even write one. However, she appears unwavering and confident and has apparently memorized whatever it is she's about to perform. It sort of terrifies me.

"I have a question," she says before she begins.

Shit. What the hell could she possibly need to ask? She left so angry last night, I wouldn't be surprised if she outs me right here and now. Hell, she's probably about to ask me if I kick *all* my students out of my house after I make out with them. I nod, giving her the go-ahead for her question . . . but all I really want to do is run to the bathroom and puke.

"Is there a time minimum?"

Jesus Christ. She's actually asking a normal question. I breathe a sigh of relief and clear my throat. "No, it's fine. Remember, there are no rules."

"Good," she says. "Okay, then. My poem is called *Mean.*"

The blood rushes from my head and pools in my heart as soon as the title flows from her mouth. She turns toward the room and begins.

According to the thesaurus . . .
and according to *me* . . .
there are over thirty different meanings and
substitutions for the word
mean.

(SHE RAISES HER voice and yells the rest of the poem, causing me to flinch.)

Jackass, jerk, cruel, dickhead, unkind, harsh, wicked,
hateful, heartless, vicious, virulent, unrelenting,
tyrannical, malevolent, atrocious, bastard, barbarous,
bitter, brutal, callous, degenerate, brutish, depraved,
evil, fierce, hard, implacable, rancorous, pernicious,
inhumane, monstrous, merciless, inexorable.
And *my* personal favorite—*asshole.*

MY PULSE IS pounding almost as fast as the insults are flying out of her mouth. When the bell rings, I sit stunned as most of the students make their way past my desk. *I can't believe she just did that!*

"The date," I hear Eddie saying to her. The word "date" snaps me back into the moment. "You said you'd have to ask your mom?" Eddie says. They're standing next to Lake's desk and Eddie has her back turned to me.

"Oh, that," Lake says. She looks over Eddie's shoulder and directly at me. "Yeah, sure," she says. "Tell Nick I'd love to."

I've never had a problem with my temper before, but it's almost as if the day I met Lake, every single emotion I had was multiplied by a thousand. Happiness, hurt, anger, bitterness, love, jealousy. I'm unable to control any of it when I'm around her. The fact that she apparently had been asked out by Nick *before* our little incident last night somehow pisses me off even more. I glare at her, open my drawer, and shove my grade book inside it, then slam it shut. When Eddie spins around, startled at the noise, I quickly stand up and begin wiping the board.

"Great," Eddie says, her attention back to Lake now. "Oh, and we decided on Thursday so after Getty's we can go to the slam. We've only got a few weeks, might as well get it out of the way. You want us to pick you up?"

"Uh, sure," Lake says.

Lake could have at least had the decency to agree to a date when she's not standing five feet from me. As much as I want her to be pissed at me, I never thought I'd be pissed at her. But she seems intent on ensuring that that happens. Once Eddie leaves the classroom, I drop the eraser and turn back toward Lake. I fold my arms across my chest and watch as she gathers her things and heads toward the door, not once looking in my direction. Before she exits, I say something I regret before I even say it.

"Layken."

She pauses when she gets to the door, but doesn't turn around to face me.

"Your mom works Thursday nights," I say. "I always get a sitter for Thursdays since I go to the slams. Just send Kel over before you leave. You know, before your *date*."

She doesn't turn around. She doesn't yell. She doesn't throw anything at me. She simply walks out the door, leaving me feeling as though I'm every single one of those names she just yelled in my classroom.

After fourth period, I sit at my desk and stare at nothing at all, wondering what the hell has gotten into me. I usually go to the teachers' lounge for lunch, but I know I can't eat right now. My stomach is in knots thinking about the last two hours. Actually, the last *twenty-four* hours.

Why would I say that to her? I know her poem stirred something in me unlike anything I've ever felt. It was a mixture of embarrassment, anger, hurt, and heartache. But that wasn't enough for her—she had to go and add *jealousy* on top of all that. If there's one thing I've learned about today, it's that I don't handle jealousy well. At all.

I know I thought the best way to help her get over me was to make sure she hated me, but I just can't do it. If I want to keep my own sanity, I can't let her hate me. I can't let her love me, though, either. *Shit!* This is so screwed up. *How the hell am I going to make this right?*

WHEN I REACH their table in the lunchroom, she's not even joined in on the conversation taking place around her. She's staring down at her tray, oblivious to the world. Oblivious to me. Eddie and I both try to get her attention. When she finally snaps out of her trance and looks up at me, the color runs from her face. She slowly rises from the table and follows me to the classroom. When we're safely inside I close the door and walk past her to my desk.

"We need to talk," I say. My head is spinning and I have no

idea what I even want to say to her. I know I want to apologize for the way I reacted earlier in class, but the words aren't coming. I'm a grown man acting like a blubbering fourteen-year-old boy.

"Then talk," she snaps. She's standing across the room glaring at me. Her current attitude coupled with the fact that she just agreed to go out on a date with another guy right in front of me infuriates me. I know everything about our situation is my fault, but she's not doing anything to help it.

"Dammit, Lake!" I spin away from her, frustrated. I run my hands through my hair and take a deep breath, then turn back to face her. "I'm not your enemy. Stop hating me."

I swear she chuckles under her breath right before her eyes fill with fury. "Stop *hating* you?" she says, rushing toward me. "Make up your freaking *mind*, Will! Last night, you told me to stop loving you, now you're telling me to stop *hating* you? You tell me you don't want me to wait on you, yet you act like an immature little boy when I agree to go out with Nick! You want me to act like I don't know you, but then you pull me out of the lunchroom in front of everyone! We've got this whole façade between us, like we're different people all the time, and it's exhausting! I never know when you're Will or Mr. Cooper and I *really* don't know when I'm supposed to be Layken or Lake."

She throws herself into a chair and folds her arms across her chest, letting out a rush of frustrated breath. She's eyeing me sharply, waiting for me to say or do something. There isn't anything to say. I can't refute a single word she just said, because it's the truth. The fact that I haven't been able to keep my own feelings in check have done more damage to her than I ever imagined.

I slowly walk around her desk and sit in the seat behind her. I'm exhausted. Emotionally, physically, mentally. I never imagined it would turn into this. If I had the slightest clue that the decision to keep my job over her would have this kind of effect on me, I would have picked her, despite whatever is going on with Julia. I *should* have picked her. I *still* should pick her.

I lean forward until I'm close to her ear. "I didn't think it would be this hard," I whisper. And that's the truth. Never in a million years did I think something as trivial as a first date could turn into something so incredibly *complicated*. "I'm sorry I said that to you earlier, about Thursday," I say. "I was being sincere—for the most part. I know you'll need someone to watch Kel and I did make the slam a required assignment. But I shouldn't have reacted like that. That's why I asked you to come here; I just needed to apologize. It won't happen again, I swear."

I hear her sniff, which only means she's crying. *Jesus.* I keep making this worse for her when all I want to do is fix it. I lift my hand to stroke the back of her hair in reassurance when the door to my classroom opens. I immediately pull my hand back and stand up, a hasty move that reeks of guilt. Eddie is standing in the doorway to the classroom holding Lake's backpack. She glances at me, then we both simultaneously look at Lake. Turning her head away from Eddie and toward me, I finally see the tears streaming down Lake's cheeks. The tears I put there.

Eddie sets the backpack in a desk and holds her palms up, backing out of the doorway. "My bad. Continue," she says.

As soon as the door is closed behind her, I begin to panic. Whatever Eddie just witnessed, it obviously wasn't a conversation between a teacher and his student. I've just added yet another shittastic thing to my list of screw-ups.

"That's just great," I mumble. How the hell do I even begin to fix all of this?

Lake rises out of her seat and begins walking toward the door. "Let it go, Will. If she asks me about it, I'll just tell her you were upset because I said asshole. And jackass. And dickhead. And bastar—"

"I get your point," I say, interrupting her before she can finish her stream of insults. She picks up her backpack and reaches the door.

"Layken?" I say cautiously. "I also want to say I'm sorry . . . about last night."

She slowly turns toward me. The tears have stopped but the residual effects of her mood are still written across her face. "Are you sorry it happened? Or sorry about the way you stopped it?"

I don't really understand what the difference is. I shrug my shoulders. "All of it. It never should have happened."

She turns her back to me and opens the door. "Bastard."

The insult cuts straight to my heart, right where she intended for it to hit.

As soon as the door closes behind her, I kick the desk over. "Shit!" I yell, squeezing the tension out of my neck with my hands. I let out a steady stream of cusswords as I pace the classroom. Not only have I screwed this up even worse with Lake, I've also screwed it up by making Eddie suspicious. I feel like I've somehow made this entire situation ten times worse. God, what I wouldn't give for my father's advice right now.

MRS. ALEX AND her pointless questions once again make me late for third period. I don't really mind being late today, though. After the interaction in my classroom yesterday with Lake, I'm still not ready to face her.

The hallways have cleared out and I'm nearing my classroom when I pass by the windows that look out over the courtyard. I stop in my tracks and step closer to the window and I see Lake. She's sitting on one of the benches, looking down at her hands. I'm a little confused, since she should be sitting in my classroom right now. She looks up at the sky and lets out a deep sigh, like she's trying not to cry. It's apparent that the last place she can be right now is two feet from me in a classroom. Seeing her out there, choosing the bitter Michigan air over my classroom, makes me hurt for her.

"She's something else, huh?"

I spin around and Eddie is standing behind me with her arms crossed, smiling.

"What?" I say, undoubtedly trying to recover from the fact that she just caught me staring at Lake.

"You heard me," she says, walking past me toward the courtyard entry. "And you agree with me, too." She walks out into the courtyard without turning back. When Lake looks up at her and smiles, I walk away.

It's not a big deal. Lake is a student skipping my class and I was looking at her. That's all. There wasn't anything happening there that Eddie could report. Despite my failed attempts at reassuring myself, I spend the rest of the day a nervous wreck.

12.

the honeymoon

"LET ME GET this straight," Lake says, glaring at me. "You were being an idiot, staring at me through the courtyard window. Eddie sees you staring at me, which only piques her curiosity at this point. But then the next weekend in your living room when Eddie figured it all out, you get mad at *me*?"

"I wasn't mad at you," I say.

"Will, you were pissed! You kicked me out of your house!"

I roll over and think back to that night. "I guess I did, huh?"

"Yes, you did," she says. "And on the worst day of my life at that." She rolls over on top of me and interlocks her fingers with mine, bringing them over my head. "I think you owe me an apology. After all, I did clean your entire house that day."

I look her in the eyes and she's grinning. I know she's not upset, but I actually do want to give her a sincere apology. The way I acted at the end of that day was purely selfish, and I've always regretted how I just kicked her out at one of the lowest points of her life. I bring my hands to her cheeks and pull her to the pillow next to me while we change positions. I lay her on her back and rest my head on my propped-up hand, stroking her face with my other hand. I run my fingers up her cheek, over her forehead, and down her nose until my fingers come to rest on her lips. "I'm sorry for the way I treated you that night," I whisper, bringing my lips to hers. I kiss her slowly at first, but the sincerity in my apology is apparently quite attractive to her, because she pushes my arm away and pulls me to her, then whispers, "You're forgiven."

"WHAT ARE YOU doing?" I ask, waking up from a nap induced by pure exhaustion. Lake has her shirt on and is pulling her jeans up.

"I need some fresh air. Wanna come?" she says. "They've got a really nice pool area and it doesn't close for another hour or so. We can sit on the patio and have coffee."

"Yeah, sure." I roll out of bed and search for my clothes.

Once we're outside, the courtyard is empty, as is the pool, even though it's heated. There are several lounge chairs, but Lake takes a seat at a table with bench-style chairs so we can sit together. She curls up next to me and rests her head against my arm, holding her coffee cup between her hands.

"I hope the boys are having fun," she says.

"You know they are. Grandpaul took them geocaching today."

"Good," she says. "Kel loves that." She brings her coffee cup to her lips and sips from it. We watch the moon's reflection on the surface of the water, listening to the sounds of the night. It's peaceful.

"We had a pool back in Texas," she says. "It wasn't as big as this one, but it was nice. It gets so hot there that the water in the pool would feel like it was heated, even when it wasn't. I bet Texas water on its coldest day is still hotter than this heated pool."

"Are you a good swimmer?" I ask her.

"Of course. I lived in that pool half the year."

I lean in and kiss her, distracting her from the fact that I'm taking the coffee cup out of her hands. I slowly lean over her, hooking my arm underneath her knees. She's used to my public displays of affection, so she's none the wiser. As soon as she runs her hands through my hair, I lift her onto my lap and stand up, heading for the water. She pulls her lips from mine and darts her eyes to the pool, then back at me.

"Don't you dare, Will Cooper!"

I laugh and keep walking toward the pool as she starts struggling to get out of my arms. When I reach the deep end of the pool, she's clinging to my neck for dear life.

"If I go, you go," she says.

I smile and kick off my shoes. "I wouldn't have it any other way."

As soon as I toss her into the water, I jump in after her. When she emerges, she swims toward me laughing. "These are my only clothes, you jerk!"

When she reaches me I wrap my arms around her and she pulls her legs up, wrapping them around my waist. She hooks her arms around my neck and I swim backward until my back meets the tile siding of the pool. I put one arm on the concrete ledge to hold us up and my other arm I secure around her waist, holding her against me.

"I'll have to throw this shirt away now. The chlorine probably just ruined it," she says.

I slide my hand underneath her shirt and up her back, then press my lips against the area of skin right below her ear. "If you throw this ugly shirt away, I'm divorcing you."

She throws her head back and laughs. "Finally! You love my ugly shirt!"

I pull her against me so close that even the water can't pass between us. I bring my forehead to hers. "I've *always* loved this shirt, Lake. This is the shirt you were wearing the night I finally admitted to myself that I was in love with you."

The corner of her lip curls up into a grin. "And what night was that?"

I tilt my head back until it rests against the concrete siding and look up to the sky. "Not a good one."

She kisses me at the base of my throat. "Tell me anyway," she whispers.

i *love* her

"CAULDER, ARE YOU sure Julia said it was okay for you to stay the night?" He's rummaging through his dresser looking for socks while Kel loads a bag with their toys.

"Yeah. She said I can't come over tomorrow night because they're having family night, so I should spend the night tonight."

Family night? I wonder if that means Julia is finally telling Lake she's sick. A knot forms in my stomach and I instantly become nervous for her. "I'll get your toothbrush, Caulder."

I'm in the bathroom packing a bag for Caulder when I hear yelling coming from outside. I immediately run to the living room window and see Lake storming out of her house toward Eddie's car. I can't hear what she's saying, but it's obvious she's pissed. Her face is almost the same shade of red as the shirt she has on. She swings open Eddie's back door and turns around, still yelling.

That's when I see Julia.

The look on her face makes my heart sink. Eddie's car pulls out of the driveway and Julia is left standing at the edge of the yard crying as she watches them pull away. As soon as the car is gone, I swing open the front door and run across the street.

"Is everything okay? Is she okay?" I say when I reach her. Julia looks up at me and shakes her head.

"Did you tell Lake that I'm sick?" she asks.

"No," I answer immediately. "No, I told you I wouldn't."

Julia stares down the street, still shaking her head. "I think she knows. I don't know how she found out but she knows. I should have told her sooner," she says, still crying.

The front door to my house slams shut and I spin around to see Kel and Caulder making their way out the front door. "Boys!

You guys are staying with me tonight instead. Go back inside," I yell. They roll their eyes and groan, and then head back into the house.

"Thank you, Will," Julia says. She turns to head back to her house and I follow after her.

"Do you want me to stay with you until she gets back?"

"No," she says quietly. "I just want to be alone for a while." She walks inside and closes the door behind her.

I spend the next two hours debating whether to text Gavin. It's killing me not knowing if Lake is okay or not. I wait on the couch with the living room curtains wide open, watching for her return. It's after eleven o'clock now, and I can't wait a second longer. I throw caution out the window and grab my phone to text Gavin.

> Is Lake okay? Where are you guys? Is she spending the night
> with Eddie or coming home tonight?

I don't have to wait long before he replies.

> Yes. Movies. No.

What the hell? Could he not elaborate a little?

> How can she be okay? And why the hell would you guys take
> her to a movie when she's this upset?

Two minutes go by without a response, so I text him again.

> Is she still crying? When are you guys bringing her home?

I wait a few more minutes without a response, then begin texting him again. Before I hit send, my phone rings.

"Hello?" I say, almost desperately.

"What the hell are you *doing*, Will?" Gavin yells into the phone. "You're acting like a psycho boyfriend."

"Is she with you right now?" I ask.

"The movie just let out, she's in the restroom with Eddie. I came outside to call you because I think you might need a reminder that you're her *teacher.*"

I grip my cell phone and shake it out of frustration, then put it back to my ear.

"That doesn't matter right now. I saw her leaving after she found out about her mom's cancer. I just need to know that she's okay, Gavin. I'm worried about her."

I get nothing but silence. Gavin doesn't respond, but I can hear background noise so I know we're still connected. "Gavin?"

He clears his throat. "Her mom has cancer? Are you sure?"

"Yes, I'm sure. Has Lake not told you guys why she was crying when she got in your car? Julia doesn't know how, but Layken somehow figured it out."

Gavin is silent again for a few more seconds, then he sighs heavily into the phone. "Will," he says, his voice lower than before. "Layken thinks her mom has a new boyfriend. She has no idea she has cancer."

I fall onto the couch, but it feels like my heart falls straight through the floor.

"Will?" Gavin says.

"I'm here," I say. "Just get her home, Gavin. She needs to talk to her mom."

"Yeah. We're on our way."

I SPEND THE next several minutes debating whether to go across the street and let Julia know that Layken has misunderstood everything. Unfortunately, by the time I decide to go talk to her,

Eddie's car is pulling into their driveway. I watch as Lake gets out and walks to her front door. When she goes inside, I close my curtains and turn out the light. I wish more than anything I could be there for her right now. I know the heartache she's about to experience. The fact that I'm a hundred yards away and not able to do a damn thing about it is the hardest thing of all.

I walk to Caulder's room and check on the boys. They're both passed out, so I turn the TV off and shut their door, then head to my room. I can already tell it's going to be a sleepless night. I can just imagine Lake crying herself to sleep. God, what I wouldn't give to be able to hold her right now. If I could just take all of this away from her, I would.

I'm lying with my hands under my head, my eyes focused on nothing in particular. A tear rolls down to my temple and I wipe it away. I'm torn up over the sadness I feel for this girl.

IT'S HALF AN hour later when I hear a knock on the living room door. I immediately jump out of bed and run to the living room and swing the door open. She's standing on my patio, mascara streaked down her cheeks. She's wiping her eyes with her shirt and she looks up at me. All the things I've been willing myself to do for the entire past month get shoved aside by the sheer sadness in her eyes. I put my arm around her and pull her inside, then shut the door behind her. I'm positive she knows the truth about her mom at this point, but I still proceed with caution.

"Lake, what's wrong?"

She tries to catch her breath, sucking in gasps of air between sobs. I can feel her melting, so I wrap my arms around her as she sinks to the floor. I sink with her, then pull her to me and let her cry. I rest my chin on top of her head and stroke her hair while she continues to cry for several minutes. I grasp the back of her shirt and bury my head in the crevice of her neck, fully aware of the fact that she came to me. She needed someone, and she came to *me*.

"Tell me what happened," I finally whisper.

She begins to sob, so I pull her closer. Between breaths, she says the words that I know are the hardest words she'll ever have to say. "She's dying, Will. She has cancer."

I know from experience that there are no words comforting enough to follow that. I squeeze her and give her what she needs. Silent reassurance. I pick her up and take her to my bedroom, then lay her on the bed and pull the covers over her. My doorbell rings, so I bend forward and kiss her on the forehead, then head back to the living room.

I already know it's Julia before I open the door. When I see her, she looks in just as bad shape as Lake does. "Is she here?" she says through her tears.

I nudge my head toward my bedroom. "She's lying down," I say.

"Can you get her? She needs to come home so we can talk about this."

I glance back toward the hallway and sigh. I don't want her to go. I know how much she needs this time to absorb everything. I turn back to Julia and take the biggest risk I've ever taken in my life.

"Let her stay, Julia. She needs me right now."

Julia doesn't respond for a moment. The fact that I'm disagreeing with her seems to throw her off for a moment. She shakes her head. "I can't, Will. I can't let her stay the night here."

"I've been in her shoes before. She needs time to absorb this, trust me. Just give her the night to calm down."

Julia's shoulders fall and she looks down, unable to look at me. I don't know if it's because she's angry with me for wanting Lake to stay, or heartbroken because she knows I'm right. She nods, then turns and begins walking back toward her house. Her defeated demeanor makes me feel as though I just broke her heart. She thinks she's losing Lake to me and that couldn't be farther from the truth.

"Julia, wait," I say, calling after her. She pauses in my front yard and turns to face me. When we make eye contact, she immediately shifts her gaze to the ground again and puts her hands on her hips. When I reach her, she still doesn't look at me. I'm not sure what to say. I clear my throat, but have no idea what to say to her.

"Listen, Julia," I say. "I know how much your time with Lake means to you, I do. *Believe* me, I do. I want her to be there for you. The fact that she wants to be here right now instead doesn't mean anything. She just needs to process this. That's all. You won't lose her."

She runs her hands across her eyes, wiping away fresh tears. She kicks at the ground beneath her foot, giving herself a second to gather her thoughts. She eventually raises her head and looks me straight in the eyes. "You're in love with her, aren't you?"

I pause.

Am I?

I sigh and clasp my hands behind my head, not sure what to say. "I'm trying so hard *not* to be," I say quietly, admitting it to myself for the first time.

When she hears my confession, she looks up at me, her expression stoic. "Try *harder*, Will. I need her. I can't have her wrapped up in this whirlwind, forbidden romance. That's the last thing we need right now." Julia shakes her head then looks away again. Her disappointment stings. I've let her down.

I take a step closer to her and look her in the eyes, making another promise that I pray to God I'm strong enough to keep. "It doesn't matter how I feel about her, okay? I don't want her consumed by what's going on between us any more than you do. She just needs a friend right now, that's all this is."

She hugs herself and looks past me at my house. "I'll let her stay tonight," she finally says. "But only because I agree with you that she needs time to process everything." She shifts her gaze back to mine. The tears still fresh in her eyes, I can do nothing but nod in agreement. She returns my acknowledgment with her own nod, then turns to head home. "You better sleep on the couch," she says over her shoulder.

After Julia is back inside, I return to my own house and lock the front door. I walk into the bedroom but Lake doesn't acknowledge me. I slide into the bed behind her, placing one arm under her head and my other arm over her chest. I pull her to me and hold her while she cries herself to sleep

13.

the honeymoon

WE REMAIN RELAXED in the water, holding on to each other. She's resting her head on my shoulder, quiet and still. She presses her lips against my shoulder, opening them slightly, and she kisses me. I inhale as she grazes my shoulder with her lips, softly kissing along my collarbone, then up to my neck. When she reaches my jaw, she pulls back and looks at me. "I love you, Will Cooper," she says with tears in her eyes. She leans in and presses her lips to mine. She tightens her grip around my waist with her legs and places her hands on the back of my head, filling me with slow, deep kisses. I don't think she's ever kissed me with such intensity and passion before. It's like she's somehow trying to show her gratitude through her kiss.

I let her. I let her thank me for a good five minutes.

When her lips finally separate from mine, she unwraps her legs from around me and grins. "That was for loving me like you do."

She kicks off the wall and floats on her back across the pool. When she reaches the other side, she props her elbows up behind her on the concrete ledge and smiles at me from across the pool. I'm left breathless, wishing we were back in the hotel room already.

"It's too bad you like my shirt now," she says, still grinning mischievously.

"Why is that?"

She releases her grip on the ledge and brings her hand to the top button of her shirt. "Because," she says in a sexy whisper. "I'm really tired of wearing it." She unbuttons the top button, revealing the outline of her bra. As many times as I've seen that bra in the last twenty-four hours, it's a whole hell of a lot sexier right now.

"Oh," I say. As much as I want that shirt off her, we're in the courtyard of a hotel. I look around nervously to make sure no one is out here. When I look back at her, the second button is unbuttoned and her fingers are already working on the third. She hasn't taken her eyes off mine.

"Lake."

"*What?*" she says innocently. The fourth button is undone now and she's working on the fifth.

I slowly shake my head. "That's not a good idea."

She slides the shirt halfway down her shoulders, revealing the entire bra now. "Why not?"

I try to think of why it's not a good idea, but I can't. I can't think. All I want to do is help her finish getting the damn shirt off. I swim across the water and ease closer to her until our faces are just inches apart. Without taking my eyes off hers, I grasp the sleeves of her shirt and pull it the rest of the way down her arms, then yank it off completely. I throw the shirt onto the concrete patio, then lower my hands to the button on her jeans. She gasps. I lean in and whisper in her ear as I slide her zipper down. "Why stop there?"

I thought I'd called her bluff, but I should know better than that. She wraps one arm around my neck and helps me pull her jeans off with her other hand. I grab her thighs and pull her flush against me, then spin us around until I'm against the ledge again. She braces her hands against the pool wall behind my head. I sink us both lower until our chins are barely above the surface of the water.

We're pressed firmly together; the only things separating us are my jeans and her underwear, and one of these items is about to go. I slide my thumb into her waistband at the hip and begin to inch her panties down. I pull them down just far enough. "What now?" I say, moving my hand farther down as I wait for her to call retreat.

She breathes heavily against my lips as her chin submerges and re-emerges against the waves of the water. Rather than call retreat, she closes her eyes, daring me to keep going.

She gasps when I unclasp her bra with my other hand and begin to slide it off her.

"Will," she says against my lips. "What if someone comes out here?" She covers herself with her arms when the bra is completely off.

I throw it on the concrete in the spot next to her shirt and I smile at her. "You started this. Don't tell me you're about to call retreat *now*." I kiss her on the chin and trail a line across her jaw with my lips. She uncovers her chest and sinks lower into the water, then pulls me against her.

"Retreat is no longer in my vocabulary," she says, finding the button on my pants.

"You two almost done here?" someone says from behind us, causing Lake to abandon her current mission. She throws her arms around me and buries her head against my neck. I glance to the left and see a hotel employee standing just inside the gated entry, his hands on his hips. "I've got to lock up," he says.

"Oh, my god, oh, my god, oh, my god," she whispers. "Where the hell are my clothes?"

I laugh. "Told you it wasn't a good idea," I say against her ear.

I keep my arms wrapped tightly around her and look over at the man, who appears a bit too amused at our plight. "Um. Could you throw me those?" I say, pointing to Lake's shirt and bra, which are several feet away. She's got a death grip on my neck.

The hotel employee looks down at the clothes and chuckles, then looks back at Lake and smiles, almost as if I'm not even here. He walks through the gate and over to the edge of the pool and tosses us the shirt, not taking his eyes off her the entire time. I wrap the shirt over her shoulders and he's still standing there, staring.

"Do you mind?" I say to him. The guy finally takes his eyes off Lake long enough to witness my glare. He clearly reads the expression on my face and turns around to head back inside.

Lake slips her shirt back on while I retrieve her pants and swim them back to her. "You're a bad influence Mrs. Cooper," I say.

"Hey, my plan was to stop at the shirt," she says. "You're the one who had other ideas."

I let her hold on to me while I help her struggle back into her jeans. "Well, if what just happened wasn't your intention, why did you lure me into the water to begin with?" I say.

She laughs and shakes her head. "I guess I just can't resist those abs."

I kiss her on the nose and swing her around onto my back, then carry her out of the pool. We leave a sopping wet trail the entire way back to our hotel room.

• • •

LAKE IS SPRAWLED across the bed on her stomach, wearing the robe I've fallen in love with. I'm stealing that robe before we leave here. She's flipping through the channels on the TV with the remote, so I crawl onto the bed next to her and take the remote from her hand.

"My turn," I say. I flip it to ESPN and she grabs the remote back from me.

"It's *my* honeymoon," she says. "I should get to watch what I want." She turns her attention back to the TV.

"*Your* honeymoon? What am I? An afterthought?"

She continues to stare at the TV without responding. She glances at me, then back to the TV. After a few seconds, she shifts her gaze in my direction again and I'm still staring at her. "What'd you say?" she teases. "Were you talking?"

I grab the remote from her and press the power button, then chuck it across the room. I grab her wrists and roll her onto her back, pinning her to the bed. "Maybe you need to be reminded who wears the pants in this family."

She laughs. "Oh, believe me, I know you wear the pants, Will. You even wear them in the bathtub, remember?"

I laugh and kiss her ear. "If I remember correctly, you wore clothes in the shower once, too."

"*Unwillingly!*" She laughs.

insanity

AFTER I FINISH cooking breakfast for the boys, I walk to my bedroom and slip inside, shutting the door behind me. The last thing I need is for them to know Lake spent the night here last night.

I sit on the edge of the bed by her feet. If I were to sit any closer, I wouldn't be able to prevent myself from reaching over and touching her or hugging her or stroking her hair. It was torture holding her last night while trying to hold back the urge to kiss away her pain. *Torture.* Not that I didn't give her a light peck after I was sure she was asleep. I might have also told her I loved her after I kissed her hair.

Torture.

"Lake," I whisper. She doesn't move so I repeat her name. She rustles slightly, but doesn't open her eyes. She looks so peaceful and serene right now. If I were to wake her up, reality would just hit her again. I stand up and decide to let her have a few more moments of peace. Before I leave the room, I walk to the head of the bed and lightly kiss her on the forehead.

"WHAT IF SHE loses weight?" Kel says.

"She doesn't need to lose weight," I say as I scoop a spoonful of eggs onto his plate. I walk back to the stove and set the pan down.

"Well, if you don't think she's fat and you like to kiss her, then why don't you want her to be your girlfriend?"

I spin around and face both of the boys. "I like *kissing* her?" I ask, afraid of his answer. He just nods and takes a bite of his food.

"You kissed her that night you took her on that test date.

Lake says you *didn't* kiss her, but I saw you. She says you can get in a lot of trouble for kissing her and that I didn't see what I thought I saw."

"She said that?" I ask.

Caulder nods. "That's what she told us. But Kel says he saw what he thought he saw and I believe him. Why would you get in trouble for kissing her, anyway?"

I wasn't expecting the third degree this early in the morning. I'm too tired to turn this into a life lesson, though. After everything that happened last night and having Lake next to me in my bed, I'm pretty sure I didn't even get an hour of sleep.

"Listen, boys," I say, walking back to them. I place my hands on the bar and come face-to-face with them. "Sometimes, there are things in life that are out of our control. I can't be Lake's boyfriend and she can't be my girlfriend. We're not going to get married, and the two of you aren't going to be brothers. Enjoy the fact that you get to be best friends and neighbors."

"Is it because you're a teacher?" Caulder asks pointedly.

I drop my head in my hands. They're relentless. And intuitive.

"Yes," I say, exasperated. "Yes. It's because I'm a teacher. Teachers cannot ask their students to be their girlfriends and vice versa. So Lake isn't going to be my girlfriend. I'm not going to be her boyfriend. We aren't going to get married. Ever. Now drop it." I walk back to the stove and place lids on all the pans to keep the food warm. I don't know when Lake will wake up, but I need to get these boys fed and out of this house before she walks out of my bedroom. How in the hell would I explain to them that teachers and students can't date, but they can sleep in the same bed?

• • •

AFTER BREAKFAST COMES and goes and she's still asleep, I walk the boys over to Julia's. Kel and Caulder rush in, but I feel inclined to knock on the door so I lag behind. When Julia opens the door, she shields her eyes from the sun and looks away.

"Sorry. Did I wake you up?"

She steps aside to let me in and shakes her head. "I don't think I've even slept," she says. She walks back into the living room, so I follow and sit on the sofa. "How is she?"

I shrug. "Still asleep. She hasn't come out of the bedroom since she got there last night."

Julia nods and leans back into the couch, then rubs her hands on her face. "She's scared, Will. She was so scared when I told her. I knew she would take it badly, but not like this. I wasn't expecting this reaction at all. I need her to be strong when we tell Kel, but I can't tell him when she's this emotional."

"It's only been seven months since her dad died, Julia. Losing a parent is hard, but the possibility of losing both of them at her age is incomprehensible."

"Yeah," she whispers. "I guess you would know."

She still doesn't seem convinced that Lake's reaction is normal. Everyone reacts differently to devastating news. I didn't even cry right away when I found out my parents died, but that's not to say it wasn't the worst moment of my life.

I was on my way to a game when I got the phone call. I was the emergency contact on their records. The person on the other line was telling me there was an accident and I needed to get to the hospital in Detroit. They wouldn't tell me anything, no matter how much I begged. I tried calling my parents' cell phones several times but never got an answer. I called my grandparents to tell them about the accident, since they were just minutes from the hospital. That was one of the hardest phone calls I've ever had to make.

I drove as fast as I could, holding my cell phone in my hand against the steering wheel, keeping a constant eye on it. All I could think of was Caulder. I just knew something terrible had happened and that my parents weren't answering their phones because they wanted to tell me in person.

When an hour passed and even my grandparents still hadn't called, I tried their phone for the fifth time. They weren't answering, either. I think it was after the sixth time I called them and they pushed it through to voicemail that I knew.

My parents. Caulder. All of them. They were all dead.

I pulled up to the emergency room and rushed inside. The first thing I saw was my grandmother doubled over in a chair, crying.

No, she wasn't crying. She was wailing. My grandfather had his back to me, but his shoulders were shaking. His entire body was shaking. I stood there and watched them for several minutes, wondering who these people were in front of me. These strong, independent people I had admired and respected and thought the world of. These people who could be broken by nothing.

Yet, here they were. Broken and weak. The only thing that can break the unbreakable is the unthinkable. I knew the moment I saw them alone in the waiting room that my worst fears were confirmed.

They were all dead.

I turned around and I walked out. I didn't want to be in there. I had to go outside. I couldn't breathe. When I reached the grass across from the parking lot, I fell to my knees. I didn't cry.

Instead, I became physically ill. Over and over, my stomach repelling the truth that I refused to believe. When there was nothing left in me, I fell backward onto the grass and stared up at the sky, the stars staring back at me. Millions of stars staring back at the whole world. A world where parents die and brothers die and nothing stops to respect that fact. The whole universe just goes and goes as if nothing has happened, even when one person's entire life is forced to a complete halt.

I closed my eyes and thought about him. It had been two weeks since I had spoken to him on the phone. I had promised him I'd come up the next weekend to take him to his football game. That was the same weekend Vaughn begged me not to go. She said midterms were in two weeks and we needed to spend time together before then. So, I called Caulder and canceled my trip. That was the last time I had talked to him.

The last time I would ever talk to him.

"Will?"

I looked up after hearing my grandfather's voice and he was standing over me, looking down. "Will, are you okay?" he asked, wiping fresh tears from his defeated eyes. I hated seeing that look in his eyes.

I didn't move. I just lay there in the grass, looking up at him, not wanting him to say anything else. I didn't want to hear it.

"Will . . . they . . ."

"I know," I said quickly, not wanting to hear the words come out of his mouth.

He nodded and looked away. "Your grandmother wants . . ."

"I *know*," I said louder.

"Maybe you should come . . ."

"I don't want to."

And I *didn't* want to. I didn't want to set foot back inside that hospital. Back inside the building that now housed the three of them. *Lifeless.*

"Will, you need to come . . ."

"I don't *want* to!" I screamed.

My grandfather—my poor grandfather just nodded and sighed. What else could he have done? What else could he have said? My entire life had just been ripped from me and I wasn't about to listen to reassurances from nurses or doctors or clergymen or even my grandparents. I didn't want to hear it.

My grandfather hesitantly took a few steps away from me, leaving me alone in the grass. Before heading back inside, he turned around one last time.

"It's just that Caulder has been asking for you. He's scared. So when you're ready . . ."

I immediately snapped my head in his direction. "Caulder?" I said. "Caulder's not . . ."

My grandfather immediately shook his head. "No, son. No. Caulder's fine."

It wasn't until those words came out of his mouth that everything hit me all at once. My chest swelled and the heat rose to my face, then my eyes. I pulled my hands to my forehead and I rolled onto my knees, my elbows buried in the grass, and I completely lost it. Sounds came from deep within me that I didn't even know I was capable of. I cried harder than I've ever cried before—harder than I've cried since. I sat on the lawn of that hospital and I cried tears of joy, because Caulder was okay.

"Are you okay?" Julia asks, breaking me out of my trance.

I nod, trying to push back the memories of that day. "I'm fine."

She readjusts her position on the couch and sighs. "I don't want her to have to raise Kel," she says. "Lake needs the chance to live her own life. I'd never burden her like that."

"Julia," I say, speaking confidently from experience, "it would burden her *not* to have him." Not having the choice to raise Kel would *kill* Lake. Just like it killed me when I thought I'd lost Caulder. It would absolutely devastate her.

Julia doesn't respond, indicating I may have crossed my boundaries with that comment. We both sit quietly on the couch for a while. I feel like neither of us has anything else to say, so I stand up.

"I'll take the boys somewhere this afternoon. I'll make sure Layken wakes up before I go so you guys will have time to talk."

"Thank you," she says, smiling a genuine smile at me. It feels good. I respect Julia's opinion and having her disappointed in me feels almost as bad as when Lake is disappointed in me.

I nod, then turn and leave. I make my way back inside the house and back into the bedroom where Lake is still sleeping. I ease onto the bed at her side and take a seat.

"Lake," I whisper, trying to wake her successfully this time.

She doesn't move, so I pull the covers off her head. She groans and pulls them back up.

"Lake, wake up."

She kicks her legs, then throws the covers off. It's well past lunchtime and she acts like she could sleep twelve more hours. She opens her eyes and squints, then finds me sitting next to her. She's got mascara smeared underneath her eyes, some of which is still on my pillowcase. Her hair is in disarray. Her ponytail holder is on the sheet beside her. She looks like hell. A *beautiful* hell.

"You really *aren't* a morning person," I say.

She sits up on the bed. "Bathroom. Where's your bathroom?"

I point to the bathroom across the hall and watch as she leaps off the bed and darts for the door. She's definitely awake now, but I can almost guarantee she needs coffee.

I go to the kitchen and make us both a cup. When she comes out of the bathroom I take a seat and place her coffee next to me.

"What time is it?"

"One-thirty."

"Oh," she says, shocked. "Well . . . your bed's really comfortable."

I smile and nudge her shoulder. "Apparently."

We drink our coffee and she doesn't say anything else. I have no idea where her head is at, so I remain silent, allowing her to think. When we finish our coffee, I put the cups in the sink and tell her I'm taking the boys to a matinee. "We're leaving in a few minutes. I'll probably take them to dinner afterward, so we'll be back around six. Should give you and your mom time to talk."

She frowns at me. "What if I don't want to talk? What if I want to go to a matinee?"

I lean forward across the bar. "You don't need to watch a movie. You need to talk to your mom. Let's go." I grab my keys and jacket and head toward the front door.

She kicks back in her chair and folds her arms across her chest. "I just woke up. The caffeine hasn't even kicked in yet. Can I stay here for a while?"

She's practically pouting, her bottom lip sticking out, pleading with me. I stare at her mouth a beat too long. I think she notices, because she pulls on her bottom lip with her teeth and her cheeks flush. I shake my head slightly, pulling my gaze away from her mouth.

"Fine," I say, snapping out of my trance. I walk over to her and kiss her on the forehead. "But not all day. You need to talk to her." I walk away, fully aware of the fact that the forehead kiss was probably crossing the line. However, the fact that she slept in my bed last night has already muddied the waters. The line isn't so black and white anymore. I'm pretty sure gray just became my new favorite color.

IT'S BEEN OVER five hours since I left with the boys, so Lake and Julia probably have had a chance to sort everything out. I tell Kel to stay the night with me to give them more time to adjust. I unlock the front door and follow the boys into the living room. We all come to a halt, not expecting to find Lake on my living room floor. There are dozens of white index cards sprawled out in front of her.

What the hell is she *doing*?

"What are you doing?" Caulder says, verbalizing my exact thoughts.

"Alphabetizing," she replies without looking up.

"Alphabetizing *what*?" I say.

"Everything. First I did the movies, then I did the CDs. Caulder, I did the books in your room. I did a few of your games, but some of those started with numbers so I put the numbers first, then the titles." I point to the piles in front of me. "These are recipes. I found them on top of the fridge. I'm alphabetizing them by category first; like beef, lamb, pork, poultry. Then behind the categories I'm alphabetizing them by—"

"Guys, go to Kel's. Let Julia know you're back," I say, without looking at them.

The boys don't move. They continue to stare at Lake. "Now!" I yell. They listen this time, opening the door and disappearing outside.

I slowly walk to the couch and sit down. I'm afraid to say anything. Something is off. She seems so . . . *chipper*.

"You're the teacher," she says. She looks at me and winks. "Should I put 'Baked Potato Soup' behind potato or soup?"

What the hell? She's in denial. *Intense* denial.

"Stop," I say. I'm not returning her smile. I don't know what happened with her mom today, but whatever is going on with her needs to stop. She needs to confront this.

"I can't stop, silly. I'm halfway finished. If I stop now you won't know where to find . . ." She picks up a random card off the floor. "Jerk Chicken?"

I glance around the living room and notice the DVDs have all been arranged next to my television. I stand and slowly walk to the kitchen, eyeing the surroundings. Did she clean the damn *baseboards*? I knew I shouldn't have left her today. Good God, I bet she cleaned the entire house and never even went to talk to her mother. I walk to my bedroom and my bed is made. Not only is it made; it's *perfect*. I hesitate before opening my closet door, afraid of what I might find. My shoes have all been rearranged. My shirts have all been moved to the right side of the closet and my pants are on the left. The way they're hung, their colors move from light to dark.

She color-coded my *closet?* I'm afraid to complete the inspection. There's no telling what all she did to this house. She probably left nothing untouched.

Shit. I rush to the bed and open the nightstand. I pull the book out and open it, but the receipt for her chocolate milk doesn't look like it's been touched. I breathe a sigh of relief, glad she didn't see it, then put the book back where it was. How embarrassing would that have been?

I walk back into the living room, more aware of the spotless condition of my house than before. She's been a little too busy, which can only mean one thing. She's still avoiding her mother.

"You color-coded my closet?" I say. I'm glaring at her from the hallway entrance. She shrugs and smiles, like this is any other day.

"Will, it wasn't that hard. You wear, like, three different color shirts." When she giggles, it makes me wince. She has to *stop* this. Her denial isn't good for her, and it certainly isn't going to be good for Kel when Julia tells him. I walk swiftly across the room and bend down to snatch up the cards. We're about to have a serious sit-down.

"Will! Stop! That took me a long time!" She begins to grab the cards as I pick them up. I realize we aren't getting anywhere, so I throw down the cards and try to pull her up off the floor. I need her to look me in the eyes and calm down.

That doesn't happen.

She actually starts kicking at me. She's literally *kicking* me. She's acting like a damn child.

"Let me go!" she yells. "I'm . . . not . . . done!"

I let go of her hands as she asked, and she falls back to the floor. I walk to the kitchen and grab an empty pitcher from under the sink and fill it up with water. I know I'll regret this, but she needs to snap out of it. I walk back to the living room and she doesn't even acknowledge me. I extend my arm and flip the pitcher upside down on top of her head.

"What the hell!" she screams. She throws her hands up in shock, then looks up at me with pure hatred. I realize once she lunges at me that perhaps this wasn't the best idea. Not enough water, maybe?

When she stands up and tries to hit me, I grab her arm and

wrap it behind her back, then move behind her while I push her toward the bathroom. Once we're inside, I wrap my arms around her and forcefully pick her up. There's no other way to do it. She's doing her best to attack me and she's almost succeeding. I hold her against the wall of the shower with one arm and turn the water on with the other. As soon as the water splashes across her face, she gasps.

"Jerk! Jackass! Asshole!"

I adjust the faucet and look her in the eyes. "Take a shower, Layken! Take a damn shower!" I release my hold and back away from her. When I shut the bathroom door, I hold the doorknob in case she tries to get out. Sure enough, she tries.

"Let me out, Will! Now!" She beats on the door and jiggles the knob.

"Layken, I'm not letting you out of the bathroom until you take off your clothes, get in the shower, wash your hair, and calm down."

I continue to hold the doorknob until I hear the shower curtain close a minute later. When I'm confident she isn't going to try to get out again, I put my shoes on and walk across the street to grab her some extra clothes.

"Is she okay?" Julia asks as soon as she opens the door. She motions behind her to let me know Kel and Caulder can hear our conversation.

"A little *too* okay," I whisper. "She's acting strange. Did you guys talk today?"

Julia nods, but doesn't elaborate. It's obvious she doesn't want to risk being overheard by Kel. "She's in the shower. I came to get her a change of clothes," I say, skirting the subject.

Julia nods and steps aside, then walks toward the kitchen.

"You can grab some out of her bedroom. Last door on the right," she says. "I'm in the middle of washing dishes." She returns to the sink and I hesitate, a little uncomfortable at the thought of going into Lake's bedroom.

I walk down the hallway and slowly open her door. When I do, it's not what I expect. I don't know if I thought it would be a typical teenager's bedroom, but I'm pleasantly surprised that there aren't posters on the walls and black lights on the ceiling. It's surprisingly mature for an eighteen-year-old. I walk to her dresser and pull the top drawer open, removing a tank top. When I open the next drawer to look for pants, I'm met with a drawer full of bras and panties. I feel somewhat guilty, knowing that she has no idea I'm in her room right now. I tell myself to just grab a pair and shut the drawer, but I begin scrolling through all of the contents, imaging what they would look like on her.

Dammit, Will! I grab a pair on top and slam the drawer shut, then search until I find some pajama bottoms. When I shut the last drawer, the tank top falls out of my hands and lands on the floor. I bend over to pick it up and a barrette catches my eye. It looks like a child's hair barrette. I pick it up and hold it between my fingers, curious why she would keep something so old.

"She used to think it was magic," Julia says from the door-way. I whip my head around, startled by her voice.

"This?" I say, holding up the barrette.

Julia nods, then walks into the bedroom and sits on the bed. "When she was a little girl her dad walked in right after she had cut a huge chunk of her bangs off. She was crying, scared I would be mad at her, so he brushed some hair over and snapped the clip in place. He told her it was magic and that as long as she kept that clip in her hair, I wouldn't notice."

I laugh, trying to imagine Lake with a chunk of her bangs missing. "I guess you noticed?"

Julia laughs. "Oh, it was so obvious. Horribly obvious. She cut a three-inch strip right out of the front of her hair. Her dad called to warn me and told me not to say anything. It was so hard. It took her hair months to grow back out and she looked ridiculous. But I couldn't say anything because every single day she woke up, the first thing she did was put that clip in her hair so I wouldn't know."

"Wow," I say. "She was strong-willed even then, huh?"

Julia smiles. "You have no idea. I've never met a person with a more indomitable will in my *life*."

I bend down and put the clip back where I found it, then turn back to Julia. She's looking down at her hands, picking at her nails. She looks just like Lake right now, but somehow even sadder.

"She hates me right now, Will. She doesn't understand where I'm coming from. She wants Kel, but I don't know if I can do that to her."

I don't even know if it's my place to be giving her advice, but she seems to be soliciting it. I just know I've been in Lake's shoes, and nothing could have stopped me from taking Caulder from my grandparents' house that night.

I tuck Lake's clothes underneath my arm and head to the door, then turn back toward Julia. "Maybe you should try to understand where she's coming from. Kel is the only thing she'll have left. The *only* thing. And right now, she feels like you're trying to take that away from her, too."

Julia looks up at me. "I'm not trying to take him away from her. I just want her to be happy."

Happy?

"Julia," I say. "Her father just died. You're about to die. She's eighteen and she's facing a lifetime without the two people she loves the most. Nothing you can do will make her happy. Her world is being ripped out from under her and she has absolutely no control over it. The least you could do is let her have a little bit of say-so over the only thing she'll have left. Because I can tell you from experience . . . Caulder is the *only* thing that kept me going. Your taking Kel away from her because you think it'll improve her situation? It's the absolute worst thing you could do to either of them."

Fearing I've overstepped my bounds again, I walk out of the bedroom and make my way back across the street.

I OPEN THE door to the bathroom and slip inside. I set the clothes and a towel down on the counter, then glance up to the mirror. It's mostly fogged over, but clear enough that I can see the shower in the reflection. There's a section a few inches wide where the wall should meet the shower curtain, but it's pulled slightly back. Lake's foot is propped up against the porcelain tub and she's shaving her legs. She's using my razor.

And my shower.

And her clothes are on the floor, next to my feet. Not on *her*. She's three feet from me without her clothes on.

It's one of the worst days of her life and I'm sitting here thinking about how she's not wearing anything. Ass-hole.

If I had any semblance of a decent conscience at all, I'd have never allowed her into my house last night to begin with. Now I'm watching the razor glide up her ankle, praying she's too upset to go home for at least one more night.

Just one more night. I'm not ready to let her go.

I quietly back out of the bathroom and shut the door behind me. I head straight to the kitchen sink and splash water on my face.

I grip the edge of the counter and take a deep breath, preparing my earth-shattering apology for when she comes storming out of the bathroom. She's so pissed at me right now for yelling at her and throwing her into the shower. I don't blame her. I'm sure there was an easier way I could have calmed her down.

"I need a towel!" she yells from the bathroom. I walk to the edge of the hallway.

"It's on the sink. So are your clothes." I go back to the living room and sit on the couch in a lame attempt to appear casual. Maybe if I don't seem so pissed anymore, she'll remain calm.

God, I can't stand the thought of her being mad at me for another day. The day she recited her poem in class was probably the hardest knock my heart has ever taken from a girl . . . and it happened in front of seventeen other students. I realize none of them knew I was her target, other than Gavin, but *still*. It felt like I'd taken over thirty bullets straight to the heart with each insult that came out of her mouth.

The door to the bathroom begins to open and my attempt at casual goes out the window. I jump over the back of the couch, wanting nothing more than to hold her and apologize for everything I did tonight.

When she sees me rushing toward her, her eyes grow big and she backs up to the wall. I wrap my arms around her and squeeze her tight. "I'm sorry, Lake. I'm so sorry I did that. You were just *losing* it," I say in my best attempt to excuse my actions. Rather than try to hit me, she wraps her arms around my neck, causing my chest to tighten as I attempt to hold on to my will-power before it slips away from me again.

"It's okay," she says softly. "I kinda sorta had a bad day."

I want nothing more than to stifle her words with my mouth right now. I want to tell her how much I need her. How much I love her. How, no matter how bad things get for her, I'll be by her through every second of it.

But I don't. Because of Julia, I don't. I reluctantly pull back and place my arms on her shoulders.

"So we're friends? You aren't gonna try to punch me again?"

"Friends," she says with a forced smile. I can tell she wants to be my friend about as much as I want to be hers. I have to turn away from her and head down the hallway before the words "I love you" fall helplessly from my mouth.

"How was the matinee?" she asks from behind me.

I can't make small talk. We need to get to the heart of why she's here, or I'm going to forget she's not here for me.

"Did you talk to your mom?" I ask.

"Jeez. Deflect much?"

"Did you talk to her? Please don't tell me you spent the entire day cleaning." I continue into the kitchen and grab two glasses. She takes a seat at the bar.

"No. Not the entire day. We talked."

"And?" I ask.

"And . . . she has cancer."

Damn that indomitable will.

I roll my eyes at her stubbornness and walk to the refrigera-tor, removing the milk. When I begin to pour it into her glass, she turns away from the bar and flips her head over, then pulls the towel off her head. Her hair falls around her and she brushes at the tangles with her fingers. She smoothes out the strands, working her fingers through them delicately. What I wouldn't give to touch—crap! I realize, just as she glances up, that I've poured way too much milk. It's trickling down my hand and onto the counter. I quickly wipe it up with a hand towel.

Please tell me she didn't see that.

I grab the powdered chocolate out of the cabinet and a spoon, then stir some chocolate into her cup. "Will she be okay?"

"No. Probably not."

I should know better than to ask close-ended questions with her. But I haven't asked Julia any details and I'm curious.

"But she's getting treatment?"

She rolls her eyes and looks incredibly annoyed. "She's dying, Will. *Dying.* She'll probably be dead within the year, maybe less than that. They're just doing chemo to keep her comfortable. While she dies. 'Cause she'll be dead. Because she's dying. There. Is that what you wanted to hear?"

Her response sends a surge of guilt through me. I'm doing the exact thing to her that I hated having done to me. Forcing her to talk about something she hasn't even accepted yet. I decide to drop it. She'll come to this on her own terms. I walk to the freezer and grab a handful of ice, then drop it into her cup, sliding it across the counter to her. "On the rocks."

She looks down at the chocolate milk and smiles. "Thanks," she says. She finishes her drink in silence.

When the glass is empty, she stands up from the bar and walks to the living room. She lies down on the floor and stretches her arms above her head.

"Turn the lights off," she says. "I just want to listen for a while."

I turn out the lights, then walk to where she is and lower myself onto the floor beside her. She's quiet, but the stress radiates from her.

"She doesn't want me to raise Kel," she whispers. "She wants to give him to Brenda."

I inhale a deep breath, understanding completely where her pain is coming from. I reach out across the floor until I find her hand and I hold it, wanting more than anything for her to know she's not alone in this.

MY EYES SNAP open at the sound of Eddie's voice. I sit up on the floor, shocked that I even fell asleep, and see Lake watching Eddie walk out the door.

Shit! Shit, shit, shit! What the hell was Eddie doing in my house? Why would Lake even let her *in*? I'm getting fired. That's it. I'm done.

After the door closes behind Eddie, Lake turns around and sees me sitting up on the floor. She purses her lips and tries to smile, but she knows I'm not happy.

"What the hell was she doing here?"

She shrugs. "Visiting," she mutters. "Checking on me."

She has no idea what kind of jeopardy she just put my entire career in!

"Dammit, Layken!" I push myself off the floor and throw my hands in the air, defeated. "Are you *trying* to get me fired? Are you that selfish that you don't give a crap about anyone *else's* problems? Do you know what would happen if she let it get out that you spent the night here?"

Lake's eyes dart down to the floor.

Oh, god. She knows. Eddie already knows.

I take a step closer to her and she glances up at me again. "Does she know you spent the night here?" I demand. She looks down at her lap. "Layken, what does she know?"

She doesn't look at me, which answers my question.

"Christ, Layken. Go home."

She nods, then walks to the door. She slips her shoes on and pauses before she leaves, looking at me apologetically. I'm standing in the middle of the living room with my hands clasped behind my head, watching her. As mad as I am right now, it hurts to let her go. I know she needs me, but there's so much we both need to process at this point. Besides, she needs to be home with her mother. Being here instead of at her own house isn't helping her confront her situation at all.

A tear rolls down her cheek and she quickly turns away.

"Lake," I say softly, dropping my hands to my sides. I can't let her leave with the added stress of my outburst lingering in her mind. I walk to the door where she's standing and reach down and touch her fingers, then take her hand in mine. She allows me to hold her hand, but she doesn't face me again. She keeps one hand on the front door and sniffs, her head still focused on the floor.

This girl. In love with the boy she can't have. Grieving the death of her father, only to find out she's about to grieve the death of the only adult left in her life? This girl who's being told she can't keep the only family member she has left? I squeeze her hand and rub my thumb over hers. She slowly turns to meet my eyes. Seeing the pain behind them and knowing that a lot of it is because of me reminds me of all the reasons I need to let her go.

Her mother.

My career.

Her reputation.

My and Caulder's future.

Her future.

Doing the right thing. The *responsible* thing.

Out of all the reasons I can come up with for her to go, there's only one reason I can come up with for her to stay. I love her. This one reason for her to stay is the *only* reason that derives from pure selfishness. If I continue whatever this is with her, it'll be completely selfish of me. I'll be putting everything I've worked for and everyone I love at risk, just to fulfill my own desires.

I drop her hand. "Go home, Layken. She needs you."

I turn around.

I walk away.

14.

the honeymoon

I'M HOLDING HER hand now and I have no intentions of letting her walk out of my life again.

Lake can see the regret I have over that night, so she takes my face in her hands and smiles reassuringly at me. "You do realize you are the most selfless person I know, right?"

I shake my head. "Lake, I'm not selfless. I put so much at risk every time I was around you, but I still couldn't control myself. It's like I couldn't breathe unless I was near you."

"You are *not* selfish. We were in love. *Really* in love. You warred with yourself to do the right thing and that says so much about your character. I respect you for that, Will Cooper."

I knew I married her for a reason. I grab the back of her neck and pull her forehead toward mine and kiss it.

She lays her head on my chest and wraps her arm around me. "Besides, there's no way you could have been perfect the *whole* time we were forced apart," she says. "It's just too hard to *not* love me, considering how irresistible I am."

I laugh and flip her off me and onto her back. "You got that right," I say, tickling her ribs. I try to straddle her and pin her down, but she squirms beneath me and somehow breaks free, scooting off the bed. I grab her wrist and she pulls back, yanking me forward. She turns and tries to break free but trips over the desk chair. I grab her waist just as she falls to the floor, then I slide on top of her and pin her wrists to the carpet.

"See how irresistible I am?" She laughs. "You won't even let me off the butterflying bed without you!"

My eyes drink in every inch of her from head to toe. "Maybe if you'd put on some clothes I'd feel less inclined to attack you."

She pulls one of her hands from mine and reaches to the chair above her head where her robe landed earlier. "Fine," she says, yanking it off the chair. "I'll wear this until we leave tomorrow."

I grab the robe from her hands and toss it behind me. "The *hell* you will. I told you what you were allowed to wear on this honeymoon, and that robe wasn't on the list."

"Well, everything that *was* on the list is sort of soaking wet, thanks to you."

I laugh. "That's only inconvenient for anyone who isn't *me*." As soon as I kiss her, she finds the one spot on my stomach that's ticklish and she attacks. I'm immediately off her, trying to get away from her hands. I hop back onto the bed and she jumps on top of me. Once I realize she has me pinned to the bed, I immediately give up and let her win.

Who *wouldn't*?

"Fun should have been the fourth thing on my mom's list," she says, dropping herself beside me, breathless from the effort she spent trying to attack me. I cock my eyebrow, curious about what list she's referring to. She sees I'm not following, so she elaborates. "She said there were three things every woman should look for in a man. Having fun with him wasn't on the list, but I think it should be." She sits up and scoots back to the headboard. "Tell me about a fun time. A happy time. I need a break from all the sad memories for a while."

I think back to the months after we first met, and struggle to come up with a positive one. "It's hard, Lake. There were happy moments, but not really happy times. There was so much heartache under the surface of that entire year."

"Then tell me one of your happy moments."

carving pumpkins

IT'S ALMOST FIVE, so after I unload the groceries I walk across the street to get Caulder. Julia and Lake need to talk, so I think I'll offer to take Kel for a while, too. Before I knock, I take a deep breath and prepare for whatever reaction Lake might have. I gave her detention today so I could talk to her and Eddie, then I just left her and Eddie a blubbering mess in my classroom. I'm not sure if she's pissed at me right now but I felt like I needed to make a point, which is the only reason I did it. Whether or not Lake got my point, I guess I'm about to find out.

When the door opens, I'm shocked to see Caulder. "Hey, buddy. You answering doors here now?"

He smiles and grabs my hand, pulling me inside. "We're carving pumpkins for Halloween. Come on, Julia bought one for you, too."

"No, it's fine. I'll carve mine another time. I just wanted to bring you home so they can have some family time."

I look up to see the four of them sitting at the bar carving pumpkins. I know Lake hasn't had a chance to talk with Julia, since she had to have just gotten home, so I'm a little confused at the serene family appearing in front of me.

Julia pulls out a chair and pats it, indicating she wants me to stay. "Sit down, Will. We're just carving pumpkins tonight. That's *all* we're doing. Just carving pumpkins."

It's obvious from her tone that Lake must have told her she doesn't want to talk about it again. That doesn't surprise me. "Okay, then. I guess we're carving pumpkins." I sit in the chair Julia pulled out for me, directly across from Lake. We glance at each other as I take my seat. Her expression is soft but not very telling. I don't know how she feels about what I said during deten-tion today, but if her expression is any indication, she doesn't seem angry. She almost seems apologetic.

"Why were you so late getting home today, Layken?" Kel asks. I glance away just as Lake snaps her head in his direction. I focus my attention on the pumpkin in front of me.

"Eddie and I had detention," she says matter-of-factly.

"Detention? What were you in detention for?" Julia asks.

I can feel the blood pooling in my cheeks.

Lie to her, Lake.

"We skipped class last week, took a nap in the courtyard."

That's my girl. I silently let out a sigh of relief.

"Lake, why would you do something like that? What class did you skip?" Julia asks, obviously disappointed. Lake doesn't re-spond, which causes me to look up. She and Julia are both staring at me.

"She skipped my class!" I laugh. "What was I supposed to do?"

Julia laughs and pats me on the back. "I'm buying you sup-per for that."

I WALK TO the door with Julia when the pizza arrives and take it from the delivery guy while she pays him. I set it on the counter and make the boys a plate.

"I want to try this suck and sweet Kel keeps telling me about," Julia says after we all sit down. Lake looks up at her, con-fused about what "suck and sweet" is, but she doesn't ask for an explanation.

"Good idea, I'll go first. Show you guys how it's done," I say. I take a sip of my drink and start with my suck.

"Mrs. Alex was my suck today," I say.

"Who's Mrs. Alex and why was she your suck?" Julia asks.

"She's the secretary, and . . . let's just say she *favors* me. Today I had to go turn in my absentee reports. We always place them in our boxes before the end of the day and Mrs. Alex collects them all in order to enter them into the system. When I looked at my name on my box, there were two purple hearts doodled over the Os in my last name. Mrs. Alex is the only one who writes with purple ink."

Lake and Julia both burst out laughing. "Mrs. Alex has a *crush* on you?" Lake says, laughing. "She's . . . *old*. And *married!*"

I smile and nod, a little embarrassed. I try to turn my focus back to Julia, but seeing Lake finally laughing is captivating. It's amazing how one smile from her can shift the mood of my entire day. Lake sighs and leans back in her chair. "So are you supposed to say a 'sweet' now? Is that how this works?"

I nod, unable to look away from her. Her smile meets her eyes, and even though I know she has a lot to deal with in the coming days, I feel a sense of relief just seeing her happiness break through, if only for a moment. The fact that she can still find something positive in her current situation reassures me that she'll be okay.

"My sweet?" I say, staring directly at her. "My sweet is right now."

For a moment, it's just the two of us in the room. I don't hear or think about or acknowledge anyone else around us. She smiles at me and I smile back and neither of us breaks our stare. It's as if a silent truce occurs between us and all is suddenly right in our little two-person world.

Julia clears her throat and leans forward. "Okay, I think

we know how to play now," she says, interrupting our moment. I glance at Julia and she's looking at the boys. "Kel, you go next," Julia says, pretending not to have noticed my and Lake's little "moment." I watch Kel, forcing myself to avoid looking at Lake again. If I do, I won't be able to stop myself from jumping over the bar and kissing her.

"My suck is that I still can't think of what to be for Halloween," Kel says. "My sweet is that Will agreed to take us geocaching again this weekend."

"I'm taking you geocaching?" This is the first I've heard of it.

"You are?" Kel says sarcastically. "Aww, gee, Will. That sounds like fun! I'd *love* to go geocaching this weekend."

I laugh and look over at Caulder. "Your turn."

He nudges his head toward Kel. "Same thing," he says.

"That's a cop-out," Julia says to Caulder. "You have to be original."

Caulder rolls his eyes. "Fine," he groans, setting down his pizza. "My suck today is that my best friend's suck is that he can't think of what he wants to be for Halloween. My sweet is that my best friend's sweet is that Will agreed to take us geocaching this weekend."

"You're such a smart-ass," I say to Caulder.

"My turn," Julia says. "My sweet today is that we got to carve pumpkins together." She leans back in her chair and smiles at all of us. I glance at Lake and she's staring down at her hands, folded in front of her on the table. She's picking at her nail polish, something I noticed she does when she's stressed, just like Julia. I know she's thinking what I'm thinking. That this is more than likely Julia's last time to carve pumpkins. Lake brings her hand to her eyes and it looks like she's trying to stop a tear from falling. I quickly turn to Julia to remove any focus from Lake.

"What's your suck?" I ask.

Julia continues to watch Lake when she responds. "My suck is the same as my sweet," Julia says quietly. "We're still carving pumpkins."

I'm beginning to understand that "carving pumpkins" has taken on a whole new meaning. Lake immediately stands up and grabs empty plates off the bar, completely ignoring her mother's gaze.

"*My* suck is that it's my night to do dishes," Lake says. She walks to the sink and turns on the water. Kel and Caulder begin discussing Halloween costumes again, so Julia and I help throw out a few ideas.

No one ever asks Lake what her sweet is.

15.

the honeymoon

"I DID HAVE a sweet that night," she says. "Remember the conversation we had when we took the trash out? When you told me about the first time you saw me?"

I nod.

"That was my sweet. Having that moment with you. All the little moments I got with you were always my sweets." She kisses me on the forehead.

"That was my sweet, too," I say. "That and the intense stare you gave me while we were playing suck and sweet."

She laughs. "If you only knew what I was thinking."

I cock my eyebrow at her. "Naughty thoughts?"

"As soon as you said 'My sweet is right now,' I wanted to jump across the bar and ravish you," she says.

I laugh. I never would have thought we were both thinking the exact same thing. "I wonder what your mom would have done if we had both attacked each other, right there on the bar."

"She would have kicked your ass," she says. She rolls onto her side and faces the other direction. "Spoon me," she says. I scoot closer to her and slide my arm underneath her head, wrapping my other arm tightly around her. She yawns a deep yawn into her pillow. "Tell me about *The Lake*. I want to know why you wrote it."

I kiss her hair and rest my head on her pillow. "I wrote it the next night. After we had basagna with your mom," I say. "When we all sat around the table that night and discussed how things with the boys were going to be handled during her treatments, I realized that you had done it. You were doing exactly what I wished my parents had done before they died. You were taking responsibility. You were preparing for the inevitable. You were facing death head-on, and you were doing it without fear." I put my leg over her legs and tuck her in closer to me. "Every time I was around you, you inspired me to write. And I didn't want to write about anything but you."

She tilts her head back toward me. "That was on the list," she says.

"Your mom's list?"

"Yeah. *'Does he inspire you?'* is one of the questions."

"*Do* I inspire you?"

"Every single day," she whispers.

I kiss her forehead. "Well, like I said, you inspired me, too. I knew I already loved you long before then, but that night at dinner something just clicked inside me. It's like every time we were together, all was right with the world. I had assumed, just like your mom did, that staying apart would help you focus on her, but we were both wrong. I knew that the only way either of us could have been truly happy was if we were together. I wanted you to wait for me. I wanted you to wait for me so bad, but I didn't know how to tell you without crossing some sort of boundary.

"The next night at the slam when I saw you walk in, I couldn't stop myself from performing that piece so you would hear it. I knew it was wrong, but I wanted you to know how much I thought about you. How much I really did love you."

She rolls over and scowls at me. "What do you mean when you saw me walk in? You said you didn't know I was there until you saw me leaving."

I shrug. "I lied."

the lake

AS SOON AS I step up to the microphone, I see her. She walks through the doors and heads straight for a booth, never once looking up at the stage. My heart rate speeds up and beads of sweat form on my forehead, so I wipe them away with the palm of my hand. I'm not sure if it's from the heat of the spotlight or the onslaught of nerves that have just overcome me seeing her walk through the door. I can't perform this poem now. Not with her here. *Why is she here?* She said she wasn't coming tonight.

I take a step away from the microphone to gather my thoughts. Should I do it anyway? If I do it, she'll know exactly how I feel about her. That could be good. Maybe if I go ahead and do it I could gauge her reaction and know if asking her to wait for me is the right thing to do. I *want* her to wait for me. I want her to wait for me so bad. I don't want to think about her ever allowing anyone besides me to love her. She needs to know how I feel about her before I'm too late.

I shake the tension out of my shoulders. I step up to the microphone, brush away my doubt, and say the words that will strip away everything but the truth.

I used to *love* the ocean.
Everything about her.
Her coral *reefs*, her *whitecaps*, her roaring *waves*, the
rocks they *lap*, her *pirate* legends and *mermaid* tails,
Treasures *lost* and treasures *held* . . .
And *ALL*
Of her *fish*
In the *sea.*

Yes, I used to *love* the ocean,
Everything about her.
The way she would *sing* me to *sleep* as I *lay* in my *bed*
then *wake* me with a *force*
That I *soon* came to *dread*.
Her *fables*, her *lies*, her *misleading* eyes,
I'd drain her *dry*
If I *cared* enough to.
I used to *love* the ocean,
Everything about her.
Her coral *reefs*, her *whitecaps*, her roaring *waves*, the
rocks they *lap*, her *pirate* legends and *mermaid* tails,
treasures *lost* and treasures *held*.
And *ALL*
Of her *fish*
In the *sea*.
Well, if you've ever tried *navigating* your *sailboat*
through her stormy *seas*, you would *realize* that
her *whitecaps* are your *enemies*. If you've ever tried
swimming ashore when your *leg* gets a *cramp* and
you just had a *huge meal* of *In-n-Out* burgers that's
weighing you down, and her *roaring waves* are
knocking the *wind* out of you, filling your *lungs* with
water as you *flail* your arms, trying to get *someone's*
attention, but your friends
just
wave
back at you?
And if you've ever grown up with *dreams* in your *head*
about *life*, and how one of these days you would pirate

your *own* ship and have your *own* crew and that *all* of

the mermaids

would *love*

only

you?

Well, you would *realize . . .*

Like I eventually realized . . .

That all the *good* things about her?

All the *beautiful?*

It's not *real.*

It's *fake.*

So you *keep* your *ocean,*

I'll take the *Lake.*

I CLOSE MY eyes and exhale, not sure what to do next. Do I walk to the booth where she's sitting? Do I wait and let her come find me? I slowly back away from the microphone and walk toward the side stairs, taking them one by one, afraid of what, if anything, might happen next. I know I need to see her.

When I reach the back of the room, she isn't in the booth anymore. I walk toward the front of the club, toward the stage, in case she came to find me up here. She's nowhere. After looking around for several minutes, I see Eddie and Gavin sliding into the booth Lake was seated in just moments ago.

What are they doing here? Lake said none of them were coming. Thank God they're late, I wouldn't have wanted Gavin to hear that piece. I walk over to them and attempt to appear casual, but my entire body is nervous and tense.

"Hey, Will," Gavin says. "You want to sit with us?"

I shake my head. "Not yet. Have you guys . . ." I pause, not really wanting Gavin to give me one of his looks again when he finds out I'm looking for Lake. "Have you guys seen Layken?" Gavin leans back in the booth and cocks an eyebrow.

"Yeah," Eddie says with a grin on her face. "She said she was leaving. She was headed toward the back parking lot of the club, but I just found her purse right here," she says, holding up a purse. "She'll be back as soon as she realizes she doesn't have it."

She *left*? I immediately turn and head toward the door without saying another word to either of them. If she stayed for the whole poem and just up and left, I must have pissed her off. Why did I not switch poems? Why didn't I think about how it would make her feel? I swing the door open and immediately round the corner toward the back parking lot. Frantic to catch her before she drives away, I find myself switching from a brisk walk, to a jog, then to a desperate sprint. I spot her Jeep, but she isn't inside it. I spin around searching for her, but I don't see her. I turn to walk back and check the club again and I hear her voice, coupled with someone else's. It sounds like a guy. My fists immediately clench, worried for her safety. I don't like the thought of her being out here alone with someone else, so I follow the sound of the voices until I see her.

Until I see *them*.

She's backed up against Javi's truck, her hands on his chest, his hands on her cheeks. Seeing his lips meshed with hers pulls a reaction from deep within me that I didn't even know I was capable of. The only thing running through my head at this point is how the hell to get this asshole off her. Of all the guys she could choose to help her move on from me, it sure as hell isn't going to be Javi.

Before I can even contemplate a more sane decision, my hands have hold of his shirt and I'm pulling him away from her. When he trips and falls onto his back, I drop my knee onto his chest and punch him. As soon as my fist meets his jaw, I realize it took all of three seconds to throw away every single thing I've worked for. There is no way I'm getting out of this predicament with a job.

My split-second realization is enough distraction to allow Javi to regain his footing and deliver a punch right to my eye, sending me back to the ground before I can react. I press my hand against my eye and feel the warm blood seeping through my fingers. I hear Lake yelling for him to stop. Or she's yelling for me to stop. Or maybe both of us. I stand up and open my eyes just as Lake jumps in front of Javi. She's hurled forward when Javi hits her in the back with a blow that was obviously intended for me. She gasps and falls against me.

"Lake!" I yell, rolling her onto her back. As soon as I confirm she's conscious, I'm consumed by rage.

Vengeance.

Hatred.

I want to *kill* this asshole. I grab the door handle of the car nearest me and pull myself up. Javi is making his way toward Lake, apologizing. I don't give him time to make amends. I hit him with every ounce of force behind my fist and watch as he falls to the ground. I kneel and hit him again, this time for Lake. As soon as I pull my fist back to hit him again, Gavin jerks me off him, sending us both backward. Gavin has hold of both my arms from behind and is yelling for me to calm down. I yank my arms away from him and stand up, intent on getting Lake out of here, away from Javi. She's probably beyond pissed at me right now, but the feeling is pretty damn mutual.

She's sitting up, clutching her chest, attempting to take a breath. As much as I want to yell at her, I'm immediately overcome by worry when I realize she's hurting. I just want to get her away from everyone. I take her hand and pull her up, then wrap my arm around her waist to help her walk.

"I'm taking you home."

When we reach my car, I help her inside and shut her door, then walk around to my side of the car. Before I get in, I take several deep breaths in an attempt to calm myself down. I can't imagine what possessed her to allow him to kiss her after seeing me practically confess my love for her on stage. Does she not even *give* a shit anymore? I close my eyes and inhale through my nose, then open the door and climb in.

I pull out of the parking lot, unable to form a thought, much less a coherent sentence. My hands are shaking, my heart is about to beat out of my chest, I probably need stitches, and my career is now in jeopardy . . . but the only thing I can think about is the fact that she kissed him.

She *kissed* him.

The thought consumes me the entire drive. She hasn't said a single thing, so she has to be feeling pretty guilty right now. As soon as I feel the urge to turn to her and tell her exactly what I think of her actions tonight, I choose to get out of the car, instead. It's better for both of us if I get a breather. I can't keep this all in anymore. I pull the car over to the side of the road and punch the steering wheel. I can see her flinch out of the corner of my eye, but she says nothing. I swing the car door open and quickly get out before I say something I'll regret. I start walking in an attempt to clear my head. It doesn't help. When I'm at least fifty yards away from the car, I bend down and pick up a handful of gravel, then throw it at nothing.

"Shit!" I yell. "Shit, shit, shit!" I'm not sure at this point what or why or who I'm even mad at. Lake is in no way tied to me. She can date whomever she wants. She can kiss whomever she wants. The fact that I overreacted isn't her fault at all. I should never have performed that poem. I freaked her out. We were finally in a good spot and I went and screwed it all up.

Again.

I tilt my head up to the sky and close my eyes, allowing the cold flakes of snow to fall on my face. I can feel the tightness and pressure increasing near my eye. It hurts like hell. I hope Javi is hurting worse than I am.

Asshole.

I throw another rock, then walk back toward the car. We drive home with so much that needs to be said, but not a single word spoken.

WHEN WE GET to my house, I help her onto the couch, then walk to my kitchen and grab an ice pack out of the freezer. The tension between us has never been thicker, but I can't bring myself to talk to her about it. I don't want to know why she ran after I performed. I don't want to know why she ran to *Javi* of all people. I sure as hell don't want to know why she kissed him.

Her eyes are closed when I reach the couch again. She looks so peaceful just lying there. I watch her for a moment, wishing I knew what the hell was going through her head, but I refuse to ask. I can carve pumpkins just as well as she can.

I kneel beside her and her eyes flick open. She looks at me with horror and reaches up to my eye. "Will! Your eye!"

"It's fine. I'll be fine," I say, shaking it off. She pulls her hand back and I lean forward and grasp the bottom edge of her shirt. "Do you mind?" I say, asking permission to lift her shirt. She shakes her head, so I pull the shirt up over her back. She's already got a bruise from where that asswipe punched her. I lay the icepack over her injury, then pull her shirt back down on top of it.

I walk to the front door and leave her on the couch as I make my way across the street to inform Julia. When I knock on the door, it takes her a while to finally answer. When she sees me standing there with blood on my face, she immediately gasps Lake's name.

"She's okay," I quickly say. "There was a fight at the club and she was hit in the back. She's on my couch." Before I can say anything else, Julia shoves past me and runs across the street. When I finally make my way back into my living room, she's holding Lake in her arms. Julia takes her hand and helps her up. I hold the door open as they both walk out. Lake doesn't even make eye contact with me when she leaves. I shut the door behind them, then head to the bathroom and begin cleaning my injury. When I've got it bandaged up, I grab my phone and text Gavin.

> If I come pick you up first thing in the morning, can you go with me to get Lake's Jeep and drive it back to Ypsi?

I hit send and sit down on the couch. I can't even wrap my mind around everything that's happened tonight. I feel like I'm living someone else's dream. Someone else's *nightmare.*

> How early?

> *Early. I have to be at the school by 7:30. Is 6:00 okay?*

> I'll do it under one condition. If you don't get fired tomorrow,

I'm exempt from every single assignment for the rest of the year.

See you at six.

HE OPENS THE passenger door and climbs inside. Before I've even backed out of his driveway, he lays into me.

"You realize you screwed up, right? Do you know who Javier's father is? If you even have a job to go back to today, you won't have it by this afternoon."

I nod, but don't respond.

"What the hell prompted you to kick a student's ass, Will?"

I sigh and pull onto the main road, keeping my eyes focused in front of me.

"I know whatever happened had to do with Layken. But what the hell did Javi do? You were pummeling him like he was your punching bag. Please tell me it was self-defense so you at least have a chance at keeping your job. Was it self-defense?" he asks, looking straight at me for an answer.

I shake my head no. He sighs, then leans forcefully back against his seat.

"And then you take her home! Why the hell would you let her in your car alone in front of him? That's enough to get you fired without even *kicking* his ass. Why the hell *did* you kick his ass?"

I look over at him. "Gavin, I screwed up. I realize this. You can shut the hell up now."

He nods and props his leg on the dash and doesn't say another word.

• • •

IT'S THE FIRST time I've ever made it into the office before Mrs. Alex. It's eerily quiet, and for a moment, I actually wish she were here. I walk around her desk toward Mr. Murphy's office. I glance inside and he's casually seated at his desk with the phone to his ear and his feet propped up. His face lights up when he sees me, but the illumination quickly fades when he sees the damage to my eye. He holds up a finger, so I take a few steps away from his door to give him some privacy.

I've thought about this moment so many times before. The moment I would walk into Mr. Murphy's office and resign. Of course, I always imagined the end result would be my walking out of his office and into Lake's life.

My fantasy is nothing like my current reality. Lake hates me right now and her feelings are warranted. I push her away every time she gets close to me, then every time she finally gets used to being without me, I do something to screw with her head even more. Why did I think performing that poem last night was a good idea? We were finally in a good spot. She was finally learning to balance all the negativity in her life, and I go and make it worse. *Again.*

That's all I do is make things worse for her. That's probably the reason she turned to Javi. I'd like to think she was just kissing him to make me jealous, but my biggest fear is that she was kissing him because she's completely moved on from me. It's my biggest fear, yet it's exactly what I know she needs.

"Mr. Cooper," Mr. Murphy says, walking past me. "Is this something that can wait until I get back? I've got an eight o'clock meeting."

"Uh," I stammer. "Well, actually it's pretty important."

He stops next to the wall of mailboxes and pulls the contents of his box out. "How important? So important it can't wait until ten?"

I shrug. "It can't wait," I say reluctantly. "I, um . . . sort of got in a fight last night. With a student."

Mr. Murphy stops sorting his mail and darts his head toward me. "Sort of? You did or you didn't, Mr. Cooper. Which is it?"

"Did," I reply. "Definitely did."

He turns to face me full on and leans his back against the row of mailboxes behind him. "Who?"

"Javier Cruz."

He shakes his head, then rubs the back of his neck while he thinks. "I'll have Mrs. Alex set up an appointment with his father at ten. In the meantime, I suggest you find someone to fill in for you," he says. "Be back here at ten." He walks over to Mrs. Alex's desk and writes something down. I nod, not at all surprised by his guarded reaction. I pick my satchel up and walk toward the office exit.

"Mr. Cooper?" he calls out.

"Yes, sir?"

"Were there any other students involved? Anyone who can give an accurate account of what happened?"

I sigh. I really don't want to get her involved, but it doesn't seem like I'm going to have a choice. "Yes. Layken Cohen," I say.

"Is this Javier's girlfriend?" he asks, writing down Layken's name.

The question causes me to wince, but from the looks of them last night I'd say it's a very legitimate question. "Yeah, I guess so." I exit the office, hoping they don't bring Lake and Javi in at ten. I don't know if I can keep it together in the same room with both of them.

I'M SEATED AT the table, waiting for the conference to begin. Luckily, Mr. Murphy met with Javier privately, not wanting us to have to interact. I'm supposed to meet with Mr. Murphy as soon as the conference with Javier's father is over. I'm not really that eager to share my version of events, since I'm obviously the one in the wrong here. The fact that Mr. Murphy brought in a member of campus police doesn't do anything to ease my apprehension. I'm not sure what the legal ramifications are of what occurred last night and if Javier is planning on pressing charges, but I guess I deserve whatever result my actions bring about.

The door opens and Lake walks into the room. I literally have to force myself not to look at her. I can't help the emotional reaction I have to her, and I'm afraid everyone in the room will see it. I keep my gaze focused on the table in front of me.

"Ms. Cohen, please take a seat," Mr. Murphy says. Lake takes a step forward and slides into the seat next to me. I clench my fists, fighting the tension between us that seems to have only increased since last night.

"This is Mr. Cruz, Javier's father," says Mr. Murphy. "This is Officer Venturelli," he says, motioning to both men. "I'm sure you know why you're here. It is our understanding that there was an incident involving Mr. Cooper that occurred off of school grounds," he says. "We would appreciate it if you could tell us your version of events."

I glance toward Lake just as she turns her head toward me. Her eyes search mine for guidance, so I nod, silently encouraging her to tell the truth. I could never let her lie for me. She turns back to Mr. Murphy. The exchange we just shared was no more than three seconds, but the look of concern for me in her eyes was undeniable.

She doesn't hate me. She's *worried* for me.

She clears her throat and adjusts herself in her seat. She places her hands on the table in front of her and begins picking at her nail polish when she speaks. "There was a misunderstanding between me and Javier," she says. "Mr. Cooper showed up and pulled him off me."

I can feel the heat in my face when the lies start coming out of her mouth. Why is she lying for me? Did I not make it clear that I wanted her to tell the truth about last night? I tap my knee against hers when she pauses. She glances up at me, but before I can tell her to tell the truth, Mr. Murphy interrupts.

"Can you start at the beginning, please, Ms. Cohen? We need to be clear on the entire sequence of events. Where were you and what were all of you doing there?"

"We were in Detroit at a poetry slam. It's part of a required assignment for Mr. Cooper's class. I arrived early before the other students. Something happened and I felt uncomfortable and had to leave, so I left just a few minutes after I arrived, which is when I ran into Javier outside."

"What happened that made you uncomfortable?" Officer Venturelli asks her. She flicks her gaze in my direction, but only for a moment. She looks back at Officer Venturelli and shrugs. "Maybe uncomfortable isn't the right word," she says quietly. "One of the performers . . ." She pauses and takes a deep breath. Before she continues, she touches her knee to mine and doesn't retract it, causing me to swallow a lump in my throat. The move is deliberate, and it confuses the hell out of me. "I was just really moved by one of the pieces performed last night. It meant a lot to me," she whispers. "So much that I just wanted to leave, before I got too emotional."

I lean forward and put my elbows on the table, then rest my face in the palms of my hands. I can't believe she just said those words, and she said them just for my benefit. Knowing that she's trying to tell me how my poem made her feel is making this too much to bear. I have the overwhelming urge to pull her up out of her chair and kiss her in front of everyone, then scream my resignation at the top of my lungs.

"My Jeep was parked behind the venue and on my way outside, I ran into Javier. He offered to walk me to my car. I needed to use his phone, so we were standing by his truck while it was charging. We were talking about the weather and . . ." Her voice grows quiet and she shifts uncomfortably in her seat.

"Ms. Cohen, is this something you would rather tell me in private?" Mr. Murphy asks.

She shakes her head. "No, it's fine," she says. "I was . . . I was asking him about the weather and he just started kissing me. I told him no and tried to push him away, but he wouldn't stop kissing me. I didn't know what to do. He had me pinned against his truck, and I guess that's when Mr. Cooper saw what was happening and he pulled him off me."

I have a grip on the edge of the table that is so tight, I don't even notice until Lake taps my leg and glances down at my hands. I release the table from my grasp and close my eyes, breathing slow and steady. Her confession should give me nothing but relief, knowing that my bout of jealousy will now be played off as if I were protecting her. However, I'm anything *but* relieved. I'm furious. Javier is lucky his ass isn't in here, because there would have been an extremely detailed reenactment of last night right in this office.

Lake continues sharing her version of the story, but I don't hear another word of it. I do my best to hold it together until everyone's dismissed, but it's the hardest five minutes I've ever had to contain myself. As soon as they dismiss her, Mr. Cruz and Officer Venturelli follow her out the door. I stand up in my seat and let out a breath. I pace back and forth under the intense gaze of Mr. Murphy. I'm not able to speak yet due to the rage coursing through me, so I continue to pace and he continues to silently watch me.

"Mr. Cooper," he says calmly, "do you have anything else to add or is her version accurate?"

I pause and look at him. "I wish it *wasn't* accurate," I say, "but unfortunately it is."

"Will," Mr. Murphy says. "You did the right thing. Quit being so hard on yourself. Javier was completely out of line and if you weren't there to stop him, there's no telling what would have happened to that girl."

"Is he being expelled?" I ask, stopping to grip the back of the chair.

Mr. Murphy stands and walks to the door where Officer Venturelli is outside speaking with Mr. Cruz. He closes the door and turns toward me. "We can't expel him. He's claiming it was a misunderstanding and he thought she wanted him to kiss her. We'll suspend him for a few days for the fight, but that's the extent of his punishment."

I nod, very aware that what I'm about to do is the only answer at this point. There's no way I can ever be in the same room with Javier again and not have it end badly.

"Then I'd like to resign," I say evenly.

16.

the honeymoon

"YOU *WILLINGLY* RESIGNED?" Lake asks, dumbfounded. "I thought it was a mutual agreement. They would have let you keep your job, Will. Why the hell did you *resign*?"

"Lake, there's no way I could have continued teaching there. I'd reached my breaking point. I was going to get fired one of two ways if I hadn't resigned that day."

"Why do you think that?"

"Because it's true. They would have fired me the first day Javier returned to school because I would have kicked his ass the moment I laid eyes on him. That, or they would have fired me because one more second in a room with you and I would have jumped *you*, but in a completely different way."

She laughs. "Yeah. The tension was intense. We would have lost control eventually."

"*Eventually?* We lost control that same day," I say, reminding her of our incident in the laundry room.

She frowns and closes her eyes, then sighs a deep sigh.

"What's wrong?" I ask her.

She shakes her head. "Nothing. It's just hard thinking about that night. It really hurt," she whispers.

I kiss her lightly on the forehead. "I know. I'm sorry."

laundry room

I SOMEHOW MADE it to the end of the workday without getting suspended, fired, or arrested. I'd say being transferred to Detroit to finish out my student teaching is one of the best outcomes I could have anticipated.

I pull into the driveway and the boys are helping Lake and Julia with groceries. I haven't even made it out of the car yet when Caulder meets me at the door, beaming with excitement.

"Will!" he says, grabbing my hand. "Wait till you see this!"

I walk across the street with him and grab the rest of the sacks and take them inside. When I set them down, I notice the contents aren't groceries. It looks like sewing supplies.

"Guess what we're going to be for Halloween?" Caulder says.

"Uh—"

"Julia's cancer!" he yells.

Did I just hear him right?

Julia walks into the room with her sewing machine and I give her a questioning look.

"You only live once, right?" She smiles and places the sewing machine on the bar.

"She's letting us make the tumors for the lungs," Kel says. "You want to make one? I'll let you make the big one."

I don't even know how to respond. "Uh—"

"Kel," Lake interrupts. "Will and Caulder can't help, they'll be out of town all weekend." Seeing the excitement on Caulder's face, there's nowhere I'd rather be than right here. "Actually, that was before I found out we were making lung cancer," I say. "I think we'll have to reschedule our trip."

• • •

"WHERE'S YOUR MEASURING tape?" Lake asks Julia.

"I don't know," she says. "I don't know if I have one, actually."

I have measuring tape, so I try to think of a way to get Lake to come with me to get it. I know she's dying to know what happened today and I owe her a huge apology for acting the way I did toward her last night. She had experienced what was more than likely a horrifying event alone with Javi, and I acted like a jerk the entire way home. I was trying to refrain from yelling at her last night, when I should have been consoling her.

"Will has one. We can use his," Lake says. "Will, do you mind getting it?"

I play dumb. "I have measuring tape?"

She rolls her eyes. "Yes, it's in your sewing kit."

"I have a sewing kit?"

"It's in your laundry room." She spreads the material out in front of her. "It's next to the sewing machine on the shelf behind your mother's patterns. I put them in chronological order according to pattern nu— Never mind," she says quickly. She shakes her head and stands. "I'll just show you."

Thank you.

I quickly jump up, maybe a little too eagerly.

"You put his patterns in chronological order?" Julia asks.

"I was having a bad day," Lake says over her shoulder.

I hold the door for Lake, then close it behind us. She turns around and completely loses her calm demeanor. "What happened? God, I've been worried sick all day," she says.

"I got a slap on the wrist," I say as we walk toward my house. "They told me since I was defending another student, they couldn't really hold it against me."

I jog a few steps and open my front door for her, stepping aside to let her in.

"That's good. What about your internship?" she asks.

"Well, it's a little tricky. The only available ones they had in Ypsilanti were all primary. My major is secondary, so I've been placed at a school in Detroit."

She looks up at me, her eyes full of concern. "What's that mean? Are y'all moving?"

I love the fact that the thought of our moving scares her so bad. I laugh. "No, Lake, we're not moving. It's just for eight weeks. I'll be doing a lot of driving, though. I was actually going to talk to you and your mom about it later. I'm not going to be able to take the boys to school, or pick them up either. I'll be gone a lot. I know this isn't a good time to ask for your help—"

"Stop it. You know we'll help." She grabs the tape measure and shuts the box, then walks the kit back to the laundry room. I follow her, but I'm not sure why I feel compelled to. I'm afraid she's about to head straight back to her house and I still have so much left I need to say to her. I walk into the laundry room behind her and pause in the doorway. She's staring quietly in front of her, running her fingers across my mother's patterns. She's got that distant look in her eyes again. I lean against the doorframe and watch her.

I still can't believe I thought she would willingly allow Javi to kiss her, especially after seeing my performance last night. I know her better than that, and she knows she deserves so much better than Javi.

Hell, she deserves so much better than *me*.

She reaches to the wall and flicks off the light, then turns toward me. She comes to a halt when she sees that I'm blocking the doorway. She quietly gasps and looks up at me, her beautiful green eyes full of hope again. She scrolls her eyes over my features, searching my face, waiting for me to either speak or move out of her way. I don't want to do either. All I want to do is take her in my arms and show her how I feel about her, but I can't. She stares up at me, slowly dropping her gaze to my mouth. She tugs on her bottom lip with her teeth and nervously darts her eyes to the floor.

I've never wanted to be teeth so bad in my entire life.

I take a deep breath and prepare to get out what I need to say, despite knowing I shouldn't say it. I just need her to know why I did what I did last night, and why I acted the way I acted. I fold my arms across my chest and prop my foot against the doorway, looking down at it. Avoiding eye contact with her is probably best right now, considering my lack of resolve at the moment. It's been a while since we've been alone in a situation like this. The way things have been going the past few weeks, I had myself convinced that I was stronger than I am, and that I've overcome the weakness I feel when I'm around her.

I was completely wrong.

My heart slams against my chest at record speed and I'm consumed by an insatiable desire to grab her by the waist and pull her to me. I hug myself tighter in an attempt to keep my hands to myself. I work my jaw back and forth, hell bent on finding a way to bury my urge to confess to her, but I can't. The words spill out of me before I can stop them.

"Last night," I say, my voice cracking the tension like a sledgehammer. "When I saw Javi kissing you . . . I thought you were kissing him back."

I swing my eyes to her, searching for a reaction. *Any* reaction. I know how she tries to hide what she's feeling more than any other person I've ever met.

Her eyes widen at the realization that I wasn't defending her at all last night. I was reacting like a possessive boyfriend, not her knight in shining armor.

"Oh," she says.

"I didn't know the whole story until this morning, when you told your version," I say. I don't know how I held myself together in the office this morning when I found out. All I wanted to do was lunge across the table and punch Javi's father across the jaw for raising such an asshole. Just thinking about it causes my blood to boil. I inhale a deep breath, filling my lungs to their maximum capacity before huffing out a sigh. I notice my hands are clenched into tight fists, so I relax them and run my hands through my hair, turning to face her.

"God, Lake. I can't tell you how pissed I was. I wanted to hurt him so bad. And now? Now that I know he really *was* hurting you? I want to *kill* him." I lean my head back against the doorframe and close my eyes. I have to get the thought of him out of my head. He hurt her, and I wasn't there in time to protect her. The image of him pressing his mouth to hers against her will is clear in my mind, as is the fact that his lips were the last to touch hers. She doesn't deserve to be kissed like that. She deserves to be kissed by someone who loves her. Someone who spends every waking moment trying to do everything right by her. Someone who would rather die than see her hurt. She doesn't deserve to be kissed by anyone other than me.

Her brows are furrowed and she's staring at me with a confused expression. "How did you"—she pauses—"How'd you know I was there?"

"I saw you. When I finished my piece, I saw you leaving."

She looks up at me and quietly sucks in a small breath with my admission. Her hand searches for support behind her and she takes a step back, steadying herself. Despite the darkness, I can see her eyes dance with hope. "Will, does this mean—"

I immediately take two steps forward, closing the gap between us. My chest heaves with each passing breath as I attempt to calm my desire to show her just how sincere my words were last night. I trail the back of my fingers against the smooth skin of her cheek, then hook my thumb under her chin, bringing her face closer to mine. The simple contact of her skin against my fingers reminds me of what her kiss is capable of doing to me. It hypnotizes me. Her touch completely, wholeheartedly shakes me to my core and I try to force myself to slow down.

She places her hand against my chest when I wrap my arms around her. I can feel her wanting to resist, but her need is just as strong as mine. I take a step forward until she finds solid backing and I quickly lean in and press my lips to hers before either of us has time to change our minds. When my tongue finds hers, she moans a soft moan and becomes putty in my hands, dropping her arms to her sides. I kiss her passionately, tenderly, and eagerly all at the same time.

I grip her by the waist and easily lift her up onto the dryer, taking a stance between her legs and never losing contact with her lips. She begins to pull at my shirt, wanting me closer, so I oblige by pulling her against me as she encircles me with her legs. Her nails lightly dig into the muscles of my forearms as her fingers search their way up my arms. When she reaches my neck, her hands glide through my hair, sending chills to places I didn't even know could *get* chills. She grabs tufts of my hair in her fists and pulls my head down, repositioning my mouth against the sweet skin of her neck. She takes the opportunity to catch her breath, panting and quietly moaning as my lips tease their way across her collarbone. I reach behind her and grab a handful of hair just as she did mine, then lightly tug until she leans her head back, giving me more access to the incredibly perfect skin against my lips. She does just as I'd hoped and arches her back, giving my lips silent permission to resume their pursuit as I make my way down her neck. I release her hair and slide my hand down her back, slipping my fingers between her skin and her jeans. My fingertips skim the top edge of her panties, and I groan under my breath.

Having her in my arms fills the constant void that has been in my heart since the first night I kissed her, but with every passing moment, every kiss, and every stroke of her hands, an even greater desire builds within me. I need more of her than these stolen moments of passion. I need so much more.

"Will," she breathes.

I mumble against her skin, unable to get out an audible response. I don't really feel like talking at the moment. I run my other hand up the back of her shirt until it meets her bra and I pull her against me as I work my way back up her neck toward her mouth.

"Does this mean . . ." she breathes heavily. "Does it mean we don't have to pretend . . . anymore? We can be . . . together? Since you're not . . . since you're not my teacher?"

My lips freeze against her neck with her breathless words. I want more than anything to cover her mouth with my own and make her stop talking about it. I just want to forget about it all for one night. Just for one night.

But I can't.

My incredibly irresponsible moment of weakness just gave her the wrong idea. I'm still a teacher. Maybe not *her* teacher, but I'm still a teacher. And she's still a student. And everything happening between us right now is still completely wrong, no matter how right I want it to be.

In the process of thinking about all of the potential complications of her question, I've somehow released her from my death grip and have taken a step away from her.

"Will?" she says, sliding off the dryer. She steps closer to me and the fear in her eyes makes my stomach drop. I did this to her. *Again.*

I can feel the regret and agony creep up to my face, and it's obvious she can see it, too.

"Will? Tell me. Do the rules still apply?" she says fearfully.

I don't know what to say that can make it any less painful. It's obvious I just made a huge mistake. "Lake," I whisper, my voice full of shame. "I had a weak moment. I'm sorry."

She steps forward and shoves her hands into my chest. "A weak *moment*? That's what you call this? A weak *moment*?" she yells. I flinch at her words, knowing I just said the wrong thing. "What were you gonna *do*, Will? When were you gonna stop making out with me and kick me out of your house *this* time?"

She spins on her heel and storms out of the laundry room. Seeing her walk away causes me to panic at the thought of not only upsetting her, but losing her for good. "Lake, don't," I plead, following after her. "I'm sorry. I'm so sorry. It won't happen again, I swear."

She turns to face me, tears already streaming down her cheeks. "You're damn right it won't! I finally accepted it, Will! After an entire month of torture, I was finally able to be *around* you again. Then you go and do *this*! I can't do it anymore," she says, throwing her arms up in defeat. "The way you consume my mind when we aren't together? I don't have time for it anymore. I've got more important things to think about now than your little *weak moments.*"

Her words slam me. She's absolutely right. I've gone so long trying to get her to accept things and move on so she won't be burdened by my life, but I can't even resist her long enough not to cave in to my selfish desire for her. I *don't* deserve her. I don't deserve her forgiveness, let alone to be loved by her.

"Get me the measuring tape," she says, standing with her hand on the door.

"Wh—what?"

"It's on the damn floor! Get me the measuring tape!"

I walk back into the laundry room and retrieve the measuring tape, then take it back to her, placing it in her hand. She looks down at my hand clamped over hers. She wipes away falling tears with her other hand. She refuses to even look at me. The thought of her hating me for what just happened between us terrifies me. I love her so much and I want more than anything to be able to give it all up for her.

But I can't. Not yet.

She has to know how hard this is for me, too. "Don't make me the bad guy, Lake. *Please.*"

She pulls her hand from mine and looks into my eyes. "Well you're certainly not the martyr, anymore." She walks out, slamming the door behind her.

The words "wait for me" pass my lips just as the door closes, but she doesn't hear me. "I want you to wait for me," I say again. I know she can't hear me, but the fact that I can say it out loud gives me the confidence I need to run after her and tell her to her face.

I love her. I know she loves me. And despite what Julia thinks is good for us, I want her to wait for me. We need to be together. We *have* to be together. If I don't stop her from walking away right now, I'll regret it for the rest of my life.

I swing open the door, prepared to run after her, but I pause when I see her. She's standing in her entryway, wiping away the tears that I'm responsible for. I watch as she takes a few deep breaths, trying to pull herself together before walking into her house. Seeing her effort to move past what just happened so that she can help her mother inside her own home brings it all back into perspective.

I'm the last thing she needs in her life right now. I have too much responsibility, and with how things are going for her right now, the last thing she needs is to put her life on hold for me. Everything I say or do just brings her more grief and heartache and I can't ask her to hold on to that while she waits for me. She doesn't need to focus on me. Julia's right. She needs to focus on her family.

I reluctantly walk back into my house and shut the door behind me. The realization that I need to let her go for good physically brings me to my knees.

17.

the honeymoon

"I WISH MORE than anything I had gone after you that night," I say. "I should have told you exactly what I wanted to say. It would have saved us both a world of heartache."

Lake sits up on the bed and hugs her knees, looking down at me. "Not me," she says. "I'm happy things worked out the way they did. I think we both needed that breather. And I definitely don't regret all the time I spent with my mother during those three months. It was good for us."

"Good." I smile. "That's the only reason I didn't run after you."

She releases her knees and falls back onto the bed. "But still. It was so hard living across the street from you. All I wanted to do was be with you, but I didn't want anyone to know that. It's like I spent the entire three months pretending to be happy when I was in front of other people. Eddie was the only one who knew how I really felt. I didn't want Mom to know because I felt like it would just burden her even more if she knew how sad I was."

I raise up and lean forward, crawling on top of her. "Thank God she knew how we both really felt, though. Do you think you would have showed up at the slam the night before my graduation if she didn't encourage you to go?"

"There's no way I would have shown up. If it weren't for her telling me about your conversation with her, I would have continued the rest of the year thinking you didn't love me like I loved you."

I press my forehead against hers. "I'm so glad you showed up," I whisper. "You changed my life forever that night."

schooled

I'VE SPOKEN TO Lake once in the last three months.

Once.

You would think it would get easier, but it hasn't. Especially today, since my last day of student teaching is finally over. I graduate tomorrow, which should be a day I'm looking forward to more than anything. Instead I'm dreading it, knowing Lake won't be waiting for me.

There are two emotions in this world I've learned I can handle. Love and hate. Lake has loved me at times and she's hated me at times. Love and hate, despite their polar opposites, are both feelings that are induced by passion. I can handle that.

It's the indifference I don't know how to process.

I went to her house a few weeks ago to talk to her about my new job at the junior high and she didn't seem to care one way or another. I would have taken it well if she had been happy for me and wished me good luck. I would have taken it even better if she had cried and begged me not to do it, which is what I was hoping would happen more than anything. It's the sole reason I even went to tell her about the job in the first place. I didn't want to accept it if I thought I still had a chance with her.

Instead, she didn't react either way. She congratulated me, but the indifference in her voice was clear. She was simply being polite. Her indifference finally sealed our fate, and I knew in that moment that I had messed with her heart one too many times. She was over me.

She *is* over me.

I have a two-week window in which I'll be nothing. I won't be a student. I won't be a teacher. I'll be a twenty-one-year-old college graduate. I've thought about walking straight over to Lake's house today to tell her how much I love her, even though I'm technically still a teacher, considering the contract I have with the junior high. Not even *that* would stop me if it weren't for the way she reacted to me last month with so much indifference. She seemed to have accepted our fate, and it was good to see her handling everything so well, as much as it hurt. The last thing I want to do, or *need* to do, is pull her back down with me.

God, this is going to be the hardest two weeks of my life. I need to keep my distance from her, that's a fact.

When the audience begins clapping, I snap back to reality. I'm supposed to be judging tonight, but I haven't heard a single word any of the performers have said. I hold up the standard 9.0 on my scorecard without even looking up at the stage. I don't even want to be here tonight. In fact, I don't want to be *anywhere* tonight.

When the scores are tallied, the emcee begins to announce the winners. I lean back in my seat and close my eyes, hoping the night goes fast. I just want to go home and get to bed so graduation will come and go tomorrow. I don't know why I'm dreading it. Probably because I'll be the only person there who couldn't find enough people to give my graduation tickets to. The average person never gets *enough* tickets for graduation. I have too many.

"I would like to perform a piece I wrote."

I jerk up in my seat at the sound of her voice, the sudden movement almost causing my chair to flip backward. She's standing on the stage, holding the microphone. The guy next to me laughs along with the rest of the crowd once they realize she's interrupting the night's schedule.

"Check this chick out," he says, nudging me with his elbow.

The sight of her paralyzes me. I'm pretty sure I forgot how to breathe. I'm pretty sure I'm about to die. *What the hell is she doing?* I watch intently as she brings the microphone back to her lips. "I know this isn't standard protocol, but it's an emergency," she says.

The laughter from the audience causes her eyes to widen and she spins around to look for the emcee. She's scared. Whatever she's doing, it's completely out of character for her. The emcee nudges her to face the front of the room again. I take a deep breath, silently willing her to keep calm.

She places the microphone back in its stand and lowers it to her height. She closes her eyes and inhales when the guy next to me yells, "Three dollars!"

I could punch him.

Her eyes flick open and she shoves her hand into her pocket, pulling out money to hand to the emcee. After he takes the money, she prepares herself again. "My piece is called—" The emcee interrupts her, tapping her on the shoulder. She shoots him an irritated glance. I expel a deep breath, becoming just as irritated by all the interruptions. She takes the change from him and shoves it back into her pocket, then hisses something at him that makes him retreat off the stage. She turns back toward the audience and her eyes scan the crowd.

She has to know I'm here. What the hell is she doing?

"My piece is called *Schooled*," she says into the microphone. I swallow the lump in my throat. If I wanted to move at this point, my body would fail me. I'm completely frozen as I watch her take several deep breaths, then begin her piece.

I got *schooled* this year.
By *everyone*.
By my little brother . . .

by The *Avett* Brothers . . .
by my *mother*, my *best friend*, my *teacher*, my *father*,
and
by
a
boy.
A boy that I'm *seriously, deeply, madly, incredibly,*
and undeniably in *love* with.
I got *so schooled* this year.
By a *nine*-year-old.
He taught me that it's *okay* to live *life*
a little *backward*.
And how to *laugh*
At what you would *think*
is *unlaughable*.
I got *schooled* this year
By a *band*
They taught me how to find that *feeling* of *feeling*
again.
They taught me how to *decide* what to *be*
And go *be* it.
I got *schooled* this year.
By a *cancer* patient.
She taught me *so* much. She's *still* teaching me so
much.
She taught me to *question*.
To *never* regret.
She taught me to *push* my boundaries,
Because *that's* what they're *there* for.
She told me to find a *balance* between *head* and *heart*

And then
she taught me how . . .
I got *schooled* this year
By a *foster kid.*
She taught me to *respect* the hand that I was *dealt.*
And to be *grateful* I was even dealt a *hand.*
She taught me that *family*
Doesn't have to be *blood.*
Sometimes your *family*
are your *friends.*
I got *schooled* this year
By my *teacher*
He taught me
That the *points* are not the *point,*
The *point* is *poetry* . . .
I got *schooled* this year
By my *father.*
He taught me that *heroes* aren't always *invincible*
And that the *magic*
is *within* me.
I got schooled this year
by
a
boy.
A boy that I'm *seriously, deeply, madly, incredibly,*
and undeniably in *love* with.
And he taught me the most important thing of *all*—
To put the *emphasis*
On *life.*

Utterly.

Frozen.

My eyes drop to the table in front of me when she finishes. Her words are still sinking in.

A boy that I'm seriously, deeply, madly, incredibly, and undeniably in love with.

In *love* with?

That's what she said.

In love with. As in *present* tense.

She *loves* me. Layken Cohen *loves* me.

"Hold up your scores, man," the guy next to me says, forcing the scorecard into my hand. I look at it, then look up at the stage. She's not up there anymore. I spin around and see her making her way toward the exit in a hurry.

What the hell am I doing just sitting here? She's waiting on me to acknowledge everything she just said, and I'm sitting here frozen like an idiot.

I stand up when the judges to the right of me hold up their scorecards. Three of them gave her a nine, the other an 8.5. I round the front of the table and flip the scores on all of their cards to tens. The points may not be the point, but her poetry kicked ass. "She gets tens."

I turn around and jump onto the stage. I grab the microphone out of the emcee's hands and he rolls his eyes, throwing his hands up in the air.

"Not again," he says, defeated.

I spot her as soon as she swings the doors open to step outside. "That's not a good idea," I say into the microphone. She stops in her tracks, then slowly turns around to face the stage. "You shouldn't leave before you get your scores."

She looks at the judges' table, then back to me. When she makes eye contact, she smiles.

I grip the microphone, hell bent on performing the piece I wrote for her, but the magnetic pull to jump off the stage and take her in my arms is overwhelming. I stand firm, wanting her to hear what I have to say first. "I'd like to perform a piece," I say, looking at the emcee. "It's an *emergency*." He nods and takes a few steps back. I turn around to face Lake again. She's standing in the center of the room now, staring up at me.

"Three dollars," someone yells from the crowd.

Shit. I pat my pockets, realizing I left my wallet in my car. "I don't have any cash," I say to the emcee.

His eyes shift to Lake and mine follow. She pulls out the two dollars in change from her fee and walks to the stage, slapping it down in front of us.

"Still a dollar short," he says.

Jesus! It's one freaking *dollar*!

The silence in the room is interrupted as several chairs slide from under their tables. People from all over the floor walk toward the stage, surrounding Lake as they throw dollar bills onto the stage. Everyone quickly makes their way back to their seats and Lake eyes the money, dumbfounded.

"*Okay*," the emcee says, taking in the pile of cash at my feet. "I guess that covers it. What's the name of your piece, Will?"

I look down at Lake and smile right back at her. "*Better than third.*"

She takes a few steps back from the stage and waits for me

to begin. I take a deep breath and prepare to tell her everything I should have said to her three months ago.

I met a girl.
A *beautiful* girl
And I fell for her.
I fell *hard*.
Unfortunately, sometimes *life* gets in the *way*.
Life *definitely* got in *my* way.
It got *all up* in my damn way,
Life *blocked* the *door* with a stack of wooden *two-by-fours* nailed together and *attached* to a fifteen-inch *concrete wall* behind a *row* of solid steel *bars*, *bolted* to a *titanium frame* that *no matter* how *hard* I shoved
against it—
It
wouldn't
budge.
Sometimes *life* doesn't *budge*.
It just gets *all up* in your *damn* way.
It blocked my *plans*, my *dreams*, my *desires*, my *wishes*, my *wants*, my *needs*.
It blocked out that *beautiful* girl
That I *fell* so *hard* for.
Life tries to tell you what's *best* for you.
What should be most *important* to you.
What should come *first*
Or *second*
Or *third*.
I tried *so hard* to keep it all *organized*, *alphabetized*,

stacked in *chronological order,* everything in its
perfect space, its *perfect place.*
I thought that's what life *wanted* me to do.
This is what life *needed* for me to do.
Right?
Keep it *all* in *sequence?*
Sometimes life gets in your *way.*
It gets all up in your damn *way.*
But it doesn't get all up in your damn way because it
wants you to just *give up* and let it *take control.* Life
doesn't get all up in your damn way because it just
wants you to *hand* it all *over* and be *carried along.*
Life wants you to *fight* it.
Learn how to make it your *own.*
It wants you to grab an *axe* and *hack* through the *wood.*
It wants you to get a *sledgehammer* and *break* through
the *concrete.*
It wants you to grab a *torch* and *burn* through the *metal*
and *steel* until you can reach through and *grab* it.
Life wants you to *grab* all the *organized,* the
alphabetized, the *chronological,* the *sequenced.* It
wants you to mix it all *together,*
stir it up,
blend it.
Life doesn't want you to let it *tell* you that your little
brother should be the *only* thing that comes *first.*
Life doesn't want you to let it *tell* you that your *career*
and your *education* should be the *only* thing that comes
in *second.*

And life *definitely* doesn't want *me*
To just let it *tell* me
that the *girl* I met—
The *beautiful, strong, amazing, resilient girl*
That I fell *so hard* for—
Should *only* come in *third*.
Life *knows*.
Life is trying to *tell* me
That the *girl* I *love?*
The girl I fell
So *hard* for?
There's room for her in *first*.
I'm putting *her* first.

AS SOON AS the last line escapes my lips, I set the microphone down on the stage and jump off. I walk directly to her and take her face in my hands. Tears are falling down her cheeks, so I wipe them away with my thumbs.

"I love you, Lake." I lean my forehead against hers. "You deserve to come first."

Telling her exactly how I feel about her is the easiest thing I've ever done. The honesty comes so naturally. It's the months of hiding my feelings that have been unbearable. I breathe a huge sigh of relief when the weight of holding everything back disappears.

She laughs through her tears and places her hands on top of mine, looking up at me with the most beautiful smile. "I love you, too. I love you so much."

I kiss her softly on the lips. My heart feels like it literally swells within my chest when she kisses me back. I wrap my arms around her and bury my face into her hair, pulling her tightly against me. I close my eyes, and it's suddenly just the two of us. Me and this girl. This girl is in my arms again . . . touching me, kissing me, breathing me in, loving me back.

She's not just a dream, anymore.

Lake moves her mouth to my ear and whispers, "We probably shouldn't be doing this here." I open my eyes and the concern on her face registers with me. She's still a student. I'm still technically a teacher. This probably doesn't look very good if anyone here knows us.

I reach down and take her hand, then pull her toward the exit. As soon as we're outside, I grab her by the waist and push her against the door. I've been waiting months to be with her like this. Two more seconds without touching her and I. Will. Die.

I lower my hand to the small of her back, then lean in and kiss her again. The feeling I get when my lips are on hers is something I've thought about, over and over, since the first time I kissed her. But actually being in the moment with her again, knowing my feelings for her are reciprocated, is nothing short of amazing.

She runs her hands inside my jacket and up my back, pulling me to her as she returns my kiss. I can't think of anything I'd rather do for the rest of my life than be wrapped up in her arms with her lips pressed to mine. But I know that despite what we've been through and despite how I feel about her, I've still got responsibilities. I don't know how much more waiting she's willing to do. The thought of it takes all of the excitement built up inside of me and crushes it.

I stop kissing her and wrap my hands in her hair, then pull her to my chest. I take a long, deep breath and she does the same, locking her hands together behind my back.

"Lake," I say, stroking her hair. "I don't know what will happen in the next few weeks. But I need you to know that if I can't back out of my contract . . ."

She immediately jerks her head up and looks at me with more fear in her eyes than I've ever seen. She thinks I'm telling her I might not choose her, and the fact that something so absurd is running through her mind right now makes me hurt for her. This is how I've made her feel for the past three months and she thinks I'm doing it to her all over again.

"Will, you can't do this to . . ."

I press my finger to her lips. "Shut up, babe. I'm not telling you we can't be together. You're stuck with me now whether you like it or not." I pull her back to my chest. "All I'm trying to say is, if I can't break out of my contract, it's only four months. I just need you to promise that you'll wait for me if it comes to that. We can't let anyone know we're together until I find out what I need to do."

She nods against my shirt. "I promise. I'll wait as long as you need me to."

I close my eyes and rest my cheek against her head, thankful that all the times I've pushed her away haven't made her lose faith in me completely.

"This probably means we shouldn't be standing out here like this," I say. "You want to come to my car?"

I don't wait for her to answer, because I need her to come to my car with me. I'm not ready to stop kissing her yet, but I can't keep doing it so carelessly and in public like this. I grab her hand and lead her to my car. I open the passenger door, but rather than let her get in first, I sit in the seat and pull her onto my lap, then shut the door. I pull my keys out of my pocket and reach over to crank the car so it'll warm up. She positions herself on my lap, straddling me. I acknowledge that our position is incredibly intimate, being as though I can count the number of times we've kissed on one hand, but it's the only comfortable way to make out in a car.

I take her hands and pull them up between us, then kiss them. "I love you, Lake."

She smiles. "Say it again. I love hearing you say that."

"Good, because I love saying it. I love you." I kiss her cheek, then her lips. "I love you," I whisper again.

"One more time," she says. "I can't tell you how many times I've imagined hearing you say it. I've been hoping this whole time that whatever I was feeling wasn't one-sided."

The fact that she had no idea how I felt about her makes my chest ache. "I love you, Lake. So much. I'm so sorry for putting you through everything I've put you through."

She shakes her head. "Will, you were doing the right thing. Or trying to, anyway. I get that. I just hope this is for real now, because you can't push me away again. I can't go through that again."

Her words are like a knife to my heart, but deservedly so. I don't know what I could do or say that could convince her that I'm here. I'm staying. I chose *her* this time.

Before I have the chance to convince her of that, she grabs my face and kisses me hard, causing me to groan under my breath. I slip my hands underneath her shirt and around to her back. The softness and warmth of her skin beneath my palms is a feeling I never want to forget.

As soon as my hands meet her skin, she takes my jacket in her fists and begins tugging it off me. I lean forward, still meshed to her mouth, and struggle to free myself from the jacket. Once it's off, I toss it behind me and place my hands back underneath her shirt.

Touching her, kissing her, being with her . . . it feels so natural. So right.

I move my lips to the spot on her neck that drives me crazy. She tilts her neck to the side and moans quietly. I move my hands to her waist and tighten my grip while I trail kisses along her collarbone. I slowly inch my hands up her waist until my thumbs meet her bra. I can feel her heart hammering against her chest, and it causes my own heart to try to outrace hers. As soon as I slip my right thumb underneath her bra, she pulls back, away from my lips. She gasps for air.

I immediately pull my hands out from underneath her shirt and place them on her shoulders, silently cursing myself for being so impatient. I push her shoulders back in order to give us space to breathe. I lean my head back against the seat and close my eyes.

"I'm sorry." I open my eyes and keep my head flush against the headrest. "I'm going too fast. I'm sorry. I've just imagined touching you so many times I feel like it's so natural. I'm sorry."

She shakes her head and pulls my hands away from her shoulders, holding them together between us. "It's okay," she says. "We're both going too fast. I just need a moment. But it feels right, doesn't it? It feels so right being with you."

"That's because it *is* right."

She stares at me silently, then out of nowhere, she crushes her lips to mine again. I groan and wrap my arms tightly around her, pulling her back against me. As soon as she's pressed against my chest, I place my hands on her shoulders and push her away. As soon as she's apart from me, I pull her back to me for another kiss. This happens several times and I keep having to remind myself to slow down. I eventually have to push her off my lap and onto the driver's seat. However, this doesn't help, because as soon as she leans her back against the driver's side door, I lean across the seat and kiss her again. Seeing how much I need her causes her to laugh, which makes me laugh at how pathetically desperate I'm acting right now. I somehow pull away and slump against the passenger door. I run my hand through my hair and grin at her.

"You're really making this hard," I laugh. "Pun intended."

She smiles and even in the dark I can see her blush.

"Ugh!" I run my palms over my face and groan. "God, I want you so bad." I lunge forward and kiss her, but place my hand on the doorknob. I yank it and the door opens up behind her. "Get out," I say against her lips. "Go get in your car where you're safe. I'll see you when we get home."

She nods and swings one of her legs out of the car, but I don't want her to go. I grab her thigh and pull her back in and kiss her again. "*Go*," I groan.

"I'm *trying*." She laughs, pulling away from me. She climbs out of the car and I slide across the seats, following her straight out the car door.

"Where'd you park?" I ask her. I wrap my arms around her and press my lips to her ear.

"A few cars over," she says, pointing behind her. I slide my hand into her back pocket and retrieve her keys, then walk her to her car. After I open the door for her and she climbs in, I lean in to kiss her one last time.

"Don't go inside when you get home. I'm not finished kissing you," I say.

She grins. "Yes, sir."

I shut her door and once her Jeep is cranked, I tap my knuckles against the window and she rolls it down. I place my hand on the nape of her neck and lean through her window. "This drive home is about to be the longest thirty minutes of my life." I kiss her on the temple and take a step back. "Love you."

She rolls up her window, then places her palm against the glass. I lift my hand up to mirror hers, matching our fingertips together. She mouths, "I love you, too," and begins backing away.

I wait until she's out of the parking lot, then I walk back to my car.

I don't understand it. I don't understand how I went so long without her and now I feel like she's such a vital part of me, I'll die if I'm not touching her.

I'M NOT EVEN in my car for a minute before I dial her number. I've never called her without the conversation being linked to Kel or Caulder before. It feels good calling her for her.

She's driving directly in front of me so I can see her reach for her phone when it rings. She tilts her head and holds the phone between her shoulder and her neck. "Hello?"

"You shouldn't talk on the phone while you're driving," I tell her.

She laughs. "Well, you shouldn't call me when you know I'm driving."

"But I missed you."

"I miss you, too," she says. "I've missed you for the whole sixty seconds we've been apart," she says sarcastically.

I laugh. "I want to talk to you while we drive, but I want you to put your phone on speaker and set it down."

"Why?"

"Because," I say, "it's not safe for you to drive with your head cocked to the side like that."

I can see her smile in her rearview mirror. She drops the phone and sits up straight. "Better?" she says.

"Better. Now listen, I'm about to play you an Avett Brothers song. Make sure the volume on your phone is turned all the way up." I turn on the song I've listened to on repeat since the night I fell for her and turn the volume up. When the chorus hits, I start singing along to the lyrics.

I lower my voice and continue to sing the rest of the song, then the song after that, and the song after that. She listens silently the entire drive back to Ypsilanti.

LAYKEN PULLS INTO her driveway right before I turn into mine. I rush to kill the engine and head across the street before she has a chance to open her car door. When I reach her, I swing the door open and reach in, pulling her out by her hand. I want to push her against the Jeep and kiss her crazy, but I know we've more than likely got at least three pairs of eyes on us. What I wouldn't give to have her alone in my house right now, rather than out here in the open. I kiss the top of her head and stroke her hair, accepting whatever time I can get with her right now.

"Do you have a curfew?"

She shrugs. "I'm eighteen. I don't know if she could give me one if she wanted to."

"We don't need to push our luck with her, Lake. I want to do this right." I'm lucky that Julia would even allow her to be with me at this point. The last thing I want to do is upset her.

"Do we have to talk about my mom right now, Will?"

I smile and shake my head. "No." I slip my hand behind her head and pull her mouth to mine, kissing her like I don't care *who* might be watching. Hell, I *don't* care. I kiss her crazy for several minutes until it gets to the point that my hands can't stay above her shoulders for much longer. I pull away just enough for us to catch our breath.

"Let's go to your house," she whispers.

The suggestion is so tempting. I close my eyes and pull her to my chest. "I need to talk to your mom first before I pull something like that. I need to know what our boundaries are."

She laughs. "Why? So we can push them?"

I lift her chin and pull her gaze to mine. "Exactly."

The entryway light flicks off, then back on. An indication that Julia is setting some boundaries.

"Dammit," I groan into her neck. "I guess this is goodnight."

"Yeah, I guess so," she says. "I'll see you tomorrow, though, right? What time do you have to leave for graduation?"

"Not until tomorrow afternoon. You want to come over for breakfast? I'll make you whatever you want."

She nods. "And lunch? What are you doing for lunch?"

"Cooking for you," I say.

"And dinner? I might want to have dinner with you, too."

She's so cute. "Actually, we have plans. My grandparents are coming to graduation and we're going out to dinner afterward. Will you come?"

A worried look crosses her face. "Do you think that's a good idea? What if someone sees us together? You're technically still a teacher, even though you're between jobs."

Dammit. I'm really starting to hate this new job and I haven't even started yet. "I guess I do need to figure that out tomorrow."

"I do want to come to your graduation, though. Is that okay?"

"You better," I say to her. I've wanted her there more than anyone, but until tonight I didn't think that was a possibility. "It'll be hard as hell keeping my hands off you, though."

I kiss her one last time, then back away from her. "I love you."

"I love you, too."

I turn and begin walking away. My emotions are contradicting themselves because I feel absolutely elated that we're finally together, but devastated that I have to leave her right now. I turn around to look at her one last time and when I catch sight of her watching me walk away, a satisfied smile spreads across my face.

"*What?*" she asks when she sees the look on my face.

Just seeing the smile on her face is enough to keep me satisfied for the rest of my life. Seeing her happy again is better than any feeling in the world. I never want to see her sad again. "This will be worth it, Lake. Everything we had to go through. I promise. Even if you have to wait for me, I'll make it worth it."

The smile fades from her eyes and she clutches her hand to her heart. "You already have, Will."

That. Right there. I don't deserve her.

I walk swiftly back to where she's standing and take her face in my hands. "I mean it," I say. "I love you so damn much, it hurts." I force my lips against hers, then pull away just as fast. "But it hurts in a really *good* way." I briefly kiss her again. "We thought it was hard being apart before? How the hell am I supposed to sleep after tonight? After actually getting to kiss you like this? After hearing you tell me you love me?" I kiss her again and walk her until she's against her Jeep.

I kiss her like I've wanted to kiss her since the moment I knew how perfect we were together. How much we made sense. I kiss her with abandon, knowing I'll never have to walk away from her again. I kiss her knowing that this won't be our last kiss. That it won't even be our best kiss. I kiss her knowing that this kiss is our beginning, not another good-bye.

I continue to kiss her, even when the light turns off and on several more times.

We both notice the light, but neither of us seems to care. It takes us several minutes to actually slow down and pull apart. I press my forehead to hers and look directly into her eyes when she opens them. "This is it, Lake," I say, pointing back and forth between us. "It's real now. I'm not walking away from you again. Ever."

Her eyes fill with tears. "Promise?" she whispers.

"I *swear*. I love you so much."

A tear rolls down her cheek. "Say it again," she whispers.

"I love you, Lake." My eyes scroll over every inch of her face, afraid I'll miss something if I don't take every last piece of her in before I go.

"One more time."

Before *I love you* can come out of my mouth again, the front door swings open and Julia walks outside. "We're going to have to set some ground rules," she says. There's more amusement in her voice than anger or annoyance.

"Sorry, Julia," I yell over my shoulder. I turn back to Lake and kiss her one last time, then take a step away from her. "It's just that I'm madly in love with your daughter!"

"Yeah." Julia laughs. "I can see that."

I mouth one last *I love you* before heading across the street.

18.

the honeymoon

"AND WE LIVED happily ever after," she says.

I laugh, because that couldn't be further from the truth.

"Yeah, for like two weeks," I say. "Until your mother put the brakes on things the night she walked in on us."

Lake groans. "Oh, my God, I forgot about that."

"Trust me, it's not something I wish I remembered."

point of retreat

"WHERE ARE WE going?"

I put my seat belt on and lower the volume on the radio. "It's a surprise."

It's the first night I've been able to take her out in public since we officially started dating two weeks ago. I was able to pull out of my contract with the job at the junior high when I was accepted into the Master's level teaching program. So technically, we're able to date. I'm not sure how it would look, since I was her teacher just a few weeks ago. But to be honest, I don't really care. Like I told her, she comes first now.

"Will. It's Thursday night. I have a feeling wherever you're taking me, it's not that much of a surprise. Are we going to Club N9NE?"

"Maybe."

She smiles. "Are you doing a slam for me?"

I wink at her. "Maybe." I reach over and take her hand in mine.

"We're leaving early, though. Are you actually taking me out to eat? No grilled cheese tonight?"

"Maybe," I say again.

She rolls her eyes. "Will, this date is going to be my suck for the day if you don't become a little more talkative."

I laugh. "Yes, we're going to Club N9NE. Yes, we're going to dinner first. Yes, I wrote a slam for you. Yes, we're leaving the club early so we can go back to my house and hardcore make out in the dark."

"You just became my sweet," she says.

• • •

"OUT OF ALL the restaurants in Detroit, you chose a burger joint," I say, shaking my head. I take her hand and lead her toward the club entrance. I like to give her a hard time, but I love that she chose a burger joint.

"Bite me. I like burgers."

I wrap my arms around her and nip at her neck. "I like *you*." I keep my arms wrapped around her and my lips attached to her neck as we walk through the door. She pries my fingers from around her waist and presses her palm against my forehead, pushing me away from her neck. "You need to be a gentleman in public. No more kissing until we're back in your car."

I lead her back to the exit. "Well, in that case, we're done here. Let's go."

She yanks my hand back. "No way. If you plan on seducing me on your couch later, you have to seduce me with your words, first. You promised a performance tonight and we're not leaving until I see one." She walks me toward the booth that Eddie and Gavin saved us seats in. She scoots in beside Eddie and I scoot in beside her.

"Hey," Eddie says, eyeing us curiously.

"Hey," Lake and I say simultaneously. Eddie's expression grows even more curious.

"This is weird," Eddie finally says.

Gavin nods. "It *is* weird. It really is."

"What's so weird?" Lake asks.

"You two," Eddie says to Lake. "I know you've been dating for a couple of weeks now, but this is the first time I've actually seen you with him. Like this, anyway. You know, all in love and stuff. It's just weird."

"Oh, shut up," Lake says.

"It'll take some getting used to. It just seems like you're doing something wrong. Something illegal," Eddie says.

"I'm twenty-one," I say defensively. "I'm not even a teacher anymore. What's so weird about it?"

"I dunno," she says. "It's just weird."

"It *is* weird," Gavin says again. "It really is."

I can see their point, but I think they're overreacting. Especially Gavin. He's known how I've felt about Lake for months. "What exactly is so weird?" I put my arm around Lake's shoulders. "This?" I turn and kiss Lake hard on the mouth until she laughs and pushes me away. We both turn back to Eddie and Gavin and they're still staring at us like we're a freak show.

"Gross," Eddie says, crinkling up her nose.

I pick up a sugar packet and toss it in Eddie's direction. "Go sit somewhere else, then," I tease.

Gavin picks up the sugar packet and throws it back at me. "We were here first."

"Then deal with it," I say.

The table grows quiet and it's obvious Lake and Eddie have no idea Gavin and I are only kidding around.

"Personally," Gavin says, leaning forward. "I thought you and Mrs. Alex made a much better couple."

I shrug. "She shot me down. I had to go with my second choice," I say, nudging my head toward Lake.

Lake scoffs at the same time the emcee begins speaking into the microphone.

"The sac has been preselected tonight, due to time constraints by the performer. Everyone please welcome Will Cooper back to the stage."

The crowd starts clapping and I slide out of the seat. Lake arches her eyebrow. "Time constraints?" she says.

I bend down and press my lips to her ear. "I already told you we can't stay long. We'll be really, really, really busy after this." I kiss her on the cheek and walk to the stage. I don't even give myself time to prepare. I begin my poem as soon as I reach the microphone so that I don't waste another second. "My piece is called *The Gift.* . . ."

If my *dad* were alive, he'd be sitting right there
Watching me up here, with a *smile* on his face
He'd be *proud* of the man I've become
He'd be *proud* that I stepped up to take his *place*
If my *mother* were alive, she'd be at home
Teaching my *brother* all the things she taught *me*
She'd be *proud* of the man I've become
She'd be *proud* of who I grew up to *be*
But they *aren't* here. They *haven't* been for a *while*.
It takes *time*, but it's starting to make *sense*.
I *still miss* them every time I take a *breath*.
Their absence will *never* go unnoticed.
But every *smile* on your *face* seems to *replace*
A *memory* I'd rather not *hold*
Each time you *laugh*, it fills a *void*
Each *kiss* heals another *wound* in my *soul*
If my *dad* were here, he'd be sitting with you
He'd be *hugging* you . . . saying *thank you.*
Thank you for saving my *boy.*
Thank you for bringing *light* to his *world.*

If my *mother* were here, she'd be *so* happy
To *finally* have a *daughter* in her life
She'd *love* you as much as *I* love you
She'd make me *promise* to one day *make* you my *wife*.
But they *aren't* here. They haven't been for a *while*.
But I can feel their *pride*. I can feel their *smiles*.
I can hear them say, *"You're welcome, Will."*
When I *thank* them for sending you from *heaven*.

AS SOON AS I return to the booth she's trying to thank me with a hug, but instead I grab her hand and wave over my shoulder as I pull her to the exit. "See you guys later," I say to Gavin and Eddie. I don't even wait for them to say good-bye as we make our way to the door. I remain two steps in front of Lake the entire way back to the car, practically dragging her along behind me. I can't think of anything but being alone with her tonight. We're never alone and I need some uninterrupted, alone time with her before I go crazy.

When we reach the car, I practically shove her inside, then climb into the driver's seat. I crank the car, then turn toward her and grab her shirt and pull her mouth to mine while I back out of the parking spot.

"Will, do you realize your car is moving?" she says, attempting to pull away from my grip. I glance out the rear window and cut the steering wheel to the right, then turn back to her.

"Yep. We need to hurry. You've got a curfew and that only gives us two more hours together." I press my lips to hers again and she shoves my forehead back with the palm of her hand.

"Then stop kissing me and drive. It won't be much fun making out with you when you're dead."

• • •

"PULL OVER," SHE says, several houses down from my driveway.

"Why?"

"Just pull over. Trust me."

I pull over and park the car on the side of the street. She leans across the seat and kisses me, then pulls the keys from the ignition. "If my mom sees your car, she'll know we're back. She told me to bring you to my house if we came home early. She doesn't want us alone at your house. Let's sneak in through your back door and we can come get your car later."

I stare at her in awe. "I think I'm in love with your brain," I say.

We both exit the car and run toward the back of the house we parked in front of. We make our way behind the fence, then crouch down and run across three backyards until we reach mine. I take the keys out of her hands and unlock the back door. Why do I feel like I'm breaking in? It's my house.

"Don't turn on the lights. She'll know we're back," I say as I help her make her way through the darkened doorway.

"I can't see," she says.

I put my arm around her back and bend down, scooping her legs up with my other arm. "Allow me."

She throws her arms around my neck and squeals. I walk her until we've reached the couch and gently lay her down. I take off my jacket and slip off my shoes, then reach down until I find her. I slide my hand down the length of her legs until I reach her feet, then I remove her shoes while she slips off her jacket.

"Anything else you need me to remove?" I whisper.

"Uh-huh. Your shirt."

I immediately agree with that and pull my shirt over my head. "Why are we whispering?" I ask her.

"I don't know," she whispers.

The sound of her voice when she whispers . . . knowing she's on her back . . . on my couch.

The significance of the next two hours is almost more than I can handle, knowing the things that could occur between us. I recognize that, so rather than lower myself on top of her, I kneel on the floor next to the couch. As much as I want her, I want to take it at her pace tonight, not mine. I tend to be extremely impatient when it comes to her.

I find her cheek in the dark and turn her face toward mine. When I touch her, her breath hitches. I feel it, too. I've touched her face countless times before, but somehow in the dark with absolutely no interruptions, it seems a hell of a lot more intimate.

She moves her hand to the back of my neck and I press my lips lightly against hers. They're wet and cold and perfect, but as soon as I part her lips and taste her, perfect becomes the understatement of the year.

She responds to my kiss tentatively. We're both slowly exploring our limits and I want to be sure I'm not taking it too fast this time. My hand remains on her cheek while we kiss, then I begin to slowly move it down her neck, trailing over her shoulder and down to her hip. Each movement I make only seems to encourage her, so I slip my hand underneath her shirt and grip her waist. I wait for any indication that she wants me to stop.

Or go *further.*

She presses her hands into my back, pulling me forward, indicating she wants me on the couch with her.

"Lake," I say, pulling back several inches. "I can't. If I get on this couch with you . . ." I release a deep breath. "Just trust me. I can't get on this couch with you."

She reaches down to my hand that's still gripping her by the waist. She slides my hand up her stomach and doesn't stop until my hand is covering the cup of her bra.

Holy shit.

"I want you on the couch with me, Will."

I immediately pull my hand away, but only because I need her shirt off. I practically yank it over her head and immediately join her on the couch. As soon as I lower myself on top of her and feel her pressed against my chest, I kiss her again and return my hand right where she put it. She smiles and wraps her legs around me as I kiss my way down her chin, straight to her neck.

"I can feel your heartbeat right here," I say, kissing the base of her throat. "I like it."

She takes my hand and slips it *beneath* her bra this time. "You can feel it beating right here, too."

I bury my face in the couch and groan. "Oh, my god, Lake."

I want to touch her. I want to feel *all* of her. I don't know what's stopping me. Why the hell am I so nervous?

"Will?"

I pull my face away from the couch, very aware that my hand is still tucked safely beneath her bra. My hand has never been happier. "You want me to slow down? I will, Lake. Just tell me."

She shakes her head and runs her hands down my back. "No. I want you to speed up."

My hesitation immediately disappears with those words. I slide my hand around her back and unfasten her bra, then slide it down her shoulders. I drop my mouth to her skin and as soon as the softest moan escapes her lips, my hand finds its way back to where she planted it earlier. I lower my lips, then immediately freeze at the sound of a key turning in the front door.

"Shh." About that time, the front door swings open and my living room light flicks on. I lift my head far enough to peer over the back of the couch and see Julia walking toward the hallway. I drop my head to Lake's neck. "Shit. It's your mom."

"Shit," she whispers, frantically pulling her bra back up. "Shit, shit, shit."

I clamp my hand over her mouth. "She might not notice us. Be still."

Our hearts are pounding now faster than they've ever pounded before. I know this, because my palm is still firmly planted right on top of Lake's breast. Apparently she recognizes the awkwardness of the moment, too.

"Will, move your hand. This is weird."

I pull my hand away. "What is she doing here?"

Lake shakes her head. "I have no idea."

And that's when it happens. I've heard people can see their lives flash before their eyes in the moments before death.

It's true.

Julia walks back into the room and screams.

I jump off Lake.

Lake jumps off the couch and *there* it is. My entire life flashes before my eyes the moment Julia sees Lake standing in my living room, fastening her bra.

"It's just us," I blurt out. I don't know why I chose those words to be my possible last words. Julia is standing with her hand over her mouth, staring at us wide-eyed. "It's just us," I say again, as if she doesn't already know that.

"I was . . ." Julia holds up Caulder's pillow. "Caulder wanted his pillow," she says. She looks back and forth between us and in a split second, her expression turns from fear to anger. I immediately reach down and retrieve Lake's shirt, then hand it to her.

"Mom," Lake says. She doesn't follow it up with anything else because she has no idea what to say.

"Go home," Julia says to Lake.

"Julia," I say to Julia.

"Will?" Julia says to me, cutting a warning shot in my direction. "I'll deal with you later."

As soon as the words come out of Julia's mouth, Lake's face turns from embarrassed to really, really angry. "Mom, we're adults! You can't talk to him like that!" Lake yells. "And you can't prevent us from making out! This is ridiculous."

I grab Lake's elbow in an attempt to calm her down. "Don't, babe," I say quietly.

She looks at me defensively. "She can't tell me what to do, Will. I'm an adult."

I calmly place my hand on her shoulder. "Lake, you're still in high school. You live under her roof. I shouldn't have brought you here, I'm sorry. She's right." I lean in and kiss her briefly to calm her, then I take her shirt and help her pull it over her head.

"Oh, my God!" Julia yells. "Are you kidding me, Will? Don't help her put her clothes back on! I'm standing right here!"

What the hell am I thinking?

I release the shirt and hold my palms up in the air, then back away from Lake. She looks at me apologetically and whispers, "I'm sorry," then heads toward the door.

The door doesn't even shut before Julia begins yelling at her. "You've been dating him for two weeks, Lake! What do you think you're doing going that far with him that fast?" The door finally closes and I sink back to the couch, feeling incredibly stupid. Incredibly guilty. Incredibly pathetic. Yet . . . somehow still incredibly happy.

I reach down and am picking my own shirt up when the front door swings open again. Julia has a grip on Lake's arm and marches her straight back into the living room, then positions her on the couch across from me.

"This can't wait," Julia says. "I don't even trust that y'all won't start this back up tonight as soon as I go to bed."

Lake is looking at me the same way I'm looking at her. Confused.

Julia turns to Lake. "Are y'all having sex already?"

Lake groans and covers her face with her hands.

"You *are*?"

"No!" Lake says defensively. "We haven't had sex yet, okay?"

I'm watching the conversation between them, hoping to hell I don't get involved in it.

"*Yet?*" Julia says. "So you're going to?"

Lake stands and throws her hands up in the air. "What do you want me to say, Mom? I'm eighteen! Do you want me to tell you I'll be celibate forever? Because that would be a lie."

Julia rolls her head back and looks up at the ceiling for several seconds. When she looks at me, I dart my eyes to the floor. I'm so embarrassed I can't even look at her.

"Where's your car?" she says flatly.

I glance at Lake, then to Julia. "At the end of the street," I reluctantly admit.

"Why?" she asks accusingly, and rightfully so.

"Mom, stop. This is ridiculous."

Julia turns her attention to Lake. "Ridiculous? Really, Lake?

What I find ridiculous is the fact that you two parked at the end of the street and snuck over here to have sex less than a hundred yards from your mother. You've only been dating him for two weeks! What I also find ridiculous is that you're acting like you did nothing wrong, when it's obvious you were trying to hide it by parking at the end of the damn street!"

We're all quiet for a moment. Lake leans her head against the back of the couch and closes her eyes. "What now, then? If you're going to ground me let's just get it over with so you can stop embarrassing me."

Julia sighs an extremely frustrated sigh. She walks over to the couch, taking a seat next to Lake. "I'm not trying to embarrass you, Lake. I just . . ."

Julia sighs again and drops her face into her hands.

Lake rolls her eyes again.

I groan.

Julia lifts her head from her hands and takes a deep breath. "Lake?" she says quietly. "I just . . ." She attempts to get out what she wants to say, but her eyes well up with tears. When Lake realizes Julia is crying, she sits up straight.

"Mom," Lake says, scooting closer to her. She puts her arms around Julia and hugs her. Seeing her care for her mom despite her frustration with her absolutely melts my heart. It makes me love her even more, somehow.

Julia separates from Lake and wipes at her eyes. "Ugh!" she says. "This is so hard for me. You have to understand that." She turns to Lake and takes her hands. "I don't want to play the sick card, but it's impossible not to. We're at this transition in our lives where you're becoming the grown-up. Sometime this year, as much as we don't want to admit it, you'll be raising my little boy. It breaks my heart to know that I'm responsible for you being forced to grow up so fast. I'm forcing you to become his guardian. I'm forcing you to become the head of a household at eighteen. It's not fair to you. All the other areas of your life like falling in love and enjoying high school and new boyfriends and . . . having sex? I just feel like these are the last things you have left before you're forced to grow up completely. I know I can't slow down the inevitable, but I'm taking away every other part of your youth by leaving you with all of this responsibility. Until that time comes, I guess I just want you to stop growing up. For my sake. Just stop growing up so fast."

As soon as she finishes speaking, Lake begins to cry. "I'm sorry," she says to Julia. "I get it, Mom. I'm sorry."

I feel like an ass. "I'm sorry, too," I say to Julia.

Julia smiles at me and wipes at her eyes. "I'm still mad at you, Will." She stands up and looks at both of us. "Okay. Now that we have that out of the way." She turns her attention to Lake. "I'm taking you to the doctor tomorrow. You're getting on the pill." She turns to face me. "And both of you need to think about this. There's no rush. You have the rest of your lives to be in a hurry. You both need to set good examples for these boys who look up to you. Sneaking around is not the kind of thing you want to be modeling. You think they don't notice, but they do. And you two are going to be the ones dealing with them as teenagers, so believe me. You don't want them throwing your own actions back in your faces."

She makes a terrifying, but excellent point.

"I want you both to promise me something," she says.

"Anything," I say.

"Wait one year. There's no rush. You're both still young, so young. You've been dating all of two weeks and believe me when I say this, the more you know about each other and the more in love you are, the better it'll be."

I do my best to pretend this is not coming out of my girlfriend's mother's mouth, but it doesn't help ease the awkwardness.

"Mom," Lake groans, sinking back into the couch.

"We promise," I say, standing up. I immediately regret making the promise to her, knowing what that will entail. An entire year of having to keep myself in check around Lake is like agreeing to infinity. Especially after being on that couch with her tonight.

"I'm sorry, Julia. Really. I respect Lake and I respect you and . . . I'm sorry. We'll wait. I love Lake and that's all I need from her right now. Just knowing I can love her is more than enough."

Lake sighs and I look over at her. She's smiling at me. She stands up and throws her arms around my neck. "God, I love you," she says. She pulls away from my neck and kisses me.

"Make sure that kiss is a good one, Lake, because you're grounded for two weeks."

Lake and I both snap our heads in Julia's direction.

"Grounded?" Lake says incredulously.

Julia nods. "Regardless of how much I love your boyfriend . . . you snuck over here knowing I told you I didn't want you alone at his house. So, yeah. You're grounded. I'll give you five minutes to say your good-byes and get home." Julia walks out and shuts the door behind her.

"Two *weeks*?" I say to Lake. I press my lips to hers and kiss her crazy for five solid minutes.

* * *

I MADE IT twenty-one years without her. After meeting her earlier this year, I somehow made it three months without her. Now, after finally being able to date her, I've had to go another two weeks without her. But these past two weeks have been the most unbearable two weeks without her of my entire twenty-one years.

I know it's not even eight in the morning and it might seem desperate if I show up at her door this early, but we've been waiting for these two weeks to pass for what feels like an eternity. I rush across the street and am lifting my hand to knock on the door when it swings open and she jumps into my arms, showering kisses all over my face.

"Way to play hard to get," I hear Julia say from behind Lake. I put Lake down and shake my head slightly, letting her know we need to tone it down. Lake rolls her eyes and pulls me inside.

"What are we doing today?" she asks.

"Whatever you want. I was thinking maybe we could take the boys somewhere."

"Really?" Julia says from the kitchen. "That would be great. I need a day of peace after being cooped up in this house with your mopey girlfriend for two weeks."

Lake laughs and pulls me toward the hallway. "Come to my room while I get ready." We disappear down the hallway and into her room. She shuts the door and pulls me to her bed. She falls back and I fall on top of her, our lips reconnecting after the torturous time they had to spend apart.

"I missed you so much," I whisper.

"Not as much as I missed you."

We kiss some more.

And some more.

And some more.

I wish we didn't have to leave this bedroom, because I could do this all day. She's already working her hands up the back of my shirt and I'm groaning into her neck, remembering how close I got to actually being with her two weeks ago. I want to run my hand up her shirt, or touch her waist, or pull her legs around me, but I have no idea what's safe with her now. Now that we have to wait a whole damn *year*.

Why did I agree to that? As much as I understand where Julia was coming from, I still don't know how in the hell we're going to wait an entire year. Especially considering how much it's already driving me insane.

"Babe," I say, pulling my lips away from hers. "We need to talk about this." I lift up and sit on the bed beside her.

"About what? Our plans today?"

I shake my head. "No." I lean forward and kiss her again. "*This*," I say, waving my hand up and down her body. "We need to talk about what's okay and what's not. I really want to respect the promise we made to your mother, but at the same time there's no way in hell I can keep my hands off you. I just need to know what my boundaries are before I slip up."

She smiles at me. "So you're saying we need to set limits to how far we can go?"

I nod. "Exactly. I need you to tell me when I've reached the point of retreat."

She grins mischievously. "Well, there's only one way to find out what our boundaries are. I guess we need to test them."

I smile and scoot back down beside her, slowly looking her up and down. "I like that idea." I brush away a strand of hair from her face and kiss her softly on the mouth. I run my nose across her jawline and kiss my way to her ear. "How's this? Should I retreat yet?"

She shakes her head. "Hell, no. Not even close."

I place my hand on her shoulder and slowly run my fingers down her arm, resting my hand on her waist. I lean in until my lips are barely touching hers again. "How about this?" I ask her. I part her lips with my tongue, sliding my hand beneath her shirt and across her stomach. The muscles in her stomach clench beneath my palm. "Is this your point of retreat?" I whisper.

She shakes her head slowly. "Nope. Keep going."

I lower my lips to her neck and my fingers crawl up her stomach and come to a stop where her bra usually is, if she were wearing one right now. I bury my head in her pillow and groan. "God, Lake. Seriously? Are you trying to kill me?"

She shakes her head again. "Not retreating yet. Keep going."

I raise my head away from her pillow and scroll over her lips with my eyes. My thumb grazes her breast and that's when we both lose it. Our lips crash together, and as soon as I cup her breast, she moans into my mouth and wraps a leg around my thigh. I immediately slide off her and stand up.

"I think we found my point of retreat," I say, breathing heavily. I run my hands through my hair and back up to the wall, putting a safe distance between us. "You need to get dressed so we can leave. I can't be alone in here with you right now."

She laughs and rolls off the bed, then heads to her closet. "And Lake? If you want to survive the day without being completely mauled by me, make sure you put on a bra." I wink at her and walk out of the room.

19.

the honeymoon

HER EYES ARE closed, but there's a smile spread across her lips. I lean forward and lightly kiss them. "You asleep?"

It's late and we have to drive home tomorrow. I'm not ready to go to sleep yet. I want to drag this night out as long as I can.

She shakes her head no, then opens her eyes. "Remember the first time we didn't call point of retreat?"

I laugh. "Well, considering it was just last night, then I'd say I remember it pretty damn well."

"I want you to tell me all about that," she says. She closes her eyes and cuddles up to me.

"You want me to tell you about last *night*?"

She nods against my chest. "Yeah. It was the best night of my life. I want you to tell me all about it."

I smile, more than willing to tell her what I thought about the sweetest sweet I've ever had.

honeymoon night

"THREE MORE MINUTES," she says. She reaches behind her and pulls down on the handle, swinging the door open. "Now carry me over the threshold, husband."

I bend down and grab her behind the knees and pick her up, throwing her over my shoulder. She squeals, and I push the door all the way open with her feet. I take a step over the threshold with my wife. The door slams behind us, and I ease her down onto the bed.

"I smell chocolate. And flowers," she says. "Good job, husband."

I lift her leg up and slide her boot off. "Thank you, wife." I lift her other leg up and slide that boot off, too. "I also remembered the fruit. And the robes."

She winks at me and rolls over, scooting up onto the bed. When she gets settled, she leans forward and grabs my hand, pulling me toward her. "Come here, husband," she whispers.

I start to make my way up the bed but pause when I come face to face with her shirt. "I wish you'd take this ugly thing off," I say.

"You're the one who hates it so much. You take it off."

So I do. I start from the bottom this time and press my lips against her skin where her stomach meets the top of her pants, causing her to squirm. She's ticklish there. Good to know. I unbutton the next button and slowly move my lips up another inch to her belly button. I kiss it. She lets out another moan, but it doesn't worry me this time. I continue kissing every inch of her until the ugly shirt is lying on the floor. When my lips find their way back to hers, I pause to ask her one last time. "Wife? Are you sure you're ready to not call retreat? Right now?"

She wraps her legs around me and pulls me closer. "I'm butterflying positive," she says.

I grin against her lips, hoping that this entire year of being frustratingly patient will be worth it to her. "Good," I whisper. I reach my hand beneath her and unclasp her bra, then help her slip it off. She slides her hands through my hair and pulls me against her.

By the time all of our clothes are off and we're wrapped together under the covers, I'm breathing too hard to hear the pounding in my chest anymore, but I can definitely feel it. I press my lips to her neck and inhale a deep breath.

"Lake?" My hands are exploring her and touching her and I can't decide if I ever want to stop long enough to actually consummate this marriage.

"What is it?" she says breathlessly.

I somehow find it in me to pull back and give myself enough space to look her in the eyes. I need her to know that she's not the only one experiencing something for the first time right now. "I want you to know something. I've never . . ." I pause and pull back a little bit farther and hold my weight up on my left arm. I reach up and slip my hand to the nape of her neck, then dip my head and kiss her softly on the mouth. I look her directly in the eyes and finish telling her what I need her to know. "Lake . . . I've never made love to a girl before. I didn't realize that until this very moment. You're the first girl I'll ever make love to." She smiles a heartbreakingly beautiful smile that completely swallows me up. "And you're the *last* girl I'll ever make love to," I add. I lower my head and press my forehead to hers. We keep our eyes locked together as I lift her thigh and brace myself against her.

"I love you, Will Cooper," she whispers.

"I love *you*, Layken Cooper."

I hold still against her, taking one final look at this amazing, beautiful girl beneath me. "You're the greatest thing that's ever happened to my life," I whisper. As soon as I push myself inside her, our lips collide, our tongues collide, our bodies collide, and our hearts collide. Then this girl completely shatters the window to my soul and crawls inside.

20.

the honeymoon

"I LIKE THAT version," she says.

She's wrapped up in my arms where she's been most of the weekend. I couldn't have imagined a better way to spend the last forty-eight hours. I think back on everything we've gone through . . . everything I just shared with her. Everything she learned about me and I learned about her and how, by some miracle, I'll leave this hotel room loving her just a little bit more than I did when we arrived. I kiss her on her forehead and close my eyes.

"Goodnight, wife."

"Goodnight, husband."

welcome home

I CAN'T COUNT how many times I've pulled into my own drive-way. At least once a day since I've lived here; sometimes twice. But I've never pulled into this driveway with my *wife* before. I've never pulled into the driveway of a house where I live with my own family—a family other than my mom and dad. I've never pulled into this driveway feeling so complete before.

"Are you gonna turn off the car?" Lake asks.

Her hand is on her door handle and she's waiting for me to put the car in park and turn it off, but I'm staring at the house, lost in thought. "Don't you just love this driveway? I'm pretty sure we have the best driveway in the whole world."

She lets go of the door handle and falls back against her seat. "I guess," she shrugs. "It's a driveway."

I put the car in park and reach over and grab her hands, then pull her onto my lap. "But it's *our* driveway now. That makes it the best. And it's *our* house." I slip her shirt over her head and she tries to cover herself, but I move her arms out of the way and kiss up her neck while I talk about all the things that are no longer just mine. "And the dishes in the kitchen are *our* dishes. And the couches are *our* couches. And the bed is *our* bed."

"Will, stop." She laughs and attempts to pull my hands away from her bra. "You can't take off my bra, we're in our driveway. What if they come outside?"

"It's dark," I whisper. "And it's not *your* bra. It's *our* bra and I want it off." I slip it off her, pulling her against me as I rub my hands down the length of her back, then around to the button on the front of her jeans. "And I want to take off *our* pants."

She grins against my lips and slowly nods. "Okay, but hurry," she whispers.

"I can be quick," I assure her. "But I'll *never* hurry."

AFTER CHRISTENING THE driveway, we make it inside to a completely empty, dark house. I flip on the light switch in the kitchen and there's a note on the table.

"My grandparents left a few hours ago. The boys are with Eddie and Gavin across the street."

Lake tosses her purse on the couch and makes her way into the kitchen. "Do we have to go get them right away? I sort of want to enjoy some quiet while we can. The second we tell them we're back, the honeymoon will officially be over. I'm having fun; I don't want it to end yet."

I pull her to me. "Who says it has to end? We still have rooms to christen. Where should we start?"

"Besides your driveway?"

"*Our* driveway," I correct her.

She squints her eyes, then they suddenly widen with excitement. "Your laundry room!" she says excitedly. "*Our* laundry room," she adds quickly, before I can correct her. She grabs the collar of my shirt and stands on her tiptoes, pressing her lips to mine. "Come on," she whispers, pulling me along with her while she continues to kiss me.

The front door swings open and someone runs through the living room. I squeeze my eyes shut and groan as Lake separates her mouth from mine.

"Don't mind me, we just need the ketchup," Caulder yells.

He runs past us and into the kitchen. He grabs the ketchup and glances at us as he makes his way back to the front door. "Gross," he mumbles before he pulls the door shut behind him.

Lake laughs and presses her head against my shoulder. "Welcome home," she says unenthusiastically.

I sigh. "I wonder what they're eating? You gave me a solid two-day workout and I'm hungry now."

Lake shrugs and pulls away from me. "I don't know but I'm hungry, too."

We both make our way across the street. When we reach the front door, she puts her hand on the doorknob, but pauses and turns to me before opening it.

"Should I knock? It feels weird knocking on my own door, but I don't live here anymore."

I ease past her and grip the doorknob. "Nobody else knocks, why should we?" I open the door and we make our way inside. The boys and Kiersten are seated at the table and Eddie and Gavin are both in the kitchen, filling plates with food.

"Look who's back!" Kiersten says when she spots us. "How was the honeymoon?"

Lake walks into the kitchen and as soon as Eddie sees her, she immediately takes her hand and pulls her down the hallway. "Yes, Layken. How was the honeymoon? I need details," Eddie says. They disappear into the bedroom.

I walk into the kitchen and take over the plates Eddie was working on. "The honeymoon was perfect," I tell Kiersten.

"What's a honeymoon?" Kel asks. "What do people do when they go on one?"

Gavin spits out his drink with his laugh. "Yes, Will," Gavin says, smirking at me. "I must know what people do on honeymoons so that I'm prepared for when I have mine. Enlighten us."

I pick the plates up and glare at Gavin, then walk to the table. "A honeymoon is what people have after they get married. It's when they spend a lot of time together . . . telling stories about their past. And eating. They tell stories and eat. That's it."

"Oh," Caulder says. "Like a campout?"

"Exactly," I say, taking my seat at the table across from Kiersten, who's rolling her eyes at me. She shakes her head.

"He's lying to both of you because he thinks you're still nine years old. A honeymoon is when newlyweds have sex, traditionally for the first time. But in *some* cases," she rolls her head toward Gavin, "people get ahead of themselves."

We're all staring at Kiersten with our mouths agape when Lake and Eddie return.

"Why is everyone so quiet?" Eddie asks.

Gavin clears his throat and glances at Eddie. "Suck and sweet time," he says. "Sit down, ladies."

"Me first," Caulder says. "My sweet is that me and Kel are finally brothers. My suck is that I now know what Will and Layken did during their honeymoon."

"I second that," Kel says.

Lake looks at me questioningly, so I nudge my head toward Kiersten. "Blame her."

Kiersten shoots me a glare that has become all too familiar from her. "*My* suck," she says, "is that I seem to be the only person in this room aware of the importance of sex education. My sweet is that a few months from now, thanks to Gavin's inability to wait for his honeymoon, I'll have a steady job babysitting."

Gavin spits his drink out for the second time in five minutes. "No. No *way* are you babysitting my daughter." He wipes his mouth and stands up, clinking his fork on the red plastic cup in his hand. "I'm going next because I can't wait another second to share my sweet." He turns to Eddie, seated next to him, and he clears his throat. Eddie smiles up at him and he presses his hand to his heart. "*My* sweet is that the woman I love, as of last night, has agreed to become my wife."

As soon as the word *wife* leaves his mouth, Kiersten and Lake are making high-pitched noises and hugging Eddie and jumping up and down. Eddie takes a ring out of her pocket and puts it on her finger to show the girls. Lake says something about this being her sweet and Eddie agrees, but Gavin has sat back down and all the boys are now eating while the girls are still squealing.

I look over at Lake and she's turning Eddie's hand back and forth in the light, admiring her ring. She's smiling. She looks so happy. Eddie is happy, too. The boys, aside from learning what you do during your honeymoon, are smiling. Gavin is watching Eddie and looks genuinely happy. I can't help but think back on these past two years and all we've been through. The heartache we had to endure to get here and the tears we've all shed in the process. I don't know how one minute, a person can think his life is nothing more than a barren valley with nothing left to look forward to. Then, in the blink of an eye, someone can come along and change it with a simple smile.

Lake looks at me and catches me smiling at her. She grins and leans against me as I wrap my arm around her. "You want to know my sweet?" I ask her.

She nods.

I kiss her on the forehead. "You. Always you."

The End.

epilogue

"GIVE HER SOME medicine!" Gavin yells at the nurse. He's pacing back and forth. Beads of sweat have pooled on his forehead and he lifts a hand to wipe them away. "Look at her! She's in pain, just look at her! Give her something!" His face is pale and he's gesturing toward the hospital bed. Eddie rolls her eyes and stands up, taking Gavin by the shoulders and shoving him toward the door.

"Sorry, Will. You would think he would take it better since I'm not the one in labor this time. If I don't get him out of here he'll pass out like he did when Katie was born."

I nod, but can't find it in me to laugh. Seeing Lake on that bed in as much pain as she's in has me feeling completely helpless. She's refusing medicine, but I'm about to go grab a damn needle and give her some myself.

I walk to the head of her bed and as soon as the contraction passes, the tension eases slightly from her face and she looks up at me. I take the wet rag and press it against her cheek to cool her off. "Water. I want water," she grumbles.

This is the tenth time she's asked for water in the past hour, and the tenth time I'll have to tell her no. I don't want to see the anger in her face again, so I just lie. "I'll go ask the nurse." I quickly walk out of the room and take a few steps past the doorway, then collapse against the wall with no intention of looking for a nurse. I slide to the floor and drop my face into my hands and try to focus on the fact that this is really happening. Any minute now, I'll become a dad.

I don't think I'm ready for this.

At least if Kel and Caulder turn out horrible, we can still blame my and Lake's parents. This is a completely different ballgame. This baby is our responsibility.

Oh, god.

"Hey." Kel drops down beside me and kicks his legs out in front of him. "How is she?"

"Mean," I answer truthfully.

He laughs.

It's been three years since Lake and I married, and three years since Kel moved in with me. I know that technically I'm becoming a dad for the first time today, and in so many ways it's so different, but I can't imagine loving Kel any more if he really were my own. I can honestly say when my parents died, I felt cursed that my life had to change course like it did. But now, looking back, I know I've been blessed. I couldn't imagine things any differently.

"So," Kel says. He pulls his leg up and ties his shoe, then straightens it back out again. "My mom? She left me something I'm supposed to give to you today."

I glance at him and, without having to ask, know immediately what it is. I hold out my hand and he reaches into his pocket and pulls out a star. "It was in one of the gifts she left me for my birthday last year, along with a note. In fact, she left eight of them. One for each kid y'all might have. Four blue ones and four pink ones."

I fist the star in my palm and laugh. "*Eight?*"

"Yeah, I know," he shrugs. "I guess she wanted to be covered, just in case. And they were all numbered, so that one goes with this kid."

I smile and look down at the star in my hand. "Is it for Lake too? I don't know if she's in the mood for this right now."

Kel shakes his head. "Nope. Just for you. Lake got her own." He pushes himself up off the floor. He pauses after taking a few steps back toward the waiting room, then he turns around and looks down at me. "My mom thought of everything, didn't she?"

I smile, thinking of all the advice I'm still somehow getting from Julia. "She sure did."

Kel smiles and turns away. I open the star; one of many that I incorrectly assumed would be the last.

> *Will,*
>
> *Thank you for taking on the role of father to my little boy.*
>
> *Thank you for loving my daughter as much as I love her.*
>
> *But most of all, thank you in advance for being the best father I could ever hope for a grandchild of mine to have. Because I know without a doubt that you will be.*
>
> *Congratulations,*
>
> *Julia*

I STARE AT the star in my hands, wondering how in the world she could be thanking *me* when they're the ones who changed *my* life. Her whole family changed my life.

I guess in a way, we all changed each *other's* lives.

"Will," Lake yells from inside the room. I quickly stand up and put the star in my pocket. I walk back into the room and over to the bed. Her jaw is clenched tight and she's gripping the handrail so hard, her knuckles are white. She reaches up with one hand and grabs my shirt, then pulls me to her. "Nurse. I need the nurse."

I nod and once again rush out of the room. This time to actually find a nurse.

WHEN THE WORDS "You're ready to push" come out of the doctor's mouth, I grip the rail of Lake's bed and have to hold myself upright. This is it. This is finally it and I'm not sure I'm ready. In the next few minutes I'm going to be a dad and the thought of it makes my head spin.

I am not Gavin.

I will not pass out.

The seconds turn into nanoseconds as the room fills with more nurses and they're doing things to the bed and to the equipment and to Lake and to the lights that are really, really, *really*, bright and then a nurse is standing over me, looking down at me.

Why is she looking down at me?

"You okay?" she asks.

I nod. *Why am I looking up at her?*

I've either shrunk six feet or I'm on the floor.

"Will." Lake's hand is reaching over the side of the bed for me. I grip the rail and pull myself up. "Don't do that again," she breathes heavily. "Please. I need you to suck it up right now because I'm freaking out." She's looking at me with fear in her eyes.

"I'm right here," I assure her. She smiles, but then her smile does this twisted thing where it flips upside down and turns into a mangled, demonic groan. My hand is being twisted worse than her voice, though.

I lean over the rail and wrap my arm around her shoulders,

helping her lean forward when the nurse tells her to push. I keep my eyes focused on hers and she keeps her eyes focused on mine. I help her count and I help her breathe and I do my best not to complain about the fact that I'll never be able to use my hand again. We're counting to ten for what feels like the thousandth time when the twisted sounds begin coming out of her mouth again. Except this time the noises are followed by another sound.

Crying.

I look away from Lake and at the doctor, who is now holding a baby in his hands.

My baby.

Everything begins moving in fast motion again, but I'm frozen. I want so bad to pick her up and hold her but I also want to be next to Lake and ensure she's okay. The nurse takes our baby out of the doctor's hands and turns around to wrap her in a blanket. I'm craning my neck, trying to look over the nurse's shoulder at her.

When the nurse finally has her wrapped up, she turns and walks to Lake, then lays her on her chest. I push the rail down on Lake's bed and climb in beside her, sliding my arm beneath her shoulders. I pull the blanket away from our baby's face so we can both see her better.

I wish I could explain how I feel, but nothing can explain this moment. Not a vase of stars. Not a book. Not a song. Not even a poem. Nothing can explain the moment when the woman you would give your life for sees her daughter for the very first time.

Tears are streaming down her face. She's stroking our baby girl's cheek, smiling.

Crying.

Laughing.

"I don't want to count her fingers or toes," Lake whispers. "I don't care if she has two toes or three fingers or fifty feet. I love her so much, Will. She's perfect."

She *is* perfect. So perfect. "Just like her mom," I say.

I lean my head against Lake's and we just stare. We stare at the daughter who is so much more than I could have asked for. The daughter who is so much more than I dreamt of. So much more than I ever thought I would have. This *girl*. This baby girl is my life. Her mother is my life. These girls are *both* my life.

I reach down and pick up her hand. Her tiny fingers reflexively wrap around my pinky and I can't choke back my tears any longer. "Hey, Julia. It's me. It's your daddy."

my final piece

We're born into the world
As just *one small piece* to the *puzzle*
That makes up an entire *life.*
It's up to us throughout our years,
to find *all* of our pieces that *fit.*
The pieces that connect *who* we are
To who we *were*
To who we'll one day *be.*
Sometimes pieces will *almost* fit.
They'll *feel* right.
We'll carry them around for a while,
Hoping they'll change *shape.*
Hoping they'll *conform* to our puzzle.
But they *won't.*
We'll eventually have to let them *go.*
To find the puzzle that is *their* home.
Sometimes pieces won't fit at *all.*
No *matter* how much we *want* them to.
We'll *shove* them.
We'll *bend* them.
We'll *break* them.
But what isn't *meant* to be,
won't be.
Those are the hardest pieces of *all* to accept.

The pieces of our puzzle
That just don't **belong.**
But **occasionally** . . .
Not very often at **all,**
If we're **lucky,**
If we pay enough **attention,**
We'll find a
perfect match.
The **pieces** of the **puzzle** that **slide** right **in**
The pieces that **hug** the **contours** of our **own** pieces.
The pieces that **lock** to us.
The pieces that **we** lock **to.**
The pieces that fit **so well,** we can't tell where **our** piece
begins
And that piece **ends.**
Those pieces we call
Friends.
True loves.
Dreams.
Passions.
Beliefs.
Talents.
They're **all the pieces** that complete our **puzzles.**
They **line** the **edges,**
Frame the **corners,**
Fill the **centers.**
Those pieces are the pieces that make us who we **are.**
Who we **were.**
Who we'll **one day be.**
Up until today,

When I looked at my *own* puzzle,
I would see a finished *piece*.
I had the *edges lined*,
The *corners framed*,
The *center filled*.
It *felt* like it was complete.
All the pieces were *there*.
I had everything I *wanted*.
Everything I *needed*.
Everything I *dreamt* of.
But up until today,
I realized I had collected *all*
but *one piece*.
The most *vital* piece.
The piece that completes the *picture*.
The piece that completes my *whole life*.
I held this girl in my arms
She *wrapped* her *tiny fingers* around *mine*.
It was *then* that I *realized*
She was the *fusion*.
The *glue*.
The *cement* that *bound* all my pieces *together*.
The piece that seals my *puzzle*.
The piece that completes my *life*.
The *element* that makes me who I *am*.
Who I *was*.
Who I'll *one day be*.
You, baby girl.
You're my *final piece*.

acknowledgments

I would like to thank my agent, Jane Dystel. Your work ethic is inspiring and you are doing exactly what you were born to do. Without your support, advice, and honesty, I know I wouldn't be where I am today. And to each and every person in the Dystel & Goderich offices, thank you for your constant support of the authors you represent. And a special thanks to Lauren Abramo. Thank you, gracias, dank u, merci, danke, grazie.

I would also like to thank my editor, Johanna Castillo. You have been an absolute joy to work with and I look forward to many more years together. Thank you for constantly being so positive and supportive.

It's bittersweet knowing that this is the final book in the Slammed series. On one hand, I'm happy to say goodbye to Will and Lake and the gang. They deserve their happy ending. But on the other hand, I'll miss these characters who completely changed my life. It might be a little odd to acknowledge the characters of a book, but I want to thank each and every one of them. After being inside their heads for a year and a half now, I feel like I'm saying goodbye to friends.

And the biggest thank-you of all I'm reserving for fans of this series. Those of you who read the books. Those of you who asked for a sequel. Those of you who took the time to email me and let me know how the books touched you. Those of you who were inspired to write your own books. Those of you who have supported me and have helped spread the word, simply because you want to. This has definitely been a whirlwind of a year, but each and every one of you have kept me sane. You've kept me inspired and you've kept me motivated. It's because of you that I am where I am today, and I'll never forget that.

Because of *you*.

about the author

Colleen Hoover is the *New York Times* bestselling author of three novels: *Slammed*, *Point of Retreat*, and *Hopeless*. She lives in Texas with her husband and their three boys. To read more about this author, visit her website at www.colleenhoover.com.

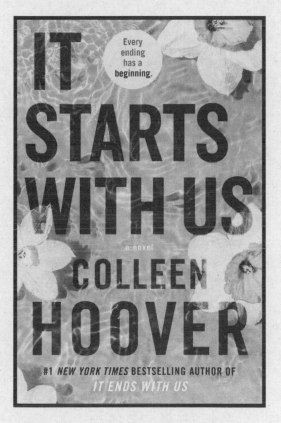